Crista smoothed it out on her lap and smiled. It was a crayon drawing, and on the bottom, scribbled letters spelled out S-A-M.

"She told me she made it for you."

"How sweet." And how sweet of him to come all the way over to give it to her in person. "It's..." She angled her head, trying to decipher the child's artwork.

His arm brushed against hers as he pointed to the stick people. "What do you think?"

Think? She couldn't think of anything except the searing heat she felt where his arm had touched hers. She was acutely aware of the man's sexuality. "I'm sorry. I'm really bad at this. Is that supposed to be you and Sam?"

"Sam told me that's a car, and these two are the people inside."

"And the line there?" She pointed to something coming from one of the stick figure's hands.

"Sam's exact words when I asked the same thing were, 'I don't know, but that's when I got blood all over Snuffy.'"

Crista's stomach dropped like an anvil. *Oh, my God. Had the little girl actually seen the shooters?*

Dear Reader,

Welcome to the third book in the WOMEN IN BLUE series about six women who met in training for the Houston Police Academy and remained friends long after. While *The Witness* stands alone, I hope you'll have the opportunity to read the five other books, too.

The Witness is Crista Santiago's story. Born and raised in one of Houston's impoverished East End barrios, Crista married at seventeen to escape an abusive stepfather. But her marriage proved to be a disaster. Determined to make a better life for herself, she left her husband and vowed never to return to the barrio. As a detective in the HPD Homicide Division, she thinks she's succeeded—until she meets Alex Del Rio, a man who forces her to come to grips with her past.

Since his wife's death, Alex Del Rio has directed all his energy toward his four-year-old daughter, Samantha, and his job. A traditional man whose values and beliefs are firmly cemented in his Latino heritage, he never dreamed he'd fall for a modern, independent woman like Crista.

I had a great time figuring out if two such polar opposites could ever get together. And I discovered that Crista and Alex's romantic story is one of self-discovery and self-love.

It was a pleasure to work with the talented authors behind the WOMEN IN BLUE series: Kay David, Sherry Lewis, Anna Adams, Roz Denny Fox and K.N. Casper. I hope you'll enjoy *The Witness* as much as I know you'll enjoy their books.

I always like hearing from readers. You can reach me at P.O. Box 2292, Mesa, AZ 85214 or LindaStyle@cox.net. Please visit my Web site at www.LindaStyle.com and www.superromanceauthors.com to read about upcoming books and other fun stuff.

Wishing you the best,

Linda Style

The Witness
Linda Style

HARLEQUIN®

TORONTO • NEW YORK • LONDON
AMSTERDAM • PARIS • SYDNEY • HAMBURG
STOCKHOLM • ATHENS • TOKYO • MILAN • MADRID
PRAGUE • WARSAW • BUDAPEST • AUCKLAND

ISBN 0-373-71243-X

THE WITNESS

This edition published by arrangement with Harlequin Books S.A.

® and TM are trademarks of the publisher. Trademarks indicated with
® are registered in the United States Patent and Trademark Office, the
Canadian Trade Marks Office and in other countries.

www.eHarlequin.com

Printed in U.S.A.

To my family
and to all the dedicated officers of the
law who make our world a safer place

My deep appreciation to those who contributed to the research for this book: Virginia Vail for lending her Spanish expertise and Jane Perrine for sharing her knowledge of the city of Houston. I'd also like to thank the Houston Police Department and the task force on gang activity. Since this is a work of fiction, I have taken liberties in some areas. Any errors are mine.

PROLOGUE

"Santiago, get up here!"

Sixty recruits in the Houston Police Academy and the instructor picks her to be the guinea pig for their first self-defense demonstration. "Yes, Sir." Crista crossed to the mat and stood at the edge.

"Okay. I'm gonna show you guys how to get away from someone who's grabbing you, regardless of your size. Santiago, pick a partner."

"Oh, pick me," Bernie Schwartz, the largest, most obnoxious man in the class, said in a girly voice and elbowed the recruit next to him.

A rash of laughter filtered through the group. "Yeah, if she wants to be in traction tomorrow," someone else said.

"Don't listen to him," Mei Lu Ling whispered.

Crista couldn't help listening. The women in the class had nicknamed Schwartz "The Mouth" because he continually harassed them. Every other word had a sexual connotation or was something related to how the women would never make it through training. So far, Crista had ignored his gibes, but she was tired of it—and there was only one way to shut a guy like that up.

Her adrenaline surged. "Okay, Schwartz. You're on."

The man grinned. "Uh, maybe you better pick

someone else, sweetheart. I wouldn't want to hurt a little thing like you."

Her nerves bunched at the condescending tone in his
voice. She wasn't sure which was bigger, Schwartz's
mouth or his inflated ego.

When she didn't back down, he glanced at the other
recruits and shrugged as if it was going to be her fault
when she got hurt.

"Get up here," the instructor ordered.

Schwartz sauntered over, so impressed with himself
Crista wanted to puke. Instead, she stood quietly with
her arms crossed and, after glancing at her friends on
the sidelines, she gave them a tiny, satisfied smile. It
was time for Bernie Schwartz to go down.

Chose your fights wisely. Crista remembered Catherine Tanner's warning. Catherine was their first instructor at the academy and had privately told the
women in the class that they might not like some of the
things that happened during training. The police department was still a brotherhood of sorts, and if the
women wanted to make it through their six months,
they'd do well to ignore a lot of things.

The thought galled Crista. She'd had enough abuse in
her life and had vowed never to get in that position again.

But right now, it was more important to protect her
future. Getting hired by the Houston Police Department was the single most significant thing she'd done
with her life, and it wouldn't mean much if she didn't
make it through the academy. Heeding Catherine's advice, she'd kept her mouth shut. All the women in the
class had done the same.

Only this time, the situation was different. She had
the perfect opportunity to make a statement without
saying a word.

"Okay, you two, over here on the mat." Their instructor, Max Wilson, pointed to where Crista and Bernie should stand, and then he explained the maneuver, point by point.

Crista considered her opponent. Broad chest and biceps that strained at the seams of his tight T-shirt, overdeveloped thighs that rubbed together when he walked. Schwartz was a bodybuilder, and bodybuilders weren't known to be fast on their feet. Certainly no match for her expertise. She wasn't a Master's level yet, but she knew she was a worthy opponent for any man.

Wilson looked at Crista. "Santiago, Schwartz is going to grab you and you're going to attempt the maneuver."

Schwartz gave a lecherous grin and did a Groucho with his eyebrows. More laughter tittered through the group.

Crista focused on her attacker. "Okay, Schwartz, do your thing."

Just as he reached out, Crista grabbed his left arm at the elbow, shoved her leg behind his and pulled hard as she turned into his body. In one quick flowing motion, she bent over, yanked his arm to bring him across her back and he landed on the floor in front of her with a thud.

A hushed "Ohh," emanated from the recruits and then—utter silence. After a moment, isolated clapping broke the air. One of her friends, no doubt. Then she heard a couple hoots and one of the guys said, "Hey, Santiago! I want you to be *my* partner." Another said, "Yeah, you can cover me on the streets anytime."

The Mouth, still flat on his back with the air knocked out of him, glared up at her. She reached out a hand to help him. "Thanks for volunteering, Bern."

Schwartz batted her hand away, rolled to a sitting position and then launched to his feet, every muscle in his body tensed for a fight.

"Okay, let's do a few more routines before we take a break." Wilson gave Crista a nod and said, "Good job, Santiago."

Later, as the larger group scattered and Crista's friends rushed to her side, she heard some of the guys ribbing Schwartz about getting taken down by a woman. Then she heard, "That bitch better watch her back."

Mei was standing next to Crista and patted her on the shoulder. "Nice work." Lucy gave her two thumbs up, Abby reached out for a hug, and Risa said, "Way to go, sister!"

Crista nodded and smiled, the rush of adrenaline still pumping through her veins.

"Did you hear him?" Abby asked. "It's gonna be tough on you to go through the rest of training with that jerk hauling his bruised ego around."

"Crista can handle Schwartz," Risa piped up.

"I made the decision, I'll live with it," Crista said softly. "Besides, I have my friends for moral support." It was true. The closeness and camaraderie they'd developed in such a short time meant a lot to Crista.

By the end of their first week at the academy, the women in the class—Risa Taylor, Lucy Montalvo, Abby Carlton, Mei Lu Ling and Crista—quickly realized they needed to support one another and had formed a sisterhood. Catherine Tanner, who'd taught the Law Enforcement Ethics class and had warned them right off to play it cool, joined, too.

In her whole life, Crista had never felt such a close bond with anyone as she did her five friends. She doubted anything could tear them apart.

CHAPTER ONE

Six years later

THE LITTLE GIRL was still alive.

Detective Crista Santiago braced one arm on the door frame of the ICU at the Texas Children's Hospital, closed her eyes and drew a breath.

Alex Del Rio, the child's father, slumped in a chair at her bedside, his dark head bowed, hands clasped and pressed against his forehead.

Crista prayed, too. Prayed the girl would live.

A moment later the man started humming, his voice barely audible. *Hush little baby, don't you cry*…a lullaby he'd probably sung to his daughter from the time she was an infant. Grief was etched in deep lines on his face as he reached out to hold the child's tiny hand.

Swallowing around a sudden lump in her throat, Crista pushed away from the door, dark memories of her own surfacing like demons from the deep, memories of another hospital—another time. Fourteen years ago.

She hurried down the hall and past the nurses chatting in hushed tones at the desk, her boot heels clicking too loudly against the tile, the sharp scent of alcohol burning her nostrils. No…she couldn't question Alex Del Rio right now. Not when he didn't know if his little girl would be okay.

As she approached the glass doors to exit, she saw her partner, Pete Richter, pacing outside.

"Finished?" he asked as the automatic doors swished open.

Crista stepped outside into the crisp autumn air, squinting in the morning sun. She shook her head, still disturbed by the image of Del Rio at his little girl's bedside. The child's name was Samantha, and whether she lived or died, Crista still had to question her father about the shooting.

"You must think I'm really good if you expected me to finish in ten minutes." Crista kept walking toward the car, her partner in step alongside.

"I would have."

"Of course. You're a much better cop than I am," she said facetiously.

"Maybe. Maybe not." The tall, blond man shrugged.

Pete hadn't gone in with her because his wife was about to have a baby and had kept him on the phone while she was experiencing false labor pains, the third time it had happened in the past two weeks. And from the dry tobacco scent in the air, Crista guessed he'd needed a cigarette, as well.

"So what's the problem?"

"The father was distraught. I couldn't question him right now."

Pete looked at her askance as she slipped into the passenger seat of the gray, department-issue sedan.

She knew the look. "I know. I know. I'm thinking like a woman, not a detective. And Englend's not going to be happy."

Pete nodded, not mentioning the most important part of the equation. Houston's mayor, Stan Walbrun, was all over their captain about the recent increase in

drive-by shootings, most of them in the tougher barrios. On Wednesday there'd been a drive-by in
Paloverde Park, and a man had died. This time the
shooters had targeted Encanto, the old but upscale Hispanic community where Alex Del Rio, one of the
mayor's staff, lived. Bottom line—the mayor wanted
the case solved and he wanted it done yesterday.

Pete pulled onto Fannin Street, the main road that
curved around the Texas Medical Center. "So where
to?"

"We've got some research to do."

Her partner popped a breath mint into his mouth and
made a quick U-turn to head back to the station. "I say
gang initiation. Open and shut."

"It appears that way, doesn't it. Or maybe one of the
gangs was claiming new turf." She was going to need
a reliable contact to find out anything about the shooting. "You know any good snitches in the barrio, Pete?"

He shook his head. "Nope. I was North Patrol before I came here. You're the one with the experience."

"Not recently." It'd been fifteen years since she'd
lived in the Paloverde barrio—a place she despised
and had vowed never to return to. How ironic that her
new assignment would take her right back. Anger
coiled in her stomach at the thought.

When she'd received the promotion to detective a
year ago, she'd put in for a job in Special Operations.
She'd heard nothing until several months later when
she was transferred to Homicide's Chicano Squad—
supposedly because she knew the culture and spoke the
language.

Lord, she was tired of being labeled. Tired of being
defined by a happenstance of birth. Her identity didn't
hinge on her heritage—only now it seemed, her job did.

"Yeah, but you have experience with the homies. Right?"

Crista had to chuckle at Pete's attempt to sound hip. "It was a long time ago. And if you talk like that in the hood, you'll be laughed off the street."

She knew there was more to her transfer to the Chicano Squad than experience. In her former unit, she'd been branded a troublemaker for speaking up for herself and for standing up for her friend Risa when she was under investigation. Voicing her opinion when it was different than most officers on her team was the same as breaking the code. The silent code every cop knew. Cops didn't make waves against the system. One cop didn't complain about another. If you had a problem, you had to suck it up. It had taken a long time on the force for Crista to learn that lesson.

She figured the powers that be, namely her old captain, wanted to show her she had to toe the line if she planned to remain on the force. In addition, she'd heard the Chicano Squad had an affirmative action quota to meet. How convenient that Crista hit two AA marks—she was a woman and a Latina.

Well, she had no plans to stay on the Chicano Squad and was going to put in for a transfer as soon as another opening in Special Ops came up. But for any transfer she needed the captain's recommendation. To get that, she had to prove herself—and solving the Encanto case seemed the perfect way to do it.

At headquarters, they cruised into the parking garage and up to the fourth floor, pulling into the space for unmarked police vehicles. Together, they headed inside to the Chicano Squad's offices, a unit separate from the rest of Homicide, located at the end of a long hall.

Crossing to her desk in the middle of the room, Crista nodded at Laura, the department clerk, ignoring the low whistle, the click of a tongue. More subtle than catcalls, yet the effect was the same.

At least she could wear pantsuits with long jackets to cover herself. But nothing stopped the guys with only one thought on the brain. Thank heaven the whole unit wasn't like that. She sat at her desk and pulled out the papers to write up her report.

"Hey, Pete. You and J.Lo crack the case?" Clyde Hanover, asked. From the suggestive tone in his voice he wasn't talking about the drive-by.

Pete gave the other detective a hand gesture. "You guys are animals."

Thank you, Pete. If she'd been there longer, she would've given Hanover a shot herself, but after all the trouble she'd had in her last unit she wasn't going to challenge something so insignificant. Before she'd arrived, the Chicano Squad had been an all-male unit, and she knew she had to gain the team's confidence before they considered her one of them. Even then, she wasn't sure it would happen.

Her first day on the job, she'd learned she was one of five Latinos on an eight-person team. An interesting mix. In addition to regular duties, the Chicano Squad provided investigative support and follow-up on homicides, serious assaults and kidnapping that required knowledge of the Hispanic culture and language.

On that same first day, the captain had made no secret of the fact that he liked his unit as it had been before her arrival—testosterone across the board. Rumor had it that he'd taken her on under the threat of demotion.

Six years of law enforcement and she still had to prove herself.

At her desk, Crista glanced at her teammates. Across the room on her right, Clyde Hanover, the loudmouth in the group, and his clone, Dylan Farrell. On her left, Jesus Garcia and David Munez, a guy who looked like he might've been a sumo wrestler in another life. David's partner, skinny Martin Vargas, sat behind Pete, whose desk butted against hers. Except for her partner, she'd made no friends yet.

She was definitely the outsider. And maybe that wouldn't matter as much if she'd still had the support of her academy friends. Until four months ago the six women, Crista, Risa Taylor, Lucy Montalvo, Abby Carlton, Mei Lu Ling and Catherine Tanner, had maintained their strong friendships. And then Risa had come under investigation for shooting her partner.

By openly supporting Risa, Crista had incurred the wrath of the guys in her old unit who'd worked with Risa's partner before. When Crista stood behind her friend even after it was confirmed the bullet had come from Risa's gun, she'd been shunned by her fellow officers. Her old academy nemesis Bernie Schwartz had led the pack.

She hadn't known how dangerous taking that lone stand would be. Until she'd been sent in as a decoy on a drug sting that went bad. She had called for backup three times, crouching behind a Dumpster, gun in her trembling hand. After the third call, she knew no backup was coming. She withdrew, made no arrests and was subsequently reprimanded for screwing up the job.

Devastated, she'd told Risa she could no longer openly support her. Crista hadn't given her friend all the ugly details, because, Lord knew, Risa had enough to worry about. Risa said she understood. But when Crista's calls went unreturned, she finally quit calling.

Each of the six friends had an opinion—and some disagreed bitterly. Lucy was convinced justice would prevail in Risa's case, but Crista knew firsthand what the system could do to a person's career.

In the end, Crista had made the only choice she could. Self-preservation. She'd worked too long and too hard to let her career slip away. And she'd learned a hard lesson in the process. Stay neutral. Never take a stand that appeared to be against a fellow officer.

When Risa was cleared and it came out that she'd been set up, Crista made another stab at resurrecting the friendship and called Risa, telling her how happy she was that the investigation was over. Risa had said thanks, and that was the end of it.

Crista felt a sharp pain in her chest just thinking about it. Four months since she'd made the decision to step back and she still wondered if she'd done the right thing. She missed her friends terribly.

Pushing the half-finished paperwork away from her, Crista looked up to see Captain Englend motioning her to his office. Embarrassed that he'd caught her day-dreaming, she got up, trooped into his office and stood facing his desk, her hands on the back of the chair in front of her.

He nodded. "Sit."

"I'm okay." At five-foot four, she'd always felt she had more leverage when she was standing. Besides that, she had too much energy to sit for very long.

The captain's eyes narrowed. "Suit yourself," he said and dropped into the black, high-backed leather chair behind his desk. All the desks in the unit were gray metal except the captain's. His was oak.

Captain William Englend oozed authority. A bull of a man with close-cropped white hair, he was all about power and control. He didn't manage his unit, he reigned over it.

"What've you got?"

"Nothing yet. The child is in intensive care. The bullet nicked her shoulder and hit an artery. She lost a lot of blood. Her condition is still questionable, so I thought it best to wait and talk to the father tomorrow."

Englend's expression never changed, but she could tell by the rigid set of his mouth that he wasn't happy with her answer.

"And if the kid doesn't get better?" Without waiting for a response he continued, "If we worried about everyone's feelings, we'd never get a case solved. Get it done, Santiago. I want someone in jail."

"I'll do what I can, Sir."

She started for the door.

"In this unit, we don't do what we can. We get the job done."

His words stopped her cold.

"If you want to stick around, forget the sentimental crap."

Gnashing her teeth, Crista stormed back to her desk. From the second he'd assigned her lead detective on such an important case, she'd thought something was fishy. She was the newest detective in the group and was partnered with a guy who, though he'd had years of experience in other units, hadn't been with the CS much longer than she had.

Until the Encanto case, the captain hadn't given her any lead assignments, and she'd found it hard to believe he was giving her a chance to prove herself. Now her gut was confirming her suspicion. She'd been given three other detectives to work with and so far none of them except Pete had done anything on the assignment.

Worse yet, the captain was demanding action— never mind that drive-bys were rarely solved unless you had hard evidence or could find a snitch or an eyewitness who could identify the perp.

And so far…she had nothing.

CRISTA GLANCED at the two-story Spanish-style home with its balconies and soaring windows and then checked Alex Del Rio's address again. Yes. Right place.

The Saturday afternoon sun glinted off the tiled rooftop, the brightness reflecting her own mood since hearing about Samantha Del Rio's improved condition. She'd called the hospital every couple of hours last night and at about 4:00 a.m., they'd given her the good news. The child was going to be okay. Thank heaven.

As she climbed the steps to the huge home, she wished her partner was with her. But Pete had thought it more productive if they interviewed separately, and he'd gone off on his own to talk to some of the neighbors.

She rang the bell and waited, her nerves drawing tight under her skin. No matter how many times she questioned victims, she never got used to it. Making someone recall a traumatic event so soon afterward was like flaying open wounds.

One of the carved double doors swung open and a matronly woman appeared, her eyes puffy, her clothes rumpled.

"*¿Puedo ayudarle?*" the woman asked.

Yes, the woman could help her. "*Sí.* Señor *Del Rio, por favor.* Detective Santiago." Crista flashed her shield. This was probably the woman who'd taken her message when Crista had called earlier to say she was going to stop by. A housekeeper maybe.

The lady motioned for her to come in and then disappeared into another room. Waiting in the foyer, Crista took inventory. A wide mahogany staircase rose directly in front of her, a sparkling crystal chandelier hung from the high ceiling decorated with faded frescoes and a statue of the Madonna rested on an ornately carved table in an alcove on the wall on her right.

She'd always admired the old homes in this neighborhood, but had never been inside one to see how truly elegant they were.

"The police were already here," a smooth bass voice came from her left. She turned to see Del Rio standing in the archway to another room, his eyes somber, his dark-as-midnight hair disheveled. He wore black dress pants and a white shirt, open in the front and left hanging out, as if he hadn't had time to get fully dressed or didn't care. His chest was smooth and muscular and under other circumstances she might have had trouble drawing her gaze away.

"Hello, Mr. Del Rio, I'm Detective Santiago. I'm sorry to barge in at this time, however, I do need to ask you some questions about the shooting last night."

"I told the other officers everything I know," he said, buttoning his shirt. He shifted, standing taller, and his shoulders seemed to broaden in the process. "I didn't see anything."

Despite his obvious weariness, the man carried himself with panache, his presence almost larger than life.

His dark eyes warned her not to get too close. Yet at the same time, the intensity of his gaze drew her in.

Crista kept her feet firmly planted. "I understand your reluctance to answer more questions, but the other officers were here to collect evidence, my job is to conduct further investigation."

Thoughtful, his gaze circled her face. "When Elena told me a detective was here, I expected a man."

"Well, as you can see, I'm not. Is there someplace we can sit?"

"Can't this wait until another time?"

"The first twenty-four hours are critical in gathering information. The longer it takes, the colder the evidence will get and it'll be difficult to find out anything." Crista pressed, "If you could go over what happened one more time with me and then answer a few questions, it would be really helpful."

"It might be more helpful if the police were out there trying to find out who shot my daughter," he said, anger vibrating in his words.

"That's what I'm here for, Mr. Del Rio. We have to know where to look."

He stared at her, and when she didn't waver, he gave a nod, motioning her inside what seemed to be both a library and an office.

Crista observed an eclectic blend of modern technology and old-world elegance, mahogany bookshelves covered one entire wall while, to her right, stood a sleek desk of glass and chrome. On the desk were an assortment of photographs and computer equipment.

To her left, a supple leather couch and two well-used Cordovan leather chairs flanked a Chicago brick fireplace with a mahogany mantel. A wine and ivory oriental rug under the couch and chairs separated the room like a demarcation between the past and the future.

Family photos, she guessed, were everywhere— walls, tables and bookshelves. Several were of the little girl and a very beautiful young woman. Probably the child's mother. Del Rio's wife.

"When we're finished, I'll need to talk with everyone who was here last night."

"Please," he said, indicating one of the chairs.

She sat, pulling out her notebook and a pen. He sat across from her, leaning forward, elbows on knees, apparently anxious to get this over with. She couldn't blame him. "Who else lives here with you?"

"Just Sam and my mother-in-law."

"And your wife?"

He took a quick breath. "My wife died two years ago. A brain aneurysm."

"Oh, I'm sorry. I didn't know."

He'd lost his wife and last night he'd almost lost his daughter. She couldn't imagine how he must've felt. At least now he knew his little girl would be okay.

"Elena has lived here since Sam was born," he said. "She was sleeping last night when it happened, and she didn't see anything, either."

"I'd still like to talk with her when we're finished."

Del Rio nodded, but she could tell he didn't like the intrusion.

"Her full name?"

"Elena Reyes-Vasquez."

Crista jotted the woman's name on her pad, then said, "Please tell me what happened as you remember it. From the beginning."

"I was in my office and heard gunshots. One came

through the window over there." He motioned toward a shattered window now taped and covered with plastic. "And the other came through Sam's window. I didn't know that at the time, but my first instinct was to go to her and make sure she was okay."

He stopped talking, rubbed his eyes with the thumb and forefinger of one hand. When he continued, his voice was hoarse, his emotions raw. "She was unconscious on the floor when I came in. I saw the blood, shouted for Elena to call 911 and applied pressure to her shoulder to stop the bleeding."

Crista kept her eyes on her notes. She wasn't supposed to feel anything. This was her job. Yet she'd never been able to dissociate when people got hurt, especially innocent children.

"She must've gotten up for some reason, otherwise…" He coughed, then continued, his voice soft, his tone bewildered. "I don't know why she was out of bed."

"Was the light in her room off or on?"

He frowned, then shook his head. "Off, I think. But there's a night-light and I saw her on the floor."

"Did you see anyone else? Out the window, maybe?"

A flash of anger swept across his face. His hands clenched into fists. "If I had…" He cracked the knuckles of one hand against the other. He inhaled deeply and a moment later, spoke with enormous control. "No, I didn't see anyone. My only concern was Sam."

He had every reason to be angry. She would probably be just as furious if she'd had a child who'd been shot.

He glanced up at her, his eyes filled with hurt and disbelief. "You know, you think your home is your sanctuary, that your family is safe and no one can harm you as long as you're together." He shook his head. "But that's not the case at all. Is it?"

She'd never known that kind of security, never had a sanctuary. It must be wonderful to feel that way. But growing up in the barrio and working a beat for five years, she knew nothing was safe. "There's no explanation for why tragic things happen, and then when they do we feel helpless."

"Yeah. That's exactly how I feel." He leaned back in his chair, drained.

He was in a world of pain, but she couldn't allow herself to be swayed by it. She had to continue the interview. Looking down at her notes, she asked, "Did your daughter see anything?"

He shook his head. "When she woke up, she was too groggy to talk much about it. Said she didn't know what happened."

Crista continued taking notes as she asked questions. "How did you know that you heard gunshots and not fireworks or something?"

"If you've ever been shot at, you don't forget the sound."

She glanced up, surprised.

He added, "I was in the Marine Corps during the Gulf War."

Yes, she could picture him in a uniform. Posture perfect, tall, muscular and imposing. Definitely marine material. "How long have you lived in Encanto?"

"Five years."

"And before that?"

"California. My family still lives there."

"Any relation to Del Rio Wines?"

A trace of interest flickered in his eyes. "Yes. My

parents bought the small vineyard fifty years ago and with a lot of hard work made it what it is today. Most of my sisters and brothers still work for the business." He gave her a studied look. "Are you a wine connoisseur?"

She suppressed an urge to laugh at the irony. Her favorite wines were Chardonnay and white Zinfandel. Beyond that, she was clueless. "No. Not at all." In her quick perusal of the room, Crista had noticed a plaque with the Del Rio Winery emblem on one of the bookshelves. She nodded toward it now.

He glanced at the bookshelf, then gave her a quick flash of a smile. "Oh. Yes."

When he smiled, just that tiny bit, he made her feel warm inside. "So why did you move to Texas when your whole family is in California?"

He frowned. "Is this information important?"

"Yes, it is. The more I know, the better I'll be able to decide where to look for pertinent information."

"Information about what? I fail to see how my past has anything to do with last night. Someone needs to get out there and find those creeps."

"Right now I'm exploring all possibilities. And one of those possibilities is that someone may have intentionally targeted you, and it might have been someone from your past. Do you know any reason why someone would want to harm you?"

A look of resignation crossed his face. "No. My family is very close."

"What about friends? Co-workers? Have you made any enemies on your job?"

He shrugged. "Not everyone likes the way I do things, but I haven't made any enemies that I know of. I create programs to get kids off the streets, and hopefully give them a sense of belonging so they don't have to get that support by joining gangs. The task force's goal is to rid the East End barrios of gangs. Most people are happy with what I do."

"Most? Who's not?"

He shook his head. "No one that I know of. You're looking in the wrong place for your evidence, Ms. Santiago. There was another shooting just two nights ago in Paloverde. Drive-by shootings are common in the barrios and most of the time there's no good reason."

"*Not* in this neighbourhood. There's never been a shooting here before, so it doesn't fit the pattern."

She stopped writing and looked at him. According to the case file, Del Rio was the director of the mayor's Anti-Gang Office and Task Force and had been since its inception. The office had only been set up a year ago at the community's insistence that the mayor do something to reduce gang-related violence and crime. But since then, the crime rate had only increased.

"What did you do before you had this job?"

"I worked for the mayor in another capacity. When the director's position came up, I applied."

"Interesting. What exactly do you do?"

"I've created a database with extensive information on the local gangs, developed some activity programs and found a building to use as a center. I've recruited some of the youth from the neighborhoods, kids I believe can persuade their peers to participate. Once they begin to get involved, I'm hoping they'll want to stick around, support the programs and spread the word." His face had brightened.

It was obvious he took pride in his work. "The kids you're recruiting…do any of them belong to gangs?"

His eyes narrowed, his hands curled into fists on his

thighs. "If you're thinking any of them would be involved in this, you're wrong." He stood.

"I'd like their names so I can talk with them."

"Most of my recruits aren't too fond of the police. And they could eat a tiny thing like you for breakfast."

Crista stood to face him. She wanted to tell him that she could take care of herself better than most men. Instead she said, "I can handle a couple of teenagers. I'm trained to do my job and I do it well."

He studied her for a moment. "Yes, I expect you do. But I'm still surprised they put a woman on a case like this."

The skin on her arms prickled. "Fortunately, your opinion doesn't count."

He looked a little surprised at her response, but didn't pursue it. It was also apparent he wasn't going to cut loose with any names. How could she blame him? She knew those kids would never trust him again if he sent the police to their homes. "Okay. If you won't give me names, then maybe you can persuade a couple of them to call me?"

"…Okay."

She heard the hesitation in his voice, but handed him a card with her office and cell phone numbers anyway. "There's a recorder, so they can call anytime—24/7." They wouldn't call, she knew that. But she had to start somewhere.

"So once again. Did you see anyone, or is there anything else you haven't mentioned?"

He hiked his shoulders again and his frown returned. "I told you everything. My word is good."

"No offense intended. It's my job to ask more than once because often people don't remember everything right away. Sometimes they remember things days or weeks later." She took the card from his hand and scribbled her home phone number on the back. "If you think of anything, I'd appreciate a call. If it's important, and if you can't get me at the other numbers, use that one."

She handed the card back to him. "Please don't give that number to anyone else."

He nodded. "Are we done?"

"*We* are." she said. "I'd like to talk to your mother-in-law before I go."

"It won't be helpful."

"Then it'll be a short conversation."

He stalked from the room and a few moments later, he returned with Señora Reyes-Vasquez.

The woman sat on the couch opposite Crista, while Del Rio stood like a sentinel behind her. Glancing at Del Rio, Crista said, "If you don't mind, it would be better if we talked privately."

His back visibly stiffened. "She speaks little English."

"That's not a problem."

His gaze locked with hers—a battle of wills, it seemed. Crista didn't look away. Finally he said to his mother-in law in Spanish, "I'll be right outside the door."

The interview with Elena Reyes-Vasquez *was* short. She'd been asleep and hadn't heard the shots, she'd only heard Alex when he'd called out to her. Listening to the older woman, Crista was pleasantly reminded of her grandmother who'd lived with the family before Crista's father died.

Despite Alex Del Rio's reluctant attitude, she decided he was a kind man to provide a home for his mother-in-law.

Alex was standing outside the door waiting when

Crista came out. "She lived through it," Crista announced.

"Encuentren a estos malvados!" Elena said, coming up behind Crista.

Crista couldn't help but smile at the older woman's spirit. Yes, Elena Reyes-Vasquez very definitely reminded Crista of her grandmother. "We'll do everything we can to find the person who did this," she answered in Spanish. "Or persons."

Crista turned to Alex. "I'd like to take a look at the bedroom, if you don't mind."

Del Rios's expression went cold.

"It'll only take a few minutes. I need to see it for my report."

Taking a breath, he nodded to Elena and asked her to show Crista the room. Apparently he couldn't bring himself to go back there yet, a response she understood only too well.

The little girl's room was pink and white, with a poufed up coverlet on her four poster bed and fluffy clouds painted on the ceiling. Crista could almost feel the love that went into creating this room. She gave a long sigh and hurried through her inspection. A single shot had come through the window. The hole was tiny and Crista was amazed the bullet could've inflicted such damage. A lighter spot on the carpet revealed where a throw rug had been removed. She knew from the case file that there had been blood on the rug and the Crime Scene Unit had taken it as evidence. She made a few notes and hurried out. The file contained the rest of the information she needed.

Coming down the stairs, Crista crossed directly to where Del Rio waited by the door, ready to escort her out. "I know this was difficult for you," she said. "But it really was helpful."

She stepped outside, then turned to face him. "Oh, one more thing. Are you planning on staying in the area? In Encanto, I mean."

"Of course," he said. "Why wouldn't I?"

She shrugged. "Living so close to the Paloverde barrio…and, well… With all that's happened and because you have family in California, I just wondered, that's all."

A puzzled expression crossed his face. "This is my home. My daughter's home. I have no intention to move anywhere."

"Not even to a different neighborhood?"

"I'm not going to run away."

Macho to the nth degree. "Admirable in principle," Crista said. "Except drive-by shooters don't care much about principles… I guess you know that already."

If he didn't, he was deluding himself. Then again, considering all his pie-in-the sky hopes for the barrios, delusion was probably the best word for it. He'd never lived in a neighborhood like Paloverde or Segundo, and he'd only worked with the Hispanic community for a year—yet he thought he knew how to fix what was wrong.

"I would move away instantly if I thought that would keep my daughter safe. But random shootings can happen anywhere. If the police apprehend the criminals, we're one step closer to a safer community." He paused for a moment, then said, "Besides, if I moved away, how credible would I be to those I'm trying to help?"

His credibility wasn't going to change anything. For eighteen hellish years she'd lived in the barrio—a place where the poverty ate at your soul and the violence kept you awake at night. She knew the only changes since

she'd left the place were more poverty and more violence.

No point in bursting his bubble, though. He'd find
out soon enough. "I see your point."

His dark gaze seemed to cut right through her. "No,
I don't think you do."

CHAPTER TWO

HE'D ACTED LIKE a jerk. Alex sat at his desk, staring at the taped-up window. He hoped the detective didn't think he was being uncooperative.

It was just that he'd been through all the questions before. And when she'd started probing his past, his family and then his job and the kids he was working with…he didn't see the point. The police should be tracking down the scumbag who did this, not wasting time with irrelevant questions about his family.

Maybe he was wrong not to give the detective the names of the boys he'd recruited, but he knew those boys. They wouldn't be at the center if they were still on the streets. Hell, if he thought for one second they might be involved and had hurt his little girl, he'd give out their names in a New York minute. But he didn't believe that. He trusted them. They trusted him. Giving the detective their names could break that trust and ruin the mayor's program he'd worked so hard to put in place.

"El te' esta listo en la cocina," Elena said from the doorway, letting him know she had tea ready in the kitchen.

"Thank you, Elena, I'll be right there." Since his mother-in-law knew little English, they always spoke in Spanish, and it drove his daughter crazy. Sam wanted to talk "American" because all her friends in preschool did, but she was forced to converse with her *abuela* in Spanish.

For him, speaking his native language was a matter of pride in his heritage. His father was a proud, hard-working man, who'd instilled the same values and beliefs in his children. *Never forget who you are and where you came from.* Alex found himself spouting his father's favorite phrase to Sam on more than one occasion. The thought made him smile. If his siblings ever heard him say that, they'd tease him unmercifully.

He pulled in a tired breath, rose to his feet and trudged to the kitchen. He needed to sleep, except right now sleep would intrude on his time with Sam. While the bullet had gone clean through the right shoulder, Sam had lost a lot of blood from the damaged artery, causing her little body to go into shock and putting her life at risk through the night. When her physician had finally given him the word that she was going to be fine, he'd collapsed in a heap. God had answered his prayers.

He'd only gone home because Dr. Rosenthal told him the medications would keep Sam out until late afternoon. But he hadn't been able to rest, and the detective had taken the brunt of his foul mood. She was there to find out who was taking potshots at his house and he'd acted like an ass.

He glanced at the table in the breakfast nook where Elena had set the teapot, then shook his head. Since Marissa died, Elena had stepped up the attention she lavished on him and Sam. He knew why. She had to do something to take her mind off her daughter's death. Unfortunately, he'd gotten used to all the fuss. Liked it, in fact. He just wished Elena would take a little time for herself. "Join me, please?"

"No, *gracias*," Elena said, explaining that she had to get things ready for Sam when she came home. He suspected Elena worried about being useless now that her daughter was gone. He'd told her many times that he and Sam needed her now more than ever, but he wasn't sure Elena believed it.

"*Gracias,*" Alex said again and, when Elena left the room, he moved the tray with the delicate china teapot, cup, saucer and cookies to the center island where he preferred to sit. He pulled up one of the wrought-iron stools and perched on the edge, going over the detective's questions.

The jangle of the phone disturbed his thoughts. He didn't feel like talking to anyone, but it could be the hospital or someone on the task force. He got up and answered, "Hello?"

"Alex, that you?" Tom Corcoran's voice bellowed from the other end.

"What can I do for you, Tom?"

"I just wanted to let you know the papers are in the works to transfer ownership of the building and everything should be completed by the end of the week."

The task force had already started work on the building despite the paperwork holdup, so Alex was relieved to hear it. "That's great, Tom. The city can't thank you enough. I can't thank you enough."

At Alex's suggestion, Tom Corcoran, Houston's largest building contractor, had agreed to donate one of his vacant buildings in the barrio for use as a neighborhood center.

Alex had had no idea who owned the property when he'd chosen it as his ideal spot. After hours of research, he'd been surprised to find that the owner of the building was none other than Tom Corcoran. Tom owned it under a corporation's name instead of his own, probably for tax purposes. And he hadn't seemed too pleased that Alex had been able to track him down.

"Well, I've been thinking about doing that for a long time. Why not put the building to good use helping the community… But I do have one requirement."

"What's that?"

"I prefer to do my charity work anonymously, if you know what I mean."

If he hadn't known before, he did then. Corcoran didn't want anyone to know he was a slumlord.

"I don't expect you'll want anything more from me."

The words were matter-of-fact, but the man's tone held a warning. Did he think Alex was going to come back for something else? That he might blackmail him? The idea of blackmail was so far removed from Alex's code of ethics it was laughable. But he found no reason to defend himself to Corcoran. The program needed the property, and he was grateful for the donation.

"You're more than generous, and of course our office will respect your wishes."

"Good. My attorney will be contacting you to finalize details."

Alex said goodbye and went back to his tea, the phone call a reminder of Detective Santiago's question, "Do you have any enemies?" He thought about Corcoran's caustic remark, then dismissed it. While the guy might not have been happy about being discovered as a slumlord, he doubted he'd hired someone to shoot at Alex's house.

The detective had asked about his family, too, but as far as family went, his brother-in-law Stan was the only one who might have an issue with him. And that was only because Alex had told him if he ever laid a hand on his sister again, he'd make sure he didn't have a hand to hit her with.

Neither Tom Corcoran nor his brother-in-law were likely suspects in a drive-by. The shooting had to be random, just like all the others in the East End barrios. Gang related. It bothered him to think the violence was spreading. He'd always felt safe in Encanto, but now he had to wonder if he was wise to keep his family here.

He pulled the woman's card from his pocket. Crista Santiago. Nice Latino name. It made sense that she'd wanted to talk to his program leaders, but he had to talk to them first. He knew a couple of them had previously been associated with local gangs, and he knew how hard it was to break away. Impossible sometimes. They'd made progress, but still had a long way to go. He didn't want to break the fragile trust they'd developed.

While he felt bad that he wasn't more help to the detective, he'd had no other choice.

When he finished his tea, he walked to the wall phone next to the kitchen door and, reading Detective Santiago's card, punched in her home number.

Saturday evening, he doubted she'd be home. He'd noticed she wasn't wearing a wedding ring, and a single woman who looked like Crista Santiago didn't sit home on a Saturday night.

"Hello."

He'd expected a message machine and was surprised to hear her voice—soft and sleepy, different from the all-business tone she'd taken with him earlier. He imagined her shiny dark hair spread on her shoulders instead of the tight bun she'd worn at his house. "Ms. Santiago. This is Alex Del Rio."

"Yes, Mr. Del Rio. What can I do for you?"

"I wanted to apologize for my rudeness earlier."

"You've been through a lot. I understand."

"There's no excuse for being rude," he said. "I also wanted you to know that after you left, I thought of a couple people who may not be too fond of me. But neither one would be involved in something like this."

"Go on."

He told her that he'd had a misunderstanding with Corcoran and then explained about his brother-in-law and that both episodes had been resolved. She must have thought the same, since she didn't seem too interested. Or maybe she thought it was an excuse to call her. He smiled. Maybe it was.

"I just wanted you to know that I'm not the boor that I must've seemed to be." He wished for just a second that he had something else to say so they could keep talking. But he couldn't think of anything else. "That's it, I guess."

"How is Samantha?"

"The doctor says she's doing great and should be able to come home soon," he responded, surprised by the question.

"Wonderful. That's good news."

Her voice rose, as if hearing about Sam's improvement was important to her. Despite her surname, he heard no trace of a Latino heritage in her speech. She didn't sound as if she was from Texas, either, and he wondered where she'd grown up.

"I'm sure you'll feel much better when she comes home."

Her empathy was refreshing. The other officers hadn't even asked about Sam. "Yes, yes I will. Thank you for your concern."

"Thank you for the information, Mr. Del Rio. Please call again if you think of anything else."

"I will if you call me Alex."

She hesitated, then said. "Okay, it's a deal—you call me with more information, and I'll call you Alex."

He laughed, the first time in two days. She was a professional all the way. He liked that. It meant she'd do a thorough investigation. She also had a sense of humor, and he liked that about her, too.

"It's a deal," he said. "And can you let me know if you get a lead?"

"I will if I can," she said, her tone all business again, ending the conversation.

SMILING, Crista leaned back on the couch and dropped the phone into the receiver. Alex's laughter, subdued as it was, was a good sign. It meant that he'd probably come out of this okay. She would have to talk to the little girl, but this was certainly not the time to mention that to the child's father. Regardless of how soon Englend wanted this case solved, some things couldn't be rushed.

She clicked on the television to watch the news, but her thoughts kept going back to the Encanto case. Finding evidence to tie it up was going to be tough. Pete wouldn't be much help, she feared, not with his wife ready to deliver at any moment. He and Sharon had waited fifteen years for this child. And Crista might as well forget the rest of the guys. It was obvious she'd have to work around the clock.

Her thoughts went round and round and eventually

she drifted off, awakening in the morning still on the sofa. She seemed to be doing more and more of that lately, finding it more comfortable to fall asleep with the television talking to her. She stretched and then rubbed her eyes. Rustling in the birdcage behind her made her sit up.

"*Awk.* What's your twenty. *Awk. Awk.*"

Crista glanced at Calvin. "I'm right here. Same location as you, silly bird."

She got up and checked the parrot's food and water.

"*Awk.* Same location as you, silly bird. *Awk. Awk!*"

Calvin hadn't said a word for the first two months after she'd rescued him from a crack house. After that he'd started spouting everything that hit the airwaves—dialogue from TV programs and commercials and things Crista said on the phone. Things she'd rather he didn't repeat, sometimes. After two years together, Calvin had an extensive vocabulary and she wasn't sure what would come out of the little guy's beak next.

Despite his large repertoire, Calvin wasn't much of a conversationalist. She sometimes tired of hearing him spout off, but mostly she was grateful for the company.

She went into the tiny L-shape kitchen, ground some coffee beans, filled the espresso pot and pressed the On button. Sitting at the kitchen table she'd bought on sale through the Ikea catalogue, she inhaled the nutty scent of freshly brewed coffee, her addiction most intense in the morning.

Crista pulled her hair back, twisting the length of it around her fingers before letting it fall again. If Alex Del Rio had come through with the names of the teens in his program, she'd have had a start. She'd already checked the department's snitch list and while she hadn't found a single reliable resource, she'd taken a few names anyway. She'd severed all her contacts in Paloverde fourteen years ago and vowed she'd never return. The thought of going door-to-door in her old neighborhood made her stomach cramp.

But it wasn't exactly true that she had no contacts. There *was* Diego.

Diego. A lump formed in her throat. Thinking of Diego sent shards of guilt and regret through her. Guilt because she'd had to leave her little brother behind. Regret that she hadn't been able to keep him from joining the Pistoles when he was twelve.

While they'd not talked in fourteen years, he was always in her thoughts. She'd planned to contact him immediately after his release a week ago, but the urgency of the Encanto case had taken over her life.

Crista sighed. Okay. If she was honest with herself, she'd admit she hadn't gotten in touch because she was afraid he might reject her again. Just as he had while he was in jail. And because Diego didn't have a phone, getting in touch meant a trip to the barrio. Two good reasons to be apprehensive, but it didn't appear she had any other choice.

She got up, poured a mug half-full of milk, added a little hazelnut flavoring and stuck the cup in the microwave. Not the best way to make a latte, but it worked for her.

After the microwave beeped, she filled the cup with espresso and sat at the table again, savoring the rich, nutty flavor and wondering if Diego would even know what was going down on the block. Ten years in jail would put anyone out of touch. She leaned against the back of the chair and closed her eyes.

On the other hand, word on the street spread fast,

and a week was plenty of time for Diego to get back into the swing of things. As it stood, any information she could get from him would be more than she had right now.

After she finished her coffee, she hurried into the bathroom and splashed water on her face. If she hustled, she'd have time to see Diego *and* go to the gym. She pulled on a pair of jeans, a black turtleneck sweater and grabbed a leather jacket to cover her gun. It was her day off and she normally wouldn't carry, but no way was she going into the hood without protection.

"HOLA, SAMITA," Alex said, entering his daughter's hospital room. She'd been moved from the ICU to the children's floor, and there was another little girl in the bed next to her.

Sam turned her head toward the door as he came in and, seeing him, her eyes lit up. She seemed so small and fragile in the hospital bed, his chest hurt just looking at her. But they'd taken the monitors off, and the doctor had assured him there would be no ill effects. The wound had been clean, the artery repaired.

"Daddy, Daddy! The doctor says I can go home."

"That's wonderful, Sam." He sat on the edge of the bed next to his little girl and gently cradled her hand in his. "I bet you're anxious, too."

"Uh-huh. I like the doctor and the nurses, but I like it at home better."

She still didn't seem to remember anything that had happened. When she'd first awakened, the medical staff had told her she'd had an accident. Though he'd asked her several times what she was doing out of bed and what she remembered, all she said was that she had to go potty and then she got an *owie.* The hospital therapist had advised him to let the child take her own time and not to frighten her by pressuring her to remember.

"That's Jenny," Sam said, pointing to the girl next to her. "She had a op-ray-shun."

"Op-er-a-tion," Alex corrected, then waved to the other child. "Hi, Jenny. Nice to meet you."

The little girl gave a limp wave back and said softly, "Hi."

"She's shy," Sam said. "Her mommy told me that."

"Then you'll just have to be extra friendly."

"Uh-huh." Sam nodded. "I want to see Snuffy."

Alex tweaked her nose. He didn't have the heart to tell her that her beloved Snuffy had been confiscated by the police as evidence. "I know you do. But first things first. We've got to get you better."

When he'd found Sam, she still had the bedraggled, blood-covered stuffed rabbit in her hands. Apparently she'd been holding the toy at the time and the bullet had gone right through it. The officer collecting evidence told him that the stuffing might include trace evidence, so they'd taken the toy. He wasn't sure he'd want her to have it back now anyway. Seeing her beloved Snuffy in that condition might be traumatic for Sam.

He'd decided to replace the animal, only he didn't know where he was going to get another. Marissa had bought the toy on a trip to Galveston before Sam was born.

"The doctor says I'm okay now," Samantha insisted.

Alex smoothed a lock of dark hair from her eye. She so resembled her mother, it made his heart ache. "You are, Punkin. But we have to get the official okay before you can come home. And the doctor tells me that won't be until tomorrow."

Sam's bottom lip protruded.

"You're a big girl, you can handle one more night. I know you can. Now let's see a smile."

Sam kept frowning, so Alex made a face, one that always made her laugh.

She broke out in giggles. "That's no fair. I didn't want to laugh."

He laughed, too. "But you did." Making faces had started out as a trick he'd used after Marissa passed away. Sam had been only two, but she kept asking for her mommy and crying. In desperation, he'd started making faces to see if he could get her to laugh. When he came up with the cross-eyed gooney bird, she'd giggled herself silly.

Later, when he was sad, Sam started making faces herself. From then on, whenever one of them was unhappy, it was the other one's job to get a laugh. It had worked every time since then.

"This way, you'll get a chance to say goodbye to all the nice nurses who took care of you."

Sam nodded, fiddling with a string on the blanket, winding it around one tiny finger. "And that other pretty lady, too?"

"What pretty lady is that?"

"That police lady with the shiny badge."

His adrenaline surged. Had Detective Santiago come here? To talk to Sam? Blood pounded through his veins. No one had the right to question his child without his permission. "What did she say to you?" He attempted to calm himself so his daughter didn't see how upset he was.

Before Sam had a chance to answer, a nurse came in to take her blood pressure. "How about if you come with me, young lady."

"Where to?" Alex asked.

"For an X ray and a couple other tests to make sure she's ready to go home tomorrow."

"Do I get another sucker?" Sam's eyes widened like dinner plates. "A red one."

"Absolutely. You might even get two. But only after lunch." The nurse turned to Alex. "She'll be busy for a couple hours, so if you have something else to do during that time…"

Yeah, he had something else to do all right! And it involved one lady detective.

CHAPTER THREE

CRISTA CRUISED down Guadalupe Street, wishing she hadn't put this off so late in the day. Apprehensive, she'd waited, having one more cup of coffee and then another. And then she'd gotten a call from her seventy-five-year-old neighbor Mrs. McGinty, who'd cut herself with a knife and had to go to the E.R. The woman had no way to get there, so Crista had taken her, glad she'd been there to help. However, the hospital stint had shot the whole afternoon.

She glanced at the dilapidated houses along the street. Fourteen years and everything looked the same. More graffiti, maybe.

She remembered her father telling her how the first Mexican settlers had contributed greatly to the economy of the burgeoning city. Paloverde Park had been one of the earliest Hispanic communities. But now the Mexican-American population seemed to have evolved into separate social classes: the long-time working-class residents, the middle-class professionals and merchants and the newly arrived, generally unskilled laborers.

The Mexicans who'd been here the longest had moved into the older upscale areas like Encanto and Idylwood and began renovating the old homes. It wasn't long before many Mexicans started identifying themselves as Latino because they didn't like the new negative connotations of the term "Mexican."

For some people in the greater Houston area, the word "Mexican" meant drugs and gangs and illegal immigrants, people who couldn't speak English and didn't pay taxes. Stereotypes that had no place in Crista's world. Hot tamale, Chiquita banana, she'd heard it all. Ironically, she'd also been called a Latina *arrepentida*—a sellout—by her so-called Latina sisters because she chose not to live in the Hispanic community.

She thought of Alex Del Rio's mother-in-law. An elegant, sophisticated woman from a wealthy family— who didn't speak English. She most definitely did not fit the stereotype. Few did.

It wasn't fair. But then life wasn't fair. Crista had known that since she was ten.

It was getting dusky and lights popped on up and down the street. A mixture of Latino and hip-hop tunes reverberated from tricked-out cars, and teens hung out on the dimly lit corners. Many of them were likely gang members looking for something to do. But there wasn't anything to do in the hood. If Alex Del Rio could find a way to get the kids off the street, more power to him.

Driving down the next block, the tiny house she'd lived in for eighteen years suddenly loomed like a behemoth. She tried not to think of anything except that she had to talk to Diego, but she felt a sharp spasm in her chest anyway.

As she pulled up in front and parked, two preteen boys gave her old Jeep a once-over. No worry there. The ten-year-old vehicle didn't have a radio and the tires were nearly smooth. Nothing any self-respecting thief would want.

She climbed from the Jeep and forced herself forward, each step more difficult than the last. Edging open the front gate, she glanced around. When her father had been alive, the place had been immaculate. He'd whitewashed the tiny house every year covering the old stucco in white so bright it was almost blinding in the afternoon sun. Her mother, a religious woman, had erected a little shrine with a flower garden around it. Now the stucco was a dingy tan, the gate practically fell off its hinges and the front steps appeared treacherous. Weeds had replaced her mother's flowers.

As she picked her way through chunks of sidewalk and slowly climbed the front steps, a pall of dread fell over her. Pain stabbed behind her eyes and she felt as if the house were pulling at her, dragging violent memories from her soul; her stepfather assaulting her mother, the beatings she'd taken herself trying to stop him, the tiny dark bedroom where she'd locked the door every night to keep her stepfather out. Her head swirled with the horror and her throat constricted—she had to fight to keep her balance.

A car backfired, jolting her to the moment. At the door, she knocked twice. No answer. She still had her own key, and unless Diego had changed the lock, she could go in and wait for him.

She had the key halfway out of her pocket when the door creaked open. Her brother stood on the other side, but he didn't say a word.

"Hi," she finally managed.

He just stood there staring at her as if she were an unwanted solicitor. "What're you doing here?"

"Can I come in?"

After a shrug, he turned and moved back, away from

the door. He didn't invite her in, but he hadn't closed
the door in her face, either.

She took that as a yes, and stepped inside. Just as
she did, a loud bang sounded behind her. She swung
around at the noise, her heart beating triple time. The
door had slammed shut, probably on a gust of wind.
She felt stupid. Man, she was on edge.

Diego dropped into an old recliner with gaping
holes in the fabric. He glared at her. "You slumming?"

"I came to see you."

Studying her, he shoved a cigarette between his lips
and took a deep drag. He was wearing faded jeans and
a white T-shirt, and Crista noticed tattoos on both his
arms. He'd also grown a couple feet since she'd last
seen him. He wasn't the skinny pimpled teenager she'd
left behind. He looked fit and muscular and his hair,
still jet-black and hanging to his shoulders, was shiny
and smooth. His complexion had always been darker
than hers, but now his skin was a smooth rich bronze.
He'd grown into a handsome man.

"Okay. You've seen me."

The chair he was sitting in, a spindly table next to it,
a lamp with a crooked shade and a sagging red vinyl hassock furnished the room. Several paintings were stacked
against the wall behind him. His paintings, she guessed.
Dim yellow light captured a layer of cigarette smoke
that floated midway between the dingy wood floor and
the low ceiling, giving the place an eerie surrealism—
as if they were actors in an old black-and-white movie.

She shoved the hassock closer to the chair with her
foot, and then sat on it, hoping she appeared relaxed.
"Your work?" she asked, pointing to the paintings.

He nodded. "Not much else to do in prison."

"From what I can see, they're very good." Diego

was a talented artist and she'd always hoped he might do something with the skill one day.

"Yeah, kinda adds a special ambiance to the place, don't ya think?"

His words were said in a casual, offhand manner, barely disguising his anger. He'd always been angry—at life, at her, their stepfather, their mother—he'd been angry at everything and everyone. Disconcerted, she kept her gaze on him.

"So what are your plans?"

He raised his chin. "What difference does it make?"

His bitter words made her wince. "I'd like to help. Maybe I can get you some secondhand furniture or something." She paused. "If you're going to stay here."

"I thought maybe I'd find you living here," he said, facetiously.

After their mother died and their stepfather moved out, she couldn't even bring herself to come near the place. She'd hired a local man to act as a rental manager, but when the fifth tenant in six months left the place in shambles, and he couldn't find any new occupants, she'd had the place boarded up. She'd mailed Diego the key the week before his release.

"I don't want any part of it. I'll sign my share over to you if you'd like."

He shrugged. "I hear you're a cop now."

"A detective."

He made a face. "You've joined the other side."

"Diego, please." His attitude was getting more annoying by the minute. "Why didn't you let me visit you when you were in prison?"

He bolted to his feet and stood over her, his body tense, hands clenched at his sides. A muscle twitched near his right eye.

On instinct, she reached to where her gun was tucked under her sweater, but the instant she made the move, she regretted it. Diego was her brother, he wouldn't hurt her.

Apparently he hadn't noticed her move for the gun. "Why should I? You're the one who disappeared and never contacted us."

Her mother knew why she'd had to flee and why Crista couldn't contact the family after that. Her mother had supported her decision—had even wished she'd done the same years before. Her mother's one wish, the thing she wanted most in the world, was for her children to leave the barrio and make good lives for themselves. And Crista had. She'd surpassed anything her mother might've wished for her.

She should feel good about that. But she didn't. Diego hadn't been told why she left. So he blamed her.

Why not? She blamed herself. If she'd stayed, she might have deflected some of her stepfather's rage and her mother's last days might have been happier.

"I had my reasons," Crista said. She wanted to tell him the truth. But she couldn't, not until she knew he'd be okay with it. Given the chip on his shoulder, she wasn't sure when that would be. "Before you start assigning blame, you better take a good look at yourself. You could've helped *Mami*. Why didn't you?"

He glanced away. "I was otherwise detained."

"I know that. But before that, you had a choice. I had a choice. They were different. My choice might've been wrong, I don't know. But I do know I can't change it now."

He turned his back and paced, his long legs eating up the tiny room in three strides, one hand jingling the change in his pocket. His agitation made her nervous.

"So what have you been doing for the past week? It is a week, isn't it?"

He dropped into the chair again. "Yeah. It's a week."

"Have you looked for a job?"

The question provoked a sarcastic bark. "Who's going to hire me? I'm an ex-con on parole. I have no skills."

"You can paint."

"Yeah, there's a lot of call for an artist around here. You think someone might pay me to do the graffiti?"

"They must've trained you to do something in ten years."

"And you must be smoking some strong weed if you think Huntsville is a job-training center. The only thing I learned was how to sleep with one eye open so I didn't get assaulted and raped during the night. I learned how to ignore the screams in the dark and the constant fear in the eyes of those smaller and weaker than me. I learned how to make my own weapons and do drug deals from the inside so I had money to keep myself alive. Basic training on how to survive in hell. Any jobs that call for those skills?"

Texas prisons were the worst. Her stomach knotted just thinking of her brother in that environment. "Maybe I can help."

"I don't need your help."

She glanced away, his words cutting to the bone. After shoring her resolve, she managed, "Okay. But I need yours."

He looked up, surprised. "That's a laugh. You never needed anyone."

She ignored the remark—one she'd heard before. Everyone she knew thought she was a loner, that she didn't need anyone. "A case I'm on... Two shootings, one on Wednesday night and another on Friday night. It seems the two might be connected. Gang-related, maybe. I was wondering if you'd heard anything?"

He stared blankly, and then anger flared in his eyes. "That's why you came here? To get information."

Oh, God. She wanted to snatch back the words, but it was too late. She shook her head. "No. I wanted to see how you're doing…see if I could do something to help. And I thought as long as I was here, I might as—"

"You're really a piece of work, you know that. For just a second there, I thought maybe…" He glanced away. "Yeah. Well, it doesn't matter what I think, does it."

She caught the slight tremor in his voice. The last thing in the world she wanted was to hurt Diego. Despite the fact they'd been estranged, she'd always trusted that he knew she cared. Apparently not.

The jangle of her cell phone cut the awful silence. Glad for the reprieve, she fished the unit from her pocket. "Crista here."

"Alex Del Rio, Detective." His voice was stern.

"What is it? Is something wrong?"

"Yes, something is very wrong. I'd like to know what the hell you were doing in my daughter's room at the hospital."

The accusation in his voice chilled her. Her hand tightened on the phone. "I was doing my job, Mr. Del Rio," she snapped, unable to keep the defensiveness from her voice. "But I can't talk to you right now. I'm with someone else. I'll call you back." She clicked off the phone, folded the unit and stuffed it into her pocket.

"Problems?"

"Uh…yeah," she mumbled and waved a shaky hand.

"The Friday drive-by in Encanto. A little girl was hit. That was her father."

Diego's eyes widened. "A kid was hit? Man, that sucks."

Maybe prison hadn't destroyed everything Crista loved about Diego. He'd always liked kids. "It's been on the news."

"I haven't been watching any news lately." He waved a hand around the sparsely furnished room.

She glanced away, still unnerved by Alex's phone call. "I have an old TV," she said, looking at him again. "You can have it if you'd like."

His mouth thinned. "I don't need any handouts."

"It's not a handout. I bought a new one, and I was going to give it away anyway." She'd planned to donate it to a shelter for battered women—the shelter that had helped her get away when she couldn't help herself. And if she didn't give it to Diego, who knows where he'd find money to buy one.

"Forget it," he said, staring at her, his gaze hard and unfeeling.

She stared back. Five years separated them in age, but it seemed a lifetime. The man sitting next to her was a stranger. She rose to her feet. "I better go."

Diego took another drag from his cigarette and blew out a string of perfectly formed smoke rings. She reached into her pocket and drew out a card, wrote her home phone number on it and handed it to him. "Here's my number if you want to talk…about anything. And the offer for the television still stands."

She moistened her lips, waiting for a response. Finally she turned and headed for the door. But as she reached for the knob, she stopped and said, "I mean it Diego. I want to help."

Silence. She closed her eyes feeling more alone than she had since she was a child. Somehow she'd always felt that as long as Diego was there, she wasn't alone in the world. But he wasn't there. She grabbed the knob, threw open the door and nearly collided with a man coming up the steps. Two men.

Marco. Marco Torres. A Pistoles gang leader she remembered from way back, and…her heart stopped. Oh, God!

Trinidad Navarro.

Trini seemed as surprised to see her as she was to see him. His black eyes raked over her like she was a piece of meat. "Hey, pretty lady. I've missed you."

He stepped closer, his face less than an inch from hers, his breath hot on her lips. She'd thought he was in prison. Twenty-five years she'd heard, which was why she'd been comfortable returning to Houston.

"Yeah, I've been away and you know it's been a long time since I had a woman. You miss me, too, *querida?*" He reached out and stroked her cheek.

A tornado of old fears ripped through her. Remembering that last horrible night, her fears switched to anger. She shoved him away. "In your dreams, *cholo.*"

Trini's eyes filled with hatred. His fist shot out to strike her, but her training kicked in first. She caught his arm, spun him around and slammed him against the house face-first. Pulling her gun at almost the same time and keeping his arm in a locked position, she jammed the Glock against his neck. With her mouth next to his ear, she said, "You want to try that again, Trini? I hope so, because then I'm going to nail your ass for assaulting a police officer. My guess is that you're on parole, so I'll tack on some other charges and you'll be going back to prison for quite a few more years."

Trini didn't say a word, but beneath her hands his body was rigid. She glanced at Marco, who, grinning like an idiot, held his hands up and spoke in heavily accented English. "Not my fight, *chica.* I'm goin' inside."

Crista tipped her head toward the door, giving him her okay. After Marco was gone, she said to Trini, "What's it going to be tough guy?" She felt his body vibrate with rage—a rage she knew all too well. "You want to try again?"

He cursed, his breathing deep and labored like he'd just run a marathon. Then after a second, he said, "I changed my mind."

"You sure about that?"

"Yeah, I'm sure," he spat out. "I'd rather take care of myself than do a bitch cop."

She held on a few seconds longer and then, releasing her hold, she shoved him away. But she kept her gun in hand.

Trini shook his shoulders out, trying to stand taller than his five-foot-seven before he yanked open the door and strutted inside. As the door closed behind him, he said, "Woman, you're gonna wish you'd never come back here."

He'd threatened her before—always right before he'd hit her. They'd only been together for a year, but even still, she couldn't remember how many punches he'd thrown. Well, this time was different and Trini had to know it. Which didn't mean he wouldn't go inside, pull out his own gun and blow her away.

She was counting on past experience that he wouldn't do that with Diego and Marco there. Trini was a coward and had always waited until he had her alone. She hurried down the steps and reached her Jeep in one piece. Holstering her weapon, she climbed inside.

As she drove away, she felt a sudden swell of pride. Up till now, she'd only imagined what she'd do if she ever ran into her ex-husband again. Now she knew.

But she'd probably fueled Trini's fire—and he wasn't the kind to forget.

Even worse, seeing both Trini and Marco at Diego's was a bad omen.

ALL NIGHT, Crista thrashed in bed, her dreams peppered with nightmares—nightmares filled with anger, guilt and shame. What bothered her most was knowing that Diego must still be with the Pistoles. Otherwise why would Marco have been there?

Relieved when narrow shafts of sunlight through the blinds signaled it was dawn, she rolled over and stretched her painfully tense muscles. She hadn't gone to the gym last night and her body was letting her know it.

Every other day for the past ten years, she'd gone to the Shao-Lin Martial Arts Studio to practice her skills in Wing Chun Kung Fu. Soon, she hoped to attain Master status.

Part of her training was spiritual. Learning to open and focus the mind. Using that internal channel to strengthen and calm the body. She closed her eyes and tried again to block last night from her memory. She couldn't. Seeing Trini had unleashed too many emotions.

Fourteen years ago, she'd escaped her ex-husband, but even then, she hadn't felt safe. Trini's possessiveness bordered on obsession, his erratic behavior and volatile personality made him a man to fear. Every waking minute became a nightmare of watching and waiting—until one of her co-workers mentioned she was taking self-defense classes. *Self-defense.* The idea intrigued Crista. If she learned to protect herself, maybe she wouldn't be such an easy target.

The next week, she'd started classes in basic self-defense, mastering the art in less than two years. She couldn't remember when exactly, but sometime during those two years, she'd realized protection wasn't her only reason for taking the classes. Knowing she could defend herself boosted her self-confidence, something she was sorely lacking. And for the first time in her life, she'd felt hopeful about the future.

At her instructor's suggestion, Crista went on to learn Wing Chun Kung Fu, a major Chinese martial art based on the theory of surviving an attack by being a better attacker than the assailant. The focus was on personal protection and street survival. Exactly what she'd needed.

When she'd returned to Houston for her mother's funeral, she was no longer the frightened teenager who'd fled the city. She was strong and confident, and that knowledge had given her the courage to stay. Knowing Trini was in jail helped, too.

But all the training in the world couldn't erase the past. She'd escaped from Trini with her life, but her unborn child hadn't been as lucky. And there wasn't a day that went by when she didn't think of her little girl.

The ugly memory was as vivid as if it had happened yesterday. Wing Chun had taught her to try to live in the moment, living each day as it came. She glanced at the clock. Almost 7:00 a.m., but if she hurried… plenty of time to go to the studio before work.

She bolted from the bed, showered, brushed her hair into a ponytail, pulled on her black instructor's level T-shirt, a pair of gray sweatpants, and, after grabbing a latte and taking care of Calvin, she was out the door.

She rarely went to the studio in the morning and was surprised to see her old friend Mei Lu Ling on her way out. Both women stopped. They'd only exchanged a few words since the rift, maybe a "Hello" as they passed each other in some official capacity, but that was it. While Crista had been close with all the women in the group, she and Mei had formed a special bond, and she regretted that loss the most.

"Hi, Mei," Crista said, feigning a perkiness she didn't feel. "I'm happy to see you're still working out."

At the academy, Mei had asked Crista to help her hone her own martial arts skills. Crista had been happy to oblige. Both women were dedicated to their careers, and they'd become close, training together, having coffee—tea in Mei's case—and talking at length about their backgrounds. They'd laughed at how they could have such different families, be raised so differently, and yet be so much alike. Especially when it came to men.

Crista's early experiences with her stepfather and ex-husband had put her off men for years, and Mei simply didn't see the need for such frivolous emotions as love. It wasn't that Mei didn't have emotions—she had plenty when it came to her family.

"I couldn't miss my workout if I wanted to," Mei responded. "You taught me well." She gave an open, friendly smile, her manner relaxed and easy.

Crista smiled back. Mei was as beautiful as ever, even in sweats and with a few wild black hairs sticking out of the bun at the top of her head. "That's good to hear," Crista said, unsure what to say next. Yet she felt compelled to say something. "If you need a sparring partner sometime, give me a call."

Mei nodded, a little hesitant herself, but she said, "Yes, let's do that. I've missed our workouts."

Crista nodded, and another awkward silence ensued.

"Well, I better go," Mei said. "I need to be at the station soon."

"Right. Me, too. I mean, I've got to work out before I go in."

Mei continued to her car and Crista went inside, hoping her friend *would* call.

Despite the unsettled feelings she'd had after talking with Mei, she managed a good workout. A stellar match always helped clear her head and her new instructor, a Master's level, was glad to take her on.

After that, she went back home to shower and put on her uniform, a navy pantsuit and white blouse. She wanted to interview a couple of Alex's neighbors Pete had missed before she went to the station.

Two hours later, she had no more information. No one had seen a thing.

At headquarters, she parked in the garage and headed straight for the CS unit. A couple of detectives from the previous shift were still working. The rest of her team either hadn't arrived yet or they were out on calls. But Captain Englend was there.

She pulled out the Del Rio file, picked up the phone and punched in Alex Del Rio's number, noting that his first name was actually Alejandro.

After several rings, the answering machine picked up. Crista started to leave a message when she heard another voice on the line. *"Hola. Residence de la Del Rio."* Elena Reyes. Crista wondered if she only answered the phone when she knew the other person spoke Spanish.

Crista asked for Alex, but learned he wasn't home and that she should call his office. Odd. He'd seemed such a doting father, she'd expected he'd spend every minute with his little girl while she recuperated.

Finally connecting with Alex at his office, he immediately asked, "What were you doing at the hospital?"

Crista's nerves tensed. "My job. I was asking the doctor about your daughter's health. Samantha awakened while I was there and we spoke for a minute."

The line was silent for too long. "Are you there?"

"Yes," he said. "Did you question her? Did you mention the shooting?"

"Of course not."

Another silence.

"I wasn't interrogating her if that's what you're thinking. Parental permission is required to interview a child. And even if I could do it without consent, I don't interrogate children. I talk with them."

Del Rio was quiet. Then he cleared his throat and said in a softer voice, "I apologize. I shouldn't have jumped to conclusions."

She took a deep calming breath herself. "If my daughter had been injured, I'm sure I'd feel the same way."

"Please accept my apology."

The man's manners were impeccable. "Apology accepted."

"Any new leads yet?"

"No. But I'm working on it." Then, since she had him on the line, she said, "I'd like to come to your office and go over some of your files."

"What files?"

"I understand you've done a lot of research on the local gangs and have statistics that might be helpful." When he hesitated, she added, "It's public information, right?"

"Yes. Most of it. But I'll have to call you back after I check my schedule. I probably won't be able to do it until Thursday or Friday since Samantha is coming home tomorrow."

"That's wonderful. I'm happy she's doing so well. Instead of bothering you and waiting till Thursday or Friday, perhaps there's someone else in your office who can help me?" Which might actually be better because she had the feeling he would censor what she was allowed to see. Or he'd be watching over her shoulder the whole time. Legally, she didn't have to wait for an appointment at all.

"No, it's best if I'm there. No one knows the program like I do and wouldn't be as much help. I'll be in touch."

He was a man who liked control and he wasn't about to relinquish it. "Fine, I'll wait to hear from you. Thanks for your time." And if he didn't come through, she'd do whatever she needed to get the information.

Hanging up the phone, she saw Captain Englend towering over her.

"Any new developments?"

"No, but you'll be the first to know when there are, Captain." She hoped he didn't hear the edge in her voice. She really had to learn to temper her words.

The captain sauntered off toward the briefing room and one-by-one, the rest of the team filtered inside. When it was time, she went in. Pete hadn't arrived yet.

"Santiago, where's your partner?" Englend bellowed, as if she had some kind of inside track on the man.

She shrugged. "I don't know. Maybe Sharon is having the baby?"

Hanover piped up, "He's taking the week off when

that happens, so I think the captain would know if that was the case. You're his partner, Santiago, how come you don't know where he is?"

Clyde was always getting on her case, trying to make her look bad, and one of these days she was going to get on his. "Because he doesn't call his partner whenever he has a hangnail, Hanover. Not like some people."

The guy couldn't function without calling his partner and it seemed he couldn't take a pee without telling the captain first. She hadn't been in the unit very long, but enough to know which cops she'd want covering her back. Hanover wasn't one of them.

"Okay, Detective Santiago. Give us the rundown on the callout in Encanto."

She'd just told Englend she had nothing, why was he asking again? She cleared her throat. "I had a lead," she said. It wasn't a blatant lie. Diego was as good a lead as any other she had at the moment. "But it didn't go down the way I wanted it to. I'm doing more interviews in the neighborhood today and meeting with the vic's father tomorrow."

"Any suspects?"

"Nothing concrete."

"Do we like anyone for the job?"

"The M.O. is consistent with the Pistoles initiation rites."

The captain's mouth formed into something between a sneer and a grimace. "Hell, it's the M.O. for every gang initiation."

Laughter scattered throughout the room.

"True," she said, feeling the heat rise in her cheeks. "CSU has some evidence that it may be the Pistoles." She'd checked with the Crime Scene Investigation Unit earlier and learned they'd picked up gang markings at the scene of the first shooting. But she was still waiting on ballistic evidence to see if the bullets from both crime scenes matched.

The captain stared at her. "You have evidence?"

"The shooter marked the first scene with the gang's colors. Beads. CSU has that on file." The Pistoles were the only local gang she knew that wore gang beads. Her brother had worn them way back when. Marco, too.

"Any names?"

"No. Not yet."

"And how do you know no other gangs use the same markings?"

"I'm getting closure on that tomorrow." That's the information she needed from Del Rio. Apparently he had a large database on gang activity in the various Houston barrios and whether he liked it or not, he was going to give it to her. If he wanted to withhold information, she'd get a subpoena. And if he still refused, he could be arrested for obstructing justice.

The captain frowned. "You file a report?"

"Of course."

"The mayor expects action within the week. If you don't think you can handle that, let me know now."

She squared her shoulders. "I can handle it."

Ignoring her answer, Englend called on Hanover to give a status report on a domestic homicide in the Idylwood neighborhood. She barely heard the report. All she could think of was that she couldn't pull evidence out of thin air.

And her job would be toast if she didn't.

CHAPTER FOUR

"THERE'S A DETECTIVE SANTIAGO here to see you, Mr. Del Rio," Alex's administrative assistant said over the intercom.

Four days since the detective's phone call, and each day he'd been more antsy, checking the calendar, making sure he hadn't gotten the date or time wrong. He realized then that he was actually looking forward to her visit.

While Crista Santiago was like none of the women he'd ever been attracted to, he was strangely intrigued by her. He'd never been with a woman who seemed to have such a firm sense of self. Never been attracted to a woman who had a man's job.

It was hard for him to think of a petite woman like her arresting criminals and putting her life on the line. He'd been brought up to believe women should be revered, taken care of. "Thanks, Adele. Send her in."

Adele, an upbeat, robust woman who reminded him of his mother, directed the detective into the room. Crista Santiago smiled courteously and extended a hand. "Thank you for making time to see me, Mr. Del Rio. Although I'm sorry to say again that we have no new leads."

He knew that. He'd called the police department to ask if they were getting any closer to finding the criminals who shot his daughter. He also knew that whoever the shooter was, he probably hadn't planned on hitting anyone. Random drive-bys were usually gang initiations, scare tactics to warn rival gangs, or a way to claim new turf. Planned hits usually took out gang members in home territory.

He reached out and shook her hand, appreciating how it fit perfectly in his. She wore dark pants and a jacket similar to what she'd worn before, but for some reason she looked different. Her blouse was unbuttoned at the collar exposing the smooth arch of her neck. "Alex. You promised to call me Alex. Remember?"

"Yes...yes, I remember...Alex." She drew her hand back.

"Do you mind if I call you Crista? I hate being so formal."

Surprise glinted in her brown eyes, but she shrugged and said, "Sure. Call me whatever you like."

He could tell by the way her shoulders stiffened that she didn't like him getting that friendly. He judged that she chose not to be disagreeable because she wanted something from him. He motioned for her to sit. "Please, make yourself comfortable." When she hesitated, he said, "If you tell me what it is you're looking for, I'll know how this office can best assist you. You mentioned statistics."

"Yes, that's one of the reasons I'm here."

He saw her glance at the chairs before sitting. They were ratty, the seat fabric an ugly gray and the metal arms scratched and dented. No one could accuse him of spending too much money on office decor. And since the task force had been forced on the mayor's office by the community, he wasn't going to kid himself that there would be money for anything new soon. "One of these days we'll get some new furniture," he said, then sat in the chair next to her rather than behind the desk.

Glancing about the room, she said, "It always amazes me how top government offices look like an interior designer was at work and the rest as if they'd scrounged the local garage sales."

Alex shrugged. "It's a workplace. It doesn't need to be fancy. I have my comforts when I go home."

Her eyes caught his. "Yes, quite nice comforts at that."

"Thank you," he said, not sure if she was being complimentary or if she thought it was inappropriate for a government employee to own such a large house.

"How is Samantha? Is she at home now?"

He smiled. "Yes, she is. She's amazing. She wants to go back to preschool right away, but I told her it wasn't going to happen until next week at the earliest."

"Children bounce back so easily, don't they?" She seemed sincerely interested, not just asking to be polite.

"Yes. I'm happy about that. She's been through a lot in the past couple years. But…you're not here to talk about my family."

She reached down, pulled a legal pad and pen from a briefcase and then leaned back in her chair. "I hear you have demographics and other more detailed information on the local gangs."

He nodded. "Yes. A lot of that information is available to the police already, and to the public on the department's Web site."

"I know. I checked. But what I want are specifics on the local gangs: names, colors, symbols, that kind of thing. Most of the stuff online is general to all gangs."

"I thought the police received some kind of special training in this area."

"They do. At the academy. But for me, that was over six years ago. I was supposed to get a refresher course when I joined the Chicano Squad, but there wasn't anything in place." She gave him a wan smile. "So I'm counting on your office to get the information I need."

"The Chicano Squad? That sounds ominous."

She laughed, a sound that was pure and natural. Infectious.

"Ominous it isn't. The unit consists of officers and detectives who have experience with the Hispanic culture and speak the language." She thought for a second, then said, "That's not entirely true. Some just speak the language, and not very well at that."

"I see. And where did you get your experience? Locally or elsewhere?"

"My grandparents came from Mexico, but I grew up here. Which I guess makes me as familiar with the culture as anyone."

Interesting. "You don't sound as if you were raised here. No Texas drawl or Latino."

A smile crossed her face. "I had a good English teacher."

"Well, whether you were raised here or not, I'm still surprised they'd give a woman this kind of duty."

The look on her face could've wilted Elena's entire rose garden.

"What surprises you? Do you think there's a difference between a man's ability to do the job and a woman's?"

Major faux pas. "No, not at all. I'm surprised because I'm aware how dangerous this investigation could be since it's more than likely gang-related."

"Uh-huh."

She wasn't buying his revised explanation.

"The job *is* dangerous sometimes," she elaborated. "But it's dangerous for all officers. Not just the women. And danger isn't confined to particular neighborhoods, either."

He hadn't explained himself very well, and he wasn't sure he could. "Doesn't your family worry about you?"

"I…I have no close family."

In his large family everyone was concerned about one another. Too concerned sometimes. He couldn't imagine what it would be like to have no one. "Everyone has someone who cares—and who worries."

Her shoulders stiffened, but she didn't answer him.

"It must be hell for the families of police officers. I can't imagine not knowing if a spouse was going to make it home each day."

"Lots of cops are married and it works out just fine. Yes, family members worry, but they usually know from the beginning what they're in for." She cleared her throat. "Since I'm not married, it's not something I think about."

"I see. If you don't get married, no one will worry."

Her mouth tightened and he could tell she didn't appreciate the comment. More points deducted.

"I'm not married because I haven't found a man I'd want to marry. And now that we've covered my personal life, I'd really like to see the statistics. Please."

He couldn't help grinning. He wanted to know more about her personal life. Just talking to her sent a jolt of energy through him that he hadn't felt since Marissa. But what he'd said was true. He couldn't imagine being married to someone whose life was in danger every

time she went out the door to work. "Sure. I've put together some things that might help." He got up and
gathered the data, which listed everything about the
local gangs. At least everything it was possible to find
out.

"Most local Hispanic gangs are aligned with the national umbrella nations La Gran Raza and La Gran Fa-
milia, but there are several renegade gangs. Hermanos
de la Frontera, aka the Border Brothers, for one. It's
mostly made up of illegal immigrants."

"I thought the umbrellas were mostly on the east
coast?"

He shook his head. "In Houston, street gangs are the
most prominent, but several organized crime and
prison gangs have taken root. The Syndicato Tejano,
the Texas Syndicate, is one of the most dangerous."

"What about the Mexican Mafia?"

He nodded. "The kids I'm trying hardest to reach are
still considering whether to join a gang or not. If I can
reach them early enough, I might be able to do some
good. My recruits so far are mostly taggers or the
younger members of street gangs. They're not hardened criminals."

"Yet."

He raised an eyebrow. "A little cynical are we?"

"Realistic."

"Then you should know how dangerous dealing with
long-time gang members can be. Most crimes are directed toward their own community, but Mexican gangs
view law enforcement as their enemy. Because many
have been victimized by the police in their own country."

"I know all that. What I'd like are specific details
that will help me decide how to go about getting the
evidence I need."

They spent the rest of the afternoon going through the files, Alex answering question after question. Exactly how many gangs are there in Houston? Which are the most violent? Did he know how many members were in each gang and their colors and signs? Who are the leaders? Mostly she asked about the Pistoles. "You ever hear of a gangster named Marco Torres in connection with the Pistoles?"

He shook his head. "You think he's responsible?"

"Not necessarily, but there are indicators pointing to the Pistoles." She drew her gaze from him. "Even so, if we can't pinpoint the crime to a specific person, we don't have a case."

"So how are you going to get that information?"

She shoved the papers on the desk away from her and leaned back in the chair. It had been a long afternoon and he could see the strain around her eyes. Eyes, the color of a smooth, expensive cognac. Oddly, he wanted to comfort her, take her in his arms and tell her everything would be okay. Which made no sense at all since she was a cop and she should be hardened to the kinds of things cops see every day.

But he didn't get the feeling that she was hardened at all. And sitting next to her he could smell clean, fresh soap…and another softer scent, too subtle to be perfume. Whether a perfume or not, it was driving him crazy.

"I don't know. I'll just keep digging and asking questions. Sooner or later someone will offer some small piece of information that will lead to another piece of evidence and another. Before you know it the case will be solved."

"Is that wishful thinking?" The success rate on solving this type of crime was low, and his gut knotted every time he thought of it. Someone needed to pay for hurting his daughter.

She exhaled. "Wishful thinking? Maybe. Right now I've got nothing. And time is running out."

That was a strange thing for her to say. "How does time run out? Either you solve it or you don't."

His comment produced a smile from Crista. "Right. Either I solve it or I don't."

She bent to pick up her briefcase, placed her notebook inside and looked directly at him. "This is probably not the time to mention this, but I will need to talk with Samantha about that night."

His protective instincts kicked in again. "That's not a good idea." He shook his head to emphasize the point. "I've asked her several times if she saw anything and she always says no. She doesn't remember what happened. She felt something hurt her and then there was blood. Right now all she knows is that she had an accident and an operation. I want to find out who did this more than anyone, but I don't want to subject Sam to questions that could traumatize or scare her."

Crista nodded. "Like I said, this might not be the right time to talk about it."

He let out a breath.

"In the meantime, I have something I'd like to give her."

He couldn't imagine what she wanted to give Sam, but didn't think it was a good idea, either. "I'll give it to her for you."

She paused briefly, then said, "Okay. It's in my car. I'll be right back."

Returning a few minutes later, she handed him a large plastic bag with paw prints on it.

"I know some things mean a lot to a child," she said.

He opened the top of the bag and peered inside. What he saw caught him off guard. He tried to say something but no words came out.

"I don't believe Samantha is going to get hers back, so I thought this little guy might be a good replacement. I used to have one just like it when I was a kid."

Alex handed the bag back to her. Finding his voice, he said, "I was wrong. I think this is something you better give to Sam yourself."

CRISTA PULLED into Alex's driveway, her pulse racing. Why she was nervous, she didn't know. No, that was a lie. Sitting with Alex all afternoon yesterday had unnerved her, and she was well aware of the reason. He was a sexy, attractive man—and she'd been attracted. No big secret there.

But that kind of attraction was all wrong.

First off, the department frowned on officers getting involved with anyone related to a case. She frowned on it herself. Business was business and she'd always kept it that way. And secondly, even if it wasn't a problem with the department, Alex Del Rio was exactly the type of man she'd vowed never to get involved with again.

For years she'd been off men altogether, and when she'd finally started dating again, she was very particular about the guys she dated. Number one on the top of her "no, thank you," list was the macho man. Which pretty much translated into, *no Latinos*.

And now she found herself attracted to Alex. Hadn't she learned anything from the past?

But Alex had only invited her over to give the stuffed animal to Sam. That was it. Even though he'd made the point that there would be no conversation about the night of the shooting, he'd insisted that she give Sam the gift herself.

So here she was, gift in hand, her nerves tingling and her heart thumping wildly. She bit her bottom lip. What was wrong with her? All she had to do was go in, give the gift to Samantha and leave. Simple as that.

She exited the Jeep, grabbed the bag from the back seat and locked the door. Taking a big breath, she climbed the steps and rang the bell. Two seconds later, the massive door swung open.

"Hi," Alex greeted her with a wide welcoming smile. "C'mon in."

He had a great smile. "Thanks." As she stepped into the foyer, Alex motioned to take her coat. Shrugging off her leather jacket, her arm got stuck in the lining of the sleeve. She shook it, struggling to get the jacket off.

"Here, let me help."

Alex moved in close and her heartbeat accelerated. His masculine scent made her stomach do a little flip. Within a second he had her out of the coat and hung it up. Placing a hand on her back, he directed her inside.

Embarrassed by her reaction to him, she concentrated on the rich scent of pastries and homemade bread that permeated the air. "Umm. Whatever you're cooking smells wonderful."

"Elena's making something for Thanksgiving."

"Almond. I smell almond. My grandmother used to make almond cookies before every holiday. And she always started baking two weeks in advance." Just thinking about it made Crista relax.

"Used to make?"

"She's been gone since I was ten." Crista had wonderful memories of her *abuela*. Memories that had dimmed with the years in between, but Elena's cooking brought it back in a flash.

"I know what you mean. My mother is a great cook, and I'm always reminded of it when Elena makes something similar."

"Where's Samantha?" Crista asked.

"Upstairs. When she found out you were coming, she got too excited, so I told her she needed to rest."

"Is she okay?"

He nodded. "You must've made quite an impression."

"I only saw her for a minute, but she told me she wanted to see Snuffy and described him for me. It was the strangest thing because I'd had the same stuffed animal when I was a child."

"Ah." He nodded. "That's why she took to you so quickly." He pointed to the bag. "That isn't your old one is it?"

Crista shook her head and laughed. "Heavens, no. Right about the time my grandmother moved out, *my* Snuffy went missing." Which was right about the time her stepfather moved in. "Funny how we bookmark events in our lives, isn't it."

"Yeah. But life goes on. Right?" His tone was wistful despite the upbeat words. She'd bet he had bookmarks of his own. The death of his wife for one.

"Let's get some cookies and milk to take up to Sam."

Crista followed Alex toward the kitchen through the formal living room off the foyer. On the other side, it opened into a family room filled with comfortable-looking furniture in dark woods and leather. A long espresso-colored sectional curved around one end of the room in perfect placement to view both a brick fireplace with bookshelves on each side and a big-screen television that dominated the wall on the left. "Sam calls this the movie room," he said, continuing through another wide archway into the kitchen.

"I can see why. Does she watch a lot of shows?"

"Not much TV. I try to get her to watch *Dora the Explorer*, but she'd rather watch Disney cartoons."

"Dora? I've never heard of it."

"It's about a little girl of Latino heritage, and the message of the show is that people should be proud of who they are."

"Oh."

"Sam is going through the *I want to be like all the rest of the kids in school* thing, so I thought the show would be good for her."

Crista knew how Sam felt. She'd always wanted to belong. Never felt she did.

"Other than that, we do watch our share of movies." He gave a low chuckle. "But if you ask me, I think Sam likes the popcorn even more than what's on the screen."

Alex was a devout father, that was obvious. "I'll bet she likes watching movies with her dad. Sharing the time together."

As they walked into the kitchen, he gave her a quizzical look, then a small grin. "I never thought of that, but I like the idea."

Elena was busy at the counter and didn't hear them enter. One by one, the older woman placed fresh, hot-from-the-oven fruit turnovers onto the counter to cool. Crista's mouth watered. *Empanadas de fruta.* Her grandmother used to make those, too.

"Elena, look who's here," Alex said in Spanish.

Elena turned to them and smiled brightly. *"Bienvenido a nuestro hogar."*

Welcome to our home. Crista felt a genuine warmth

in the woman's words—a warmth she hadn't felt when she'd been at the house the first time. Apparently Alex's mother-in-law viewed this visit differently than when Crista had come to interview them after the accident. *"Mucho gracias,"* Crista responded. "It's my pleasure."

Her earlier meetings with Alex had been more formal, though he'd lightened up a little when she was at his office. Now he seemed totally relaxed, which in turn made her more comfortable.

She reminded herself that it was okay to be here. She was here to give Samantha a gift. That was all. Really.

Alex turned to the refrigerator, a wide, stainless steel double-door job, and pulled out a gallon of milk. Elena handed him a glass and then gave Crista a plate of almond cookies.

Waiting for Alex to pour, Crista glanced around the room, noticing rich maple cabinets that matched the round table in the breakfast nook where, from the bank of windows she could see a large well-manicured yard and garden. Dark, earth-toned granite topped the center island and the counters lining three sides of the room. Everything coordinated perfectly with honey cabinets and the adobe-tiled floor. A far cry from what she'd grown up with. Hell, it was a far cry from what she ever expected she'd have.

"Okay," Alex said after putting the milk back in the refrigerator. "We're all set."

"I'll follow you," Crista said.

Alex headed for the stairs with Crista behind, and with every step, she felt Elena's assessing gaze on her back. She wondered what the woman thought of her visit. She seemed friendly enough, but her daughter *had* been married to Alex....

Upstairs, Alex stopped in front of Sam's open door.

"I thought she might want to sleep in one of the other bedrooms," Alex explained softly to Crista. "I was wrong." He motioned for Crista to go in first, but she deferred to him.

"Daddy, daddy! See what I did." Sam held up a piece of paper, a drawing with some stick people on it. "I drew you and me."

"And what a fantastic picture it is." Practically in the same breath, he said, "Look who's here. You remember Ms. Santiago, the lady at the hospital."

"Crista." Samantha beamed.

Crista saw the surprise on Alex's face. "I told her to call me Crista at the hospital," she said quickly. Alex, she could tell, was obviously from the old school—the type who would object to his child calling an adult by her first name. "I don't like being formal, either."

"Then you hafta call me Sam," the little girl said to Crista. "Not Samantha."

Alex didn't voice his opinion on the matter, but set the milk on the side table and pulled a chair to the bedside. "Go ahead," he said, indicating for Crista to take the chair. She set the cookie tray next to the milk and did as he asked. He sat on the end of the bed.

Crista leaned forward, closer to the child. "So how are you feeling?"

"I'm all better now, but my dad won't let me play and he won't let me go back to school till way next week."

"Well, dads usually know best, don't they."

The child nodded reluctantly, even though she looked as if she'd wanted Crista to side with her. "I guess so. But I still want to play."

"Maybe this will help." Crista opened the bag and pulled out the stuffed animal.

Sam's mouth dropped open. "Snuffy!" she squealed. "You got Snuffy back, and he's all clean."

Oh, dear. Crista wasn't sure what to say. Let the child think it's the same animal or tell her she bought it online and had it express-mailed to her home. She glanced at Alex for help.

He shrugged as if he didn't know what to tell her, either.

"Oh, I know," Sam said. "He had to take a bath cuz he had blood on him from the accident." She examined the animal from head to toe. "But he'll probably get all dirty again. Rabbits don't know any better."

Crista smiled. "Kinda like little girls and boys, huh?"

"Do you have any little girls or boys?"

"No…" Crista answered, surprised. "But if I did, I'd want them to be just like you."

Sam frowned. "I don't have a mommy anymore because she's in heaven. Maybe you can marry my daddy and then you'd have a little girl just like you want. And I'd have a mommy."

Crista heard a strangled cough from Alex's direction.

"Uh…why don't you have some cookies, Sam," Alex mumbled. "Better yet, let's all have some cookies." He held the tray while both Sam and Crista decided which one to take, and then he took one of his own.

"Umm. Good," Crista said, relieved that Alex had changed the subject. Some things were better left to the imagination—things like being Samantha's mommy. Like being any child's mommy. Once upon a time she used to fantasize about being happily married and having a large loving family. She'd never dreamed what was in store when she'd married Trini. Now, her days of dreaming were over.

She knew what being married to a police officer was like, had witnessed the horrors more than once.

Alex had been partially right when he'd assumed that Crista's job had something to do with her marital status. But it wasn't the only reason.

None of her reasons seemed important as she watched Alex with his loving family. Seeing their closeness made her aware of what she was missing.

Risa, Lucy, Abby, Mei Lu and Catherine used to fill that void. For the past six years, the friends had always spent some part of the holidays together. But not this year. This year she'd be alone.

"Okay," Alex said. "Time for this little girl to go to sleep."

"Yes. It's getting late and I have to go home and take care of Calvin."

"Who's Calvin?" Alex and Sam asked in unison.

"Calvin Klein. He's a parrot I rescued from an abandoned house. He's red and yellow and blue, and he repeats whatever you say to him."

"I like parrots," Sam said. "I like all animals. I want to get a puppy, but Daddy says not until I'm old enough to take care of one."

"It sounds like your daddy has some good ideas, because pets do take a lot of care."

"Does Calvin?"

"He sure does." More than she'd ever imagined. "Calvin is a Scarlet Macaw, a special kind of parrot."

"Can I see him sometime? I really, really like birds."

Crista glanced at Alex. She didn't have the heart to refuse the child. When Alex didn't object, Crista said, "Maybe. But first you need to get better."

Sam yawned. "Snuffy can help me get better." She hugged the stuffed animal in a vise grip against her chest.

Crista started to get up when Alex placed a hand on her shoulder and then said to Sam, "Aren't you forgetting something?"

The little girl looked down, as if embarrassed. "Thank you very much for bringing Snuffy back." And then she reached out her arms to Crista for a hug.

Crista's chest tightened as she leaned in and hugged Sam, hopefully not too tightly. Closing her eyes, Crista inhaled the sweet little-girl scent of bubble bath and freshly washed hair. She felt the tightness move to her throat and she wanted to hold the child indefinitely. After a moment, Crista gently pulled away. "You're very welcome," she said, her voice a whisper.

As Crista stood to leave, she felt Alex's warm hand on her arm.

"I'll walk you to the door," he said.

Crista waved at Samantha. "Get better, little one."

ALEX WAS IMPRESSED with Crista's ease with Sam. The woman had a quiet confidence about her, and he'd been both surprised and pleased when she'd supported his decision to not mention the accident to Sam. She seemed a very different woman tonight than the one he'd met the other day—and he wanted to know this woman better. Much better.

The realization caught him off guard. He hadn't had thoughts about getting to know any woman since Marissa died. He'd put all his energy into making sure Sam was safe and happy.

When he and Crista reached the door, he opened it and stepped outside with her.

"You have a wonderful daughter," Crista said.

"Thank you. I think so, too." He didn't want her to leave quite yet, so he added, "She really likes you."

"I'm sorry that I didn't know how to answer her when she asked to meet Calvin, but I suppose she'll forget about it as soon as I'm gone anyway."

"Oh, no, she won't. She remembers everything, and she's going to bug me about it."

"That's not good, is it. I'd hate to disappoint her. Maybe you can explain."

He pulled the door shut behind him. "Explain what?"

"It was an inappropriate suggestion on my part, and I imagine you don't want her going anywhere for a while."

"Not for a while. But when she's feeling better, I think she'd love to meet Calvin. If it's no trouble for you, of course."

"Uh, no. It's no trouble. And Calvin does love attention. Just let me know when she's feeling better and we can arrange something…when I have some spare time."

"So what does an unmarried detective do in her spare time?"

Crista did a double take, but she recovered quickly. "Actually, I don't have much spare time, and when I do, I go to the gym. I'm working toward a Masters level in Wing Chun Kung Fu."

"I'm impressed. I've done a little martial arts training myself, but I'm not familiar with that form of Kung Fu. Maybe you could give me a lesson or two?"

She laughed. "It isn't a casual sport. It requires dedication of both mind and body. You wouldn't learn anything unless you get the head stuff down first."

He thought he saw a glint in her eyes. Then she said, "Besides, I wouldn't want to hurt you."

At that moment, Alex could think of nothing he'd like better than getting physical with Crista Santiago. "Uh…I don't think that's a problem."

The problem was the direction his thoughts were taking. If she knew, she'd probably think he was a macho guy with nothing on the brain but sex. And at the moment…she'd be right.

"How did you get interested in such a demanding sport?" he asked, changing the subject before his body gave him away.

She backed up, one foot reaching for the step below, as if she suddenly wanted to get the hell out of here. He'd thought it a benign question, but he'd made her anxious. Maybe he was getting too personal? He couldn't help himself. He wanted to find out as much as he could about this woman before she left.

"It's not a very interesting story," she said and then turned and headed for an old red Jeep parked in the drive.

He walked alongside, his strides longer than hers. Reaching the vehicle first, he leaned against the door. "So tell me anyway. I want to know."

She gave an exasperated sigh. "I wanted to be able to defend myself. That's it. No big deal."

No big deal, Alex said to himself as he watched her drive away. Except that her reaction to the question indicated just the opposite.

CHAPTER FIVE

"*MAYBE YOU CAN BE my mommy and then you'd have a little girl just like you want.*"

Driving home, Samantha's words played over and over in Crista's head. Yes, she'd like more than anything to have a little girl just like Samantha, and if her baby had lived, she would have. There was a time when she'd longed to be a mother, and though it wasn't in the forefront of her mind anymore, many nights she still felt the need. Or was it the void she felt?

It was easy to imagine being part of Alex's welcoming family, a family where everyone seemed to care more about one another than anything else. It was easy to imagine herself married to Alex.

And wasn't that a ridiculous concept? He was interested in her, she could tell. But he'd already said he couldn't fathom being married to a cop, so his interest had to be purely physical.

Even if she'd had a sudden change of heart regarding marriage, which she didn't, Alex Del Rio was the total opposite of any man she'd even consider. He loved his community and wanted to stay there. She'd spent the past fourteen years building a new life for herself—away from the Hispanic community. A life that wasn't constrained by her gender or her heritage. She valued her hard-won independence too much to even consider a relationship with a man like Alex.

So why couldn't she get him out of her mind? Why couldn't she stop thinking about being intimate with him?

Okay. It didn't matter what her hormones were telling her, she wasn't going to get involved with Alex Del Rio and that was that. She had a case to solve and it wasn't going to get done if she was mooning over some guy like a love-struck teenager.

SITTING AT her desk two days later, Crista punched information on the Encanto case into NCIC to determine if any other local cases had a similar M.O. When the data hit the screen, she was surprised to see Diego's name come up.

But of course it would. Diego had been a member of the Pistoles and drive-by shootings were part of the gang's initiation rites. Diego had been picked up as a suspect in one of the crimes, but he'd beaten the rap because there was no evidence he was the shooter. The police had bullets, but no gun, which meant no evidence to trace the crime to Diego—or anyone. Which was the case with both crimes she was working on. Bullets but no gun. Hell, it was the same with most drive-bys.

A few years later, her brother hadn't been as lucky when he was caught breaking and entering a jewelry store. A man had died, and even though Diego hadn't wielded the gun, he'd gotten ten years anyway.

"What's going down?" Pete's voice came to her as if in a fog.

"Not much," she answered and quickly closed the computer file. No one in her office knew she had a brother, and she didn't feel the need to inform them. Personal information in the employee files was confidential and it wasn't likely anyone would make the connection even if they came across Diego's file in the course of an investigation because she'd taken a different family name after she escaped her marriage. She wasn't ashamed of Diego, but she had enough strikes against her within the department. Her past could easily cloud any major issues that might arise.

"What's up with you?" she asked Pete, knowing exactly what was up. His wife was having a baby and he couldn't think of anything else.

"Sharon is in labor. She's having pains. Real ones."

From the beaming smile on his face, Crista determined that was a good thing. "So it's really going to happen, huh?" She grinned at Pete, his happiness making her happy. They'd only been together a short time, but had formed a close bond.

"I wanted you to be the first to know."

"Thanks, I appreciate that." She wanted to give Pete a hug, but knew the razzing they'd both get if she did. "You taking vacation now?"

"Yeah. And I better get the heck out of here."

"Right. Give my love to Sharon and be sure to let me know right away if it's a boy or a girl."

Pete was practically out the door before she finished her sentence. Crista couldn't blame him. Having a baby had to be the most exciting moment in a person's life.

Crista turned back to the case. The more she read, the more she was reminded that she had to talk to Diego again—see how he was doing. Even if he didn't want her help. She'd been disappointed to see Marco at Diego's and she'd been horrified to run into Trini. She hated the thought of going to the house again.

Just then it occurred to her that if anyone knew what was going on, it was Marco. Maybe he wouldn't willingly offer information, but sometimes people gave things away without realizing it. Hell, she wouldn't know unless she tried.

She flipped through the database again. Marco had a record and it was easy to find his address and phone number, which she immediately punched in. If she could set up a meeting…

"Ese," a gruff voice answered.

"Marco?"

"¿Quién quiere saber?"

She wanted to know, that's who. "It's Detective Santiago." When there was a silence on the line, she added, "Crista. Diego's sister."

"¿Cómo estás?" he asked cheerily, almost as if he was happy to hear from her.

She knew different. He'd never be happy to hear from the police.

"I'm fine," she responded.

"You want to talk to Diego?"

"Uh…is he there?" She hadn't expected her brother to be there. She wanted to talk to Marco.

In the background she heard Marco say, "Your sister is on the phone." The next voice she heard was Diego's. "You tracking me down?"

"No. I had no idea you were there. I was calling to talk to Marco, but as long as I have you on the ph—"

"I can't talk now."

His voice was muffled, as if he'd cupped a hand over the receiver.

"I'll call you later tonight," he said.

That was a switch. "What time? I planned to go to the gym, but if it's important…"

"It's important." He hung up. No goodbye, nothing.

Just as she replaced the receiver, the phone rang again. She picked it up.

"Will you please come into my office," the captain's voice boomed into her ear.

She glanced up to see Englend sitting at his desk staring directly at her. "Sure. Be right there."

She'd barely stepped inside the room when he asked, "Where are you on the case?"

"I have a couple good leads in the Paloverde barrio."

The captain picked up a form from his desk, glanced at it and leaned against the back of his chair. "I can get you a replacement for Pete while he's gone."

Crista's stomach knotted. "Pete's only going to be gone for a week. It would take that long to get someone up to speed."

Englend frowned. "Maybe you'll do better with another partner."

The back of Crista's neck prickled. "Do better? In what way?"

"Maybe you'll get some results on the Encanto case."

"I'm getting results."

"We need a suspect."

"I'm working on it."

"Make it fast or you're off the case."

CRISTA SHOVED another batch of cookies into the oven and turned on the timer. Baking was good therapy. Baking and going to the gym. And she'd already worked out early so she'd be at her apartment for Diego's call.

She glanced at the clock again. It was already 8:00 p.m. He'd said it was important, but apparently not enough to call early.

The timer dinged and just as she went to the oven to remove the cookies, the phone rang. She answered and said, "Hold on for a sec." She rushed to take the cookie sheet out of the oven and then went back to the phone. "Sorry about that. I was in the middle of something."

"No problem."

The deep, smooth voice wasn't Diego's, but she recognized it instantly. Her stomach clenched way down low. "Alex."

"Yes. Sorry if I interrupted you."

"What's wrong?"

"Nothing is wrong. But I have something I think you should see."

"Is it about the case? I can stop by tomorrow whenever you like."

"Can we meet somewhere tonight?"

If she left, she'd miss Diego's call. "I'm sorry, I can't leave right now." What was so important it couldn't wait?

"How about if I come there?"

The request took her off guard. But if he had information about the case…and if he felt that strongly about it…

"It's about Samantha."

Samantha? A jolt of fear shot through her. "Has something happened—"

"No. Nothing has happened. But I really need to talk to you about her and I have something to show you."

Relieved to hear Sam was okay, she gave him her address. After they'd said goodbye, she wondered if she'd done the right thing. While she needed all the information she could get on the case, she knew her feelings for Alex weren't all business, and inviting him to her apartment wasn't the wisest decision in the world.

Crista had finished two batches of cookies before she heard the knock at the door. She wiped her hands on a kitchen towel and then hurried to answer, smoothing the front of her T-shirt on the way. Peeking through the security hole to make sure it was Alex, she slid off the chain and opened the door. "Hi. C'mon in."

His eyes traveled over her, his expression approving.

"I'm really sorry about barging in like this."

She stepped back and he came inside. "You're not interrupting. I'm finished what I was doing, but I'm waiting for a phone call and couldn't leave."

He sucked in a breath. "Whatever you're making smells great."

Crista grinned. "Your mother-in-law inspired me to do a little baking for the holidays."

He glanced around, apparently searching for a place to sit. Her apartment was so small the whole thing would probably fit in his living room. Well, it might not be fancy, but it served her purposes for now and allowed her to save part of her paycheck for the down payment on a house.

"Here, let me take your jacket."

He reached into a pocket and pulled out a rolled-up paper. Shrugging off his jacket, he handed it to her before sitting on the brown frizee couch she'd picked up a few years ago at a garage sale. She sat on the chair opposite him, another find that some of her friends actually thought was pretty cool—1950s modern, Catherine had said. To Crista, it was the pumpkin chair. Round and orange. She'd always meant to recover it, but good intentions didn't make it happen.

"You look different," he said.

She glanced at her clothes. "I suppose I do. I don't usually wear jeans on the job." Or a T-shirt that said Juicy across her boobs. She waved a hand over her shirt. "It's a designer name. One of my friends gave it to me as a birthday present. A joke."

He grinned. "The clothes *are* different. But I think it's the hair."

She raised a hand to touch her hair. "It's…better to wear it up for work. Not as dangerous."

"Dangerous?"

"If I got into a physical altercation with a suspect and my hair was down, that person would have an advantage."

And this would be where he'd take the opportunity to give her his opinion on the dangers of women in law enforcement again. Crista braced herself. But, surprisingly, he didn't. Instead, he said, "You have nice hair. I like it better this way."

She shifted in the pumpkin chair. It felt good to get a compliment even though it embarrassed her a little. "Thank you," she said. "What did you want to show me?"

He handed her the rolled paper, his expression immediately sober.

Crista smoothed out the paper on her lap, then smiled. It was a crayon drawing, and on the bottom, scribbled letters spelled out S-A-M.

"She told me she made it for you."

"How sweet." And how sweet of him to come all the way over to give it to her in person. "It's…" she angled her head, trying to decipher the child's artwork. He motioned for her to sit next to him. Though hesitant, she went over and sat, holding out the picture so he could explain. The drawing consisted of two stick people on top of a black box, which was next to another pink box with a roof on top. A house maybe.

His arm brushed against hers as he pointed to the stick people. "What do you think?"

Think? She couldn't think of anything except the searing heat she felt where his arm had touched hers. She was acutely aware of his sexuality. "I'm sorry, I'm really bad at this. Is that supposed to be you and Sam?"

"Sam told me that's a car, and these two—" he waved his hand over the stick figures "—are the people inside."

Crista's nerves pinched. "And the line there?" She pointed to something coming from one of the stick figures' hands.

"Sam's exact words when I asked the same thing were, 'I don't know, but that's when I got blood all over Snuffy.'"

Crista's stomach dropped like an anvil. The look in Alex's eyes sent an ominous shiver up her spine. *Ohmygod.*

"I think it's what she saw the night of the shooting."

The thought was so awful, Crista couldn't find any words. Had Sam actually seen the shooters?

Alex launched to his feet, his anger vibrating as he paced across the tiny living room. "What happened was bad enough, but now this…" He dropped down onto the couch next to her again, his hands on his knees. "I didn't know what to do with the picture, and when Sam said she wanted me to give it to you, I realized that she was right. I also realized she's probably more affected by the shooting than I imagined."

Crista reached out and placed her hand over his. "That's not necessarily true, Alex. I've had other cases involving child witnesses. When children don't understand what they've seen, they aren't usually affected by it. You've given her love and security. That should help in her recovery."

He looked at her hand on his and then caught her gaze. His eyes filled with appreciation. "Thank you for that," he said, then placed his other hand over hers and tightened his grip. "I hope that's the case with Sam. I had no idea she saw the whole thing. I never explained anything to her except to say she'd had an accident. I didn't want her to remember anything."

"It might help if she talked with a professional. I can give you the name of a child psychiatrist who's very good."

"Thanks. But I've already got a call in to someone. She helped us after Marissa died."

"Are you sure Sam actually saw something?"

His eyes narrowed.

"No, I don't know if she did. I was so upset, I just assumed…" His hands balled into fists. "Damn. I just want Sam to grow up happy."

"She will, Alex. She's a loving, well-adjusted child. She'll be fine."

She hoped Sam would be fine. Now it was even more urgent that she talk to the child—to find out if she actually saw the shooters and if she could identify anyone. Alex wouldn't like it, but if the child was really a witness, she could be in danger.

He stood, as if to go.

With utmost seriousness, she said, "About Samantha."

"What about her?"

"I'll need to talk with her."

Alex's eyes locked with Crista's. "I know. I knew the second I saw the picture."

"I'm sorry, Alex," Crista said, studying the picture again. "This *could* mean she witnessed the crime, and because of that—"

"I'm aware of that," he interrupted. "All too aware."

"I won't tell her anything you don't want her to know. I can work around almost anything."

He nodded again. "I trust you."

Crista felt warm inside. *I trust you.* He didn't like that she had to question his daughter, but he trusted her to do it gently.

"I trust you. *Awk. Awk.*" Calvin squawked, breaking the seriousness of the moment.

They looked at each other in shared amusement, then laughed. She'd covered Calvin's cage before Alex arrived and had thought the bird was asleep. When Alex glanced at his watch, Crista looked at hers and was amazed at how quickly the time had passed. It was ten o'clock. Her brother hadn't called yet.

Alex gave her a grateful smile and said, "I suppose I had better go."

"But first…let me give you some cookies to take home to Samantha for tomorrow." She rose to her feet.

"Sam would like that." He was smiling, but the worry lines around his mouth were still there.

"I'll be right back." At that, Crista hustled into the kitchen where Alex couldn't see her. Where he couldn't see how much he had affected her.

Inappropriate as her feelings were where Alex was concerned, she seemed to have no control. Whenever he was around, all she could think about was being with him. She dreamed about it.

"How about me?"

Alex's voice behind her made her jump like a skittish cat. She caught her breath and did a one-eighty. He was so close she almost couldn't breathe, but she managed to sound casual. "Sure. I'll put some in for Elena, too, though the Mexican wedding cookies she makes are probably much better than this. I haven't done much baking in the past couple of years."

"I have a better idea," he said. "Why don't we sit down and have some right now. Together." With that he pulled out two kitchen chairs.

She couldn't help laughing. Was this guy sure of himself or what! That kind of cocky behavior usually turned her off. But on Alex, the self-confidence seemed sincere and, strangely, made him even more appealing. "Okay. How about some coffee or cocoa with your cookies."

"How about milk," he said as he sat in one of the chairs. "I'm still a kid at heart."

Crista went to get the glasses, sensing his eyes following her every step of the way. Handing him the glasses, she said, "Okay, then you can get the milk while I put some cookies on a plate."

He launched to his feet and walked to the fridge. His backside was toward her as he poured the milk so she took the opportunity to appreciate his finer qualities. He looked different tonight, too. His hair was messier, not his usual combed-back do. In faded Levi's and a black mock-turtleneck T-shirt, he looked imposing and…a little dangerous.

She liked this new casual Alex, the way his jeans hugged his backside. Not tight, but fitted enough to show his assets. Her gaze traveled upward from his trim hips to where his shoulders broadened nicely. This was a guy who had to spend time working out. Maybe he wasn't kidding when he said he had some martial arts skills?

Just then he turned and, catching her in the act, gave her a slow, sexy, smile. He held up the glasses. "Milk's ready."

Heat burned her cheeks. She cleared her throat. "Good," she mumbled and quickly placed a half-dozen cookies on the plate, brought them to the table and sat. Alex set a glass in front of her and grabbed a cookie before his butt hit the chair. "I haven't had a good wedding cookie in a long time."

"I haven't made them for a long time, either, so you better reserve judgment."

He bit off an end and chewed slowly—very slowly—as if doing a taste test. The rest he wolfed down in one bite. "Delicious. The best I've ever had."

"Don't overdo it," she joked, then bit into a cookie herself. She had to admit, they were pretty good.

For the next hour they ate cookies and talked. Mostly they talked. Alex started to tell her more about his work, but she wanted to know more about Alex, the man. "Is the job why you left California?" she asked.

He smiled thoughtfully. "No, it wasn't. I left California to get married."

"Oh." Crista hadn't expected that answer, but wasn't sorry she asked. She didn't want to open old wounds, but she did want to know more.

"Marissa grew up in Houston. She couldn't bear to leave her home, so we stayed. Her roots were in Encanto, and now, so are mine and Sam's."

Which was why he'd said he'd never leave. There was more of a tie than just belonging to the community. He had memories. Memories of his wife. "Do you miss California?"

"Sure. At first I missed it a lot. Then Marissa got me involved with the community and everything changed."

How ironic. She'd spent her life running away from the place where she grew up, and he was more committed to it than many who'd been there all their lives.

Even though he wasn't realistic about the changes he could affect in the barrio, she admired his conviction. If anyone *could* make a difference, it would be Alex.

"So how about you?"

"Me?"

"How'd you get into law enforcement?"

Crista worried her bottom lip between her front teeth. "It's a long story."

"Okay, how about the short version?"

"It's a boring story, short or long."

"Not to me," he said in a low husky tone.

Her nerves tense, she clasped her hands tightly in her lap. "I was living in Plano and working as an administrative assistant at the local police department when a co-worker suggested that with all my martial arts training, I should try for a job as a police officer. I thought about it. And when I came home for my mother's funeral seven years ago and saw a posting for openings at the Houston P.D., I applied. I never expected to get hired."

Interest sparked in his eyes.

"I guess you'd say the martial arts training was my springboard to the job."

"And how did you get involved with martial arts in the first place? It seems an unusual hobby for a woman."

For a woman. Sometimes it was hard not to think Alex was a chauvinist.

Apparently recognizing his blunder, he quickly added, "I mean it's usually considered a guy thing."

She'd never told anyone the real reason she'd become involved in the sport and she didn't want to divulge it now. "It was an evolution," she said. "The same co-worker had signed up for a basic self-defense course and suggested I come, too. I was a fast learner and was good at it. The specialization in Wing Chun grew from that basic course a few years later."

"Uh-huh."

She liked that he didn't dig any deeper and she allowed herself to relax against the back of her chair. She felt a comfort level with Alex that she'd not felt with a man in a very long time.

If ever.

"Have you ever been married?"

"Once for about twenty minutes. I was very young and it didn't work out."

"A steady boyfriend?"

She shook her head. "No steady boyfriend."

"But you do date."

"My friends fixed me up on a blind date once and the guy was...uh, let's just say it wasn't meant to be."

"The same friends who gave you the shirt?"

She couldn't help but smile. "Yes. Six of us trained together at the police academy and we've been friends ever since. One is now the chief of police," Crista said proudly. She glanced away. "We haven't had much time to spend together for a while. We're all really busy with our jobs."

Thinking about the broken friendships made her sad and she didn't want to talk about it any longer. She gulped down the last swallow of milk.

"I better go," Alex said, rising. "I've taken up enough of your evening."

Crista stood, too. "I'm glad you brought the picture over. You did the right thing."

In the living room, Alex reached around her for his jacket, brushing against her as he did.

"I'll go out with you," Crista said. If Diego hadn't called by now, he wasn't going to.

Her building had no elevator and three floors later, they reached the front door. Crista stepped outside with Alex, glad to breathe in the crisp fresh air. The evening had been emotionally taxing, but it had also been fun.

As they stood quietly together, she felt as if something had passed between them tonight. Their new intimacy was…exciting.

Alex reached out and, with two fingers, tilted her chin up. "Despite my reason for coming, I enjoyed spending time with you," he said.

Arousal grew low in Crista's groin. And standing there with Alex gazing into her eyes, she wished he'd kiss her. And just as she wished it, his lips brushed hers.

Her heart leaped, and she was seized by a physical need so intense she thought she might combust at any second. She brought her arms up and clung to Alex, deepening the kiss, letting him know she enjoyed the evening as much as he had.

More. She'd enjoyed it more.

At that moment, it didn't matter that he was the worst possible man in the world for her. The only thing that mattered was how she felt right now. And when he crushed her in his strong arms, she knew he felt the same. She couldn't think. She couldn't breathe and all she could hear was her heart thumping in time with his.

A loud screech of tires broke the spell.

POP! POP! POP! A trio of gunshots ripped through the air.

Crista threw Alex to the pavement and, covering his body with hers, she glanced up to see if she could I.D. the vehicle, a license plate. Anything.

But the moonless night and the dim street lighting were good cover. All she could see was an old dark-colored truck speeding away.

A dark truck. Like the one in Sam's drawing?

CHAPTER SIX

"10-38. OFFICER NEEDS ASSISTANCE," Crista said calmly into Alex's cell phone after she'd practically ripped it from his hand.

As she spoke, Alex heard the wail of sirens and with lightning speed, three squad cars descended on them. Within minutes, a dozen officers were on the scene. He'd never seen anything like it.

"Let me handle this," Crista said, handing him back the phone.

Alex stiffened. "I can speak for myself."

She glared at him, her attitude subzero. "I meant the police stuff."

Okay. He should have known that's what she meant. But after getting shot at for the second time in a week, he was a little shaken and had automatically taken the remark as a stab against his masculinity. And who wouldn't? She'd brushed him aside like he was nothing when she went over to talk to one of the other officers.

He was still steaming when, a few minutes later, she told him, "The captain wants to talk to you."

"I thought you were going to handle it?" he said, unable to keep the sarcasm from his tone.

"I did. But he wants your version. Everyone sees things differently."

He wondered if she'd told them what they were doing before they were shot at. "I didn't see anything."

She frowned. "He still wants to talk to you."

"Okay." He agreed, but then had to ask, "Does it matter that I didn't see anything because I was busy doing something else?"

She glanced away. "No, I didn't mention that. It wasn't important. Just talk to them. Tell them what you saw—or didn't see."

It wasn't important. He felt like a kid being told to go play so he wouldn't be in the way. Hell, he'd only asked because it occurred to him she might get in some kind of trouble for fraternizing with someone involved in a case she was working on. Though irked at her behavior, he nodded his okay. After all, it was his fault she'd been in that position in the first place.

"Excuse me, Mr. Del Rio. Don't leave," one of the officers called out from a few yards away. "I'll need to talk to you."

The man wore plain clothes with a badge on his lapel.

"Sure," Alex said. He motioned to Crista to come with him to talk to the guy, but she didn't budge.

"Go ahead," she said. "He just wants your version of what happened."

Alex waited a second, then, impatient, walked over to where the detective was standing. "I'm Alex Del Rio. You wanted to talk to me?"

"I'm Captain Englend, Mr. Del Rio, and yes, I need to ask you some questions."

"I doubt I can add anything to what Detective Santiago told you. I had my back to the street."

"Why was that?"

Surprised at the sharp tone in the captain's voice, Alex straightened his shoulders. He didn't like the guy already. "We were talking."

"About what? What were you doing at Detective Santiago's apartment?"

And now he felt like a criminal under interrogation. "I came by to give her some information about the case."

"What kind of information?" The captain picked at something between his teeth, his manner crude and disgusting.

Alex planted his feet apart and crossed his arms.

Englend wrote something on a pad.

"Specifically, I came over to show her one of Samantha's drawings because I thought it might be important to her investigation. I was just leaving. We were standing on the steps when it happened and, as I said, my back was to the street and—"

"You didn't see anything. But what happened then?"

"We hit the ground."

The captain's gaze lifted from his paper. "I meant, what did you hear?"

The back of Alex's neck prickled. Why didn't the guy just ask the right question in the first place? "I heard a car, then a round of gunshots. Three of them. We ducked down and I heard the squeal of tires as they sped away."

"I thought you didn't see anything."

"I didn't."

"Then how do you know it was a car and not another type of vehicle."

"I don't. I just assu—"

"Yeah. I know," the captain said. "Everyone does that." He tapped his pen against his pad. "That's it?"

"That's it."

The captain wore an expression of complete boredom, but the questions in his eyes said he didn't believe Alex was telling him everything. Tough. Alex didn't give a damn what the guy believed. It was up to Crista to tell her boss the personal stuff—if she wanted to. He'd said why he was here and it was the truth.

After that, the captain went into all the same questions that Crista had after the first shooting. Did he have any enemies? Did he know anyone who might want to harm him, etcetera, etcetera.

Just as quickly as the police came, they were gone. Alex turned to Crista with a bewildered shrug. "What just happened?"

"Not a helluva lot," she answered, her voice laced with irritation. "Until they know otherwise, they have to consider it a random act. They can't do anything without concrete evidence."

"And what do you think?"

"I think we'll know more when we get information from Ballistics. They found two of the bullets."

Crista didn't believe for a second that the shooting had been another random act. Two drive-bys, both involving Alex, could only mean one thing. Alex had to know what it meant, too. "We need to talk about this, Alex. And I need to talk to Samantha as soon as possible."

He ran a hand through his hair. "I can talk now if you want. But Sam's in bed."

"Tomorrow is okay." Actually, Crista had to look at the file and put her information together. She needed to get the results from Ballistics as soon as she could. They might have something.

"I'm worried. What if Sam saw the shooters and they know she did. She could be in danger."

"Has anything happened to make you think that?"

"No. Nothing. I'm just worried."

She nodded. "I know how you feel. But until I talk to Sam, we have to go on the assumption that because her bedroom light was out they didn't see her. Has she heard anyone talking about the night of the shooting?"

"I don't know. Elena and I have had conversations, but not when Sam is around."

"Not that you know of, anyway."

"What are you implying?"

Crista took a deep breath. "Sometimes children hear people talking and say what they think their parents want them to say. They make things up."

"Sam wouldn't do that."

"I didn't say she would. But it happens. Kids have vivid imaginations."

He tipped his head back and closed his eyes. When he opened them he said, "She does have that."

"If you're worried about Sam's safety, I can come over and stand watch."

Alex did a double take, looking at her as if she'd suddenly grown two heads. "I'm not going to have you put yourself in danger."

"Excuse me? I do it all the time. It's my job to serve and protect. I protected you tonight."

He looked surprised, then admitted, "Yeah, you did. I guess I owe you a thank-you for that."

"Thanks aren't necessary. It's all in the line of duty."

"You weren't on duty."

"I'm always on duty if something happens that requires an officer of the law."

He shook his head and exhaled noisily. Purposefully. He gave her a wry grin. "Doesn't seem right to me. It goes against the laws of nature or something."

He might have said the words with humor, but she knew there was truth in what he said. "If you don't want me to stand watch, I can give you the name of someone who can."

"Thanks for the offer," he said. "I'll take care of Sam myself."

Crista didn't know what that meant, but she knew he wasn't going to accept her help.

"And I better go do that right now. I'll call you in the morning so you can talk to her." He turned to go.

"Be careful," she said. When he was gone, Crista hurried back upstairs to her apartment. She knew Alex was worried about Sam, but after tonight she was fairly certain it wasn't Sam who was in danger. Only she couldn't do anything about it. Her suspicions weren't evidence, and she'd be way off base to tell Alex what she thought until she had that evidence.

Reaching the door, she suddenly felt emotionally and physically exhausted. She stuck her key in the lock, but as she started to turn it, she realized it didn't catch. The door wasn't locked. A chill crawled up her spine. The door was weighted to automatically latch when she closed it.

Stepping inside the apartment, her gaze darted from corner to corner. Nothing seemed out of place. She took out the gun she kept hidden in the front closet, then she did a quick search of the three small rooms and bath. Everything seemed fine and she felt a little foolish. Maybe she hadn't pulled the door tight when she and Alex went outside? That had to be it. She went to Calvin's cage and lifted his cover.

"What do you think, Calvin?" She reached in and took him out.

Calvin was silent when usually he repeated everything she said. She checked his feathers, brushing his back as she did. "You okay little bird? What's the matter?"

"What's the matter?" Calvin suddenly repeated. "Are you mute? Dumb bird."

Though glad to hear him say something, Crista puzzled over where he'd heard that particular line. She didn't remember watching any TV shows that referred to a mute or dumb bird. But then she'd fallen asleep in front of the television more than once and wouldn't know anyway. She set him back in his cage and went to the kitchen to get a glass of wine. She enjoyed a glass of wine once in a while, and tonight she needed it.

Chardonnay in hand, she sat on the couch, slipped off her shoes and put her feet on the laminate coffee table. Too much had happened in just a few short hours and she was overtired. Imagining things.

She took a sip of wine, mentally cataloguing the events. She'd learned Sam was a possible witness to the crime, and then someone had taken shots at them while they were standing outside. To her, it was obvious that someone wanted to hurt Alex.

Which made her wonder if Alex knew more than he'd told her. How could he not know if someone wanted to do him harm? How could he not know who his enemies were?

She knew her enemies. She'd met the most dangerous one face-to-face at Diego's. A sick feeling settled in her stomach at the thought. But she quickly dispelled it. She'd handled the meeting with Trini. Maybe not well, but she'd stood her ground. And it had felt damn good.

Remembering the incident reminded her again that Diego hadn't called when he said he would. She hoped nothing had happened to him and debated driving to his house to see if he was okay. She nixed the idea. God knew who she might run into over there, and she didn't need any more surprises tonight.

After finishing her wine, Crista showered and attempted to meditate—to no avail. She went to bed and tried to sleep, but all she managed to do was worry. Sam. Alex. Diego. Her job. It was almost overwhelming.

Just as she started to drift off, a sharp ringing jerked her awake again. Groggy, Crista fumbled in the dark and snatched the receiver on the third ring. "Hello," she croaked. "Santiago, here."

"Sorry to call so late, but I couldn't get to a phone before now."

Hearing her brother's voice, Crista pushed to a sitting position. "That's okay. What is it you wanted to talk about?"

"I don't want to do it over the phone. Can you meet me for lunch tomorrow?"

Without hesitation she said, "Sure. Where and when?"

"Dave's Diner at two o'clock. It should be quiet then."

"Okay—" Crista barely got the syllables out when she heard a muffled sound on the other end and then the drone of the dial tone.

Bewildered, she slowly replaced the receiver and tried to go back to sleep. But how could she sleep when someone had tried to kill Alex tonight? She didn't have any proof, but given that he'd been shot at before, she had to consider the worst-case scenario. And then there was Samantha's drawing.

A new kind of fear pulsed through Crista. Both Alex and Sam might be in danger.

Or they might not. Like a carousel, her thoughts went around and around. It was all speculation on her part, but she did have good reason to believe what she did, and she had to do something about it. Maybe Alex didn't want her help, but she knew a couple guys, former cops who did security work after they retired....

She drifted off, only to awaken again in the wee hours with something else on her mind.

Alex had kissed her. With everything that had happened, she'd put it out of her mind. She touched her mouth with her fingertips. Alex had kissed her and she'd enjoyed every second. Just thinking about it, she could almost feel the heat of his lips against hers.

How had she let that happen? Getting personally involved in a case was unprofessional. For her, it could be career suicide.

Crista rolled over and jammed the pillow over her head, wishing she had someone to talk to because she sure could use some advice about now. A familiar pang jolted through her, reminding her once again how much she missed her friends—and how much she needed them.

She awoke in the morning groggy from a disturbed sleep, and first thing out of bed, she went for her latte. The coffee gave her the jolt she needed to get into the shower and, a half hour later, she was at the station. She hung up her leather coat and went directly to Captain Englend's office. The team's response last night had been reassuring. More than reassuring. Given her previous experience, she truly appreciated the speedy backup support and had to let Captain Englend know how she felt—regardless of any other issues she might have with him.

Englend was sitting at his desk reading the paper when she reached his door. Even though she knocked, he didn't lift his head. She went in and stood behind one of the chairs until he finally said, "Detective Santiago. What can I do for you?"

He seemed on edge, his tone annoyed.

Drumming her fingers against the chair, she said, "I just wanted to say thanks for the team's quick response last night. I thought maybe you could let everyone know that."

Englend shrugged as if to say it was nothing, or simply part of the job. He gave her a studied look, and leaning back in his chair, steepled his fingers. "So what really happened?"

Taken aback by the question, Crista's breath caught. Was he implying she hadn't told him everything? She didn't know what he was referring to, but answered anyway. "In my opinion, the shooting was not another drive-by."

The captain's passive expression remained fixed, but his brows raised mechanically—two straight, dark lines that contrasted markedly with his silver hair and looked as if they'd been drawn on with a black marking pencil.

"And what evidence do you have to support that opinion?"

"Two drive-bys involving the same person. In my book, that's no coincidence."

"It's also not evidence."

"My neighborhood isn't the greatest, but as far as I know, it doesn't get many drive-bys. I think the hit was planned, I think someone wants to harm Alex Del Rio."

"Your opinion isn't evidence, either."

Crista gritted her teeth. "Right. But hopefully we'll have that evidence soon."

"Good. Come talk to me when you have it."

She turned to leave when he added, "How close are you to wrapping up the case?"

How close? Not even. "I don't have the results from Ballistics yet. It will be a week or so before I do. It's going to take time."

The captain's lips thinned. The cords in his neck suddenly popped out like a bas-relief road map. He leaned forward, both hands on the desk as he rose to his feet.

She cringed a little inside. It was obvious her statement rubbed him the wrong way. Hard as it was, she had to watch what she said. Especially now.

"We don't have more time, so I suggest you figure out how to get those results and get it done. One way or another."

On her way out, the captain repeated himself. "One way or another, Santiago."

What did that mean? He didn't expect her to arrest just anyone, did he? Not without evidence. But the more she thought about the urgency in his voice, she realized that maybe he did expect her to arrest some-one—anyone. If they had a suspect in custody, it would appear as if they'd solved the case—or were close to solving it.

The very idea went against everything Crista stood for. Her stomach knotted, her anger impossible to disguise. She stormed back to her desk. How the hell was she supposed to arrest anyone when the evidence results hadn't come back yet? All those TV shows that portrayed detectives sweet-talking other departments to get information sooner than they could pump it out, was a lot of fiction. It didn't happen that way in real life.

The captain knew that. Which meant he was telling her to fudge the case. Arrest anyone so Englend could let it be known his department had a suspect in custody.

Too riled to sit when she reached her desk, Crista shoved a stack of files aside, causing them to nearly topple off her desk. *Wrap it up. One way or another.*

She couldn't do it. Not even if it meant her job.

At that moment, realization dawned. Given the captain's unreasonable demands on the Encanto case, and that he'd never wanted a woman on his team, that may have been the plan all along. Assign her a difficult, time-sensitive case, show she can't do the job and then get rid of her.

Despite the fact that she didn't want to be working with the Chicano Squad, being forced out, for any reason, wasn't what she wanted, either. She felt anger so strong and deep it made her tremble.

She shoved a stray hair from her face and glancing around, saw Hanover's weasle eyes on her. Did he know what was going on? He and the captain went way back.

She shuffled some papers, pretending she was trying to find something, and then she sat down. She didn't know why, but she got the feeling Hanover liked to see her squirm.

Too bad. She wasn't going to squirm for anyone. She was going to do something. If she only knew what. File a complaint and break the code of silence? What proof did she have? She closed her eyes, remembering how she'd been shunned when she went against her team to support Risa. She couldn't imagine going through that again.

She girded her reserves and opened the Encanto file. Whatever the outcome, she wasn't going to let this case be her downfall.

CHAPTER SEVEN

"IT'S A GIRL!" Pete's voice reverberated.

Crista pulled the receiver away from her ear before her eardrum split. She was glad she'd stayed in the office and delayed her lunch in order to meet Diego at two o'clock. "Mary Elizabeth Richter. Six pounds, ten ounces and she has a really healthy set of lungs."

Crista chuckled. "How's Sharon?"

"Great. After all those false labor pains, she breezed through it in only six hours."

"Wonderful," Crista said. "And how's dad doing?"

Pete let out a blast of air. "I'm fine now. But I was a basket case before. How are things at the station?"

God, she wished Pete were here. He was the only person she'd been able to confide in these past two months. The only person in her unit she trusted. But she wasn't about to spoil his euphoria. "Fine," she said.

"You don't sound fine."

"I'm fine. Really."

He was silent on the other end of the line. "Okay, things could be better, but it's no big deal," she said hunching over and talking softly so Hanover couldn't hear. Most of the guys were out, either on cases or at lunch, but Hanover was working in today.

"Better? How so?"

Crista hedged. She hated complainers and didn't

want to become one herself. Problems were part of the job. "It...it's nothing."

Pete was silent for a moment, then said, "I don't think so. And I'm not hanging up until you tell me."

Knowing he meant what he said, she told him, "Alex brought me some information last night and when I was saying goodbye to him on the front steps, someone took potshots at us."

"Are you okay?" His voice was raised, concern edging his words.

"Yes. I'm fine. No one was hurt. But I'm worried. I think the shooting has to be connected with the Encanto case, but since I have no evidence, it's just a hunch."

"Sounds like a good hunch to me. Unless you've made some enemies yourself."

She had a few of those—her ex for one. And more than a few criminals she'd arrested and who'd vowed to get even. She wasn't number one with a couple of the guys she used to work with, either. But none of that was anything new.

"What does Englend say?"

Crista gave a scornful laugh. "He wants the Encanto case wrapped up and has threatened to take me off the assignment if I don't arrest someone immediately. I know the mayor is on his back, but I can't make a collar if I don't have a suspect."

Pete was quiet again, so she asked, "Any suggestions?"

He cleared his throat. "I think...you should watch your back."

Surprised, Crista said, "That's a joke. Right?"

"No, it's not."

He was serious. And while she hated herself for getting into it, today of all days, she had to ask. "What's going down?"

He was quiet again and she realized that even if Pete had heard something, he wouldn't tell her. He'd never break the code of silence. He was that kind of a cop. But what he'd said was a warning for sure.

"Take my advice, okay? Just do your job and stay on Englend's good side."

Stay on Englend's good side. As far as she was concerned, he didn't have a good side. "Thanks for the advice, Pete. I appreciate it."

"You'll be fine. I know. I've seen you in action."

She wished she felt as sure as he did. She heard some voices in the background and a muffled sound like a hand over the receiver. Then Pete said, "Hey, I hate to rush off, but I gotta go see Sharon and the baby. I'll get in touch when we get home."

"You'll be busy. Don't worry about it. And give my best to Sharon, will you? A healthy baby is a wonderful early Christmas present."

"It is, isn't it," he said. "A family for Christmas. That's the best present anyone could get."

Letting the receiver drop slowly into the cradle, she felt a familiar ache in her chest. One she'd felt every holiday season for fourteen years. Diego was her only family and time and circumstance had destroyed whatever closeness they'd once shared. More than anything, she wanted to repair the years of damage, but she didn't know if it was possible. Especially not if Diego was involved with the Pistoles again. Gang culture dictated that members break from their loved ones so the gang became their new family.

She glanced at her watch one more time. Still too early to meet her brother, but it was difficult to think of anything else. If what he had to tell her was important enough to make a lunch date, it had to be significant.

She picked up the phone. Maybe Diego was at Marco's house. Maybe she could get him to meet her now?

ALEX SIGNED IN at the front desk in Homicide's Chicano Unit. The officer in charge cleared him and then directed him to the main area where uniformed and plainclothes officers milled about; some were standing and some sitting behind a sea of desks butted against one another. A man, dirty and ragged, sat dejectedly at an officer's desk, apparently not happy to be there. One of the homeless, maybe.

Crista's desk was in the middle of the room, but she was on the phone with her back turned to him. Another clerk led him to Captain Englend's office.

"Mr. Del Rio is here to see you," the girl said, then left him standing at the door.

"Come in, Mr. Del Rio."

Alex noted the captain seemed friendlier than last night, and he went inside and sat in the chair the captain indicated with a wave of his hand. No handshake this time.

"Thank you for coming, Mr. Del Rio."

"No problem. My office isn't too far from here."

The silver-haired man nodded. "I know. I understand you're an invaluable asset to Mayor Walbrun's team."

Alex gave him a tight smile. "The task force is making progress. The mayor can be proud of everyone involved."

"Which brings me to the reason I asked you to come in. I thought you might talk a little more freely in private than last night with so many people around."

Surprised, Alex shrugged. "I told you everything I saw last night."

"Right. But now that I've had a chance to go over my notes, I have a few more questions."

"Okay. I'll do what I can to answer."

The captain went right to it. "The information you brought for Detective Santiago. What did you do with it?"

"I gave it to her. It was a picture my daughter drew about the night of the shooting. Samantha asked me to give it to Detective Santiago, and since she's the investigator on the case, it seemed the thing to do."

"You thought it was important?"

"I didn't think anything except that Sam asked me to show it to Crist—Detective Santiago. And I was worried the picture might indicate that she'd seen something that night."

"You think she saw the shooter? Do you think she could she identify him in a lineup?"

A lineup? Astounded, Alex drew back. "She's four years old," he said incredulously. "I don't know what she really saw, if anything. It was dark, and even if she did see something, I'd have to think about it long and hard before I'd subject her to such a responsibility."

Captain Englend nodded as if in agreement. "Kids make up a lot of stuff. It's hard to depend on a child as an eyewitness to any crime. Prosecutors have difficulty with that because no matter how certain a kid is, when the child gets into court, it's always another story. That's why kids under five aren't swearable as witnesses."

Well, Alex had news for him. It didn't matter what Captain Englend, or the court, or anyone else wanted. Samantha wasn't going to do anything Alex didn't feel was right for her. Including picking someone out of a lineup. He wouldn't allow it.

But as quickly as the captain finished his sentence, he changed the subject. "Based on the evidence we have so far, we suspect that both shootings were by the same person."

"Really?" Alex said, again a little surprised. Crista had told him they had no evidence. What was that all about?

"Statistically, most crimes against an individual are committed by someone they know. So we're looking close to home."

Crista had said the same thing, and his data bore out the statement. But drive-by shootings usually involved gang activity and were in another category altogether.

"So what can you tell me about the people you've recruited for your programs. Would any of them want to harm you?"

They were back to that again. "Of course not. And I gave that answer more than once. Not only to you, but to Detective Santiago."

"Okay," Englend drawled. "If something comes up...if you remember anything, give me a call."

Alex frowned again. "Are you saying I should call you and not Detective Santiago?"

"No, but I'd like you to call me first."

"Okay." But even though he'd agreed, Alex felt as if he'd be going behind Crista's back if he did that. Maybe Crista knew about it already. "And if you get a lead or make an arrest, I'd appreciate it if you could let me know, too."

The captain nodded. "We'll tell you what we can."

"Thanks," Alex said, feeling as if the captain was giving him lip service. Most of all, he didn't understand the purpose of his visit, other than the captain telling Alex he should call him first if anything came up. He reached out, shook the captain's hand and turned to leave. On his way out of the office, he glanced toward Crista's desk. Her head came up and she waved him over.

"What are you doing here?"

He sat in the chair next to her desk. "The captain asked me to come down for more questions."

"Really. What kind of questions?"

"He asked if Sam saw the shooters—if she could identify them. After that, he asked all the same stuff as before." Suddenly Alex wasn't sure who he should tell what. Crista had told him they had no evidence, but the captain had said they did. Englend had also said Alex should notify him first if he had any new information. What was that about? Didn't he trust his own officer to do the job? Disappointment flashed in Crista's eyes, and Alex realized she knew he was holding out on her.

He felt like a rat. He was beginning to care about her, and if he cared at all, he couldn't keep secrets. Besides, the captain never indicated theirs was a private conversation. "Does the captain usually get information on the evidence before you?"

She looked surprised at the question. "Why do you ask?"

He shrugged. "He said there was evidence that both shootings had been by the same person."

For a moment, she just sat there. Then she said, "I hadn't heard that yet, but I imagine the information will come down to me soon."

"He also asked that I call him first if I have any new information."

Crista's breath hitched. She didn't have a response

to that. She didn't know what to make of Alex's asser-
tions. He obviously felt uncomfortable about his conversation with the captain or he wouldn't have
mentioned it. It made her uncomfortable, too. Why did
the captain want to be called first? Why hadn't he mentioned the new evidence? It was her case, and she
needed all the facts to be able to solve it.

But these were her problems, no concern to Alex.
"Have you thought about setting up a time for me to
talk to Samantha? It should be soon."

"She's at preschool right now, but tonight would
work. I'd like to get this over with so we can get on with
our lives."

"Okay. Tell me when and where?"

"How about coming for dinner? I can let Elena
know we're having a guest."

"Oh, I don't—"

"It would make things easier for Sam. She could get
comfortable with you before you start questioning her."

That made sense—even though she couldn't launch
into a formal interview with a four year old anyway.
There were major considerations when questioning a
child, especially since children were easily led by inter-
viewers. "Okay. I'm all for making Sam comfortable.
What time?"

"I can pick you up after work."

Not knowing how long her meeting with Diego
would take, she shook her head. "I have some things
to take care of and I don't know where I'll be. It's
probably best if I just drive over."

His gaze softened as he looked at her. "Darn. I was
hoping to spend more time with you myself."

She could tell by the glint in his eyes that he was
teasing, but was there a note of truth there, too.

"But after last night, I guess that's no surprise, is it?"

She glanced around, hoping no one had heard. Hanover, the office gossip, would have a field day with that kind of information—even if she had no interest in seeing Alex again. But she *was* interested in seeing Alex again. Too interested. She'd be lying to herself if she denied it.

Apparently seeing her discomfort, Alex lowered his voice. "How about six o'clock then? We usually have dinner early because Sam can't wait much longer than six."

"Fine. Six o'clock it is," she said with a quick glance at her watch. She had to leave immediately to meet Diego. "I'm sorry, but I have another appointment right now."

Alex stood to leave. "I understand. I shouldn't have interrupted you like this."

"It's okay. I wanted to talk to you, too." She glanced around, then added, "About Samantha."

The look in his eyes said he knew what she meant— and she wasn't fooling anyone, except maybe herself.

"Okay. I'll see you tonight then."

CRISTA OBSERVED the restaurant from across the street. The parking lot was deserted, the writing on the pink adobe facade faded and chunks of stucco peeled away from the walls like layers from an onion. Frozen in time, the building was a relic of the past when the neighborhood had bustled with life. Now the only people she saw were two raggedy men and a woman crouched outside on the concrete. Homeless people, she guessed. Hungry and waiting for a handout.

She headed toward the door, peering through the glass as she came closer to see if Diego was there and hoping he wouldn't stand her up.

"Got a cigarette?" One of the street people reached out to her as she came closer.

She shook her head.

"Can you help out with a dollar?" another asked.

"Sorry," Crista said as she pulled open the door to go inside. If she gave one person money, she'd have to give them all money. She stopped. "But there's a shelter one street over where you can warm up and get some food."

All three waved her off, so she went inside. They probably knew where the shelters were better than she did. A quick scan of the room told her the place was ready to fold. Even so, it was clean, and the man behind the counter said, "Have a seat, Ma'am. Anywhere."

"Thanks," she muttered as hope plummeted. No Diego. He'd said it was important. If he screwed up again…

"Hey," a deep voice came from behind her. "I've been waiting for you."

She swung around. She must have missed her brother where he sat in a corner booth. "Diego." Crossing to meet him, she noticed his gaze darting nervously around the room.

Her coat was bulky, so she shrugged it off and laid it on the bench before she sat across from him.

"What's good?" She picked up the menu. "Lunch is on me."

Diego didn't respond, but glanced at the menu himself. Then he said, "It's been a while. I don't know what's good."

At that point the man behind the counter came over with two glasses of water. He wore an apron that looked as if it had done a stint in an E.R. room, a hairnet that covered his Donald Trump comb-over and a name tag on his shirt that read Dave. "I make the best hamburgers in town. Best chili, too."

Crista was tempted not to order anything and just have coffee, but she wanted to keep Diego here as long as she could. "I'll have the chili and a cup of coffee."

Diego set down the menu. "Same here."

Dave left and an awkward silence ensued. How should she start? He was the one who'd wanted to talk to her, so it made sense that she let him go first.

The waiter/cook brought them two coffees and a small creamer. "It's not cream. It's milk," he said. "The rest is comin' up in a minute."

Crista poured a liberal amount of milk into her coffee, then finally said, "I hope you're getting settled okay."

Diego raised his chin. "I'm doing all right. Nobody's knockin' at my door to give me a job, but I didn't expect anything different."

Every time she looked at Diego, her chest hurt. He had such potential and it was all going down the tubes if he didn't change his life soon. If only she could do something to help. If only he'd let her.

He'd always been proud, even as a boy, unwilling to take help from anyone. "No one ever came to my door, either. I've had to work hard for everything I have."

Eyes narrowed, his sharp gaze cut into her. "Why'd you disappear?"

She cupped her coffee tightly with both hands. Should she tell him? As a boy, Diego had idolized Trini, and after seeing them together last week, things obviously hadn't changed. If she told him what had happened between her and Trini, would he even believe her? It might alienate him even more.

"It didn't work out between me and Trini. I couldn't stay. It—it's a long story."

"I've got time."

"Maybe you should tell me first why Marco and Trini were at your place?"

"They're my friends."

"Well…" she said. "In my opinion, you keep the wrong kind of friends."

His chin came up again. "No one asked for your opinion."

"Maybe not, but I'm giving it anyway. You could do so much if you tried. Your paintings are wonderful, you could exhibit them somewhere. Sell them. You can't throw all that talent away just because you had a bad start in life."

Surprise registered in Diego's eyes. His attitude seemed to soften a little. "I care about you, Diego. I want what's best for you."

As she spoke, the cook brought their chili and some crackers, and Diego, obviously uncomfortable with the conversation, dug right in as if he hadn't eaten for a week. But he didn't look hungry or deprived. Physically, he looked just the opposite. Despite ten years in the worst prison in Texas, Diego was the picture of good health and fitness.

She gazed at him with wonder. It felt so good to see her little brother again. Talk to him. Even if their relationship was strained, it was better than not having a relationship at all. As she watched him eat, she made a commitment to herself that she would help him turn his life around—whether he wanted her to or not.

But lecturing him wasn't the way to start. "I guess the chili's good, huh?"

He glanced up. "Better than what I've had recently. Try it."

"Okay." She tasted a spoonful. "Umm. Very good."

"You hurt a lot of people by disappearing like that. *Mami*, Trini…"

The chili lodged in her throat. He didn't say he was hurt, too, but she could tell that Diego had been hurt the most. Why else would he be so bitter about it?

"I'm sorry, Diego. I really am. I had good reason to leave, and even better reasons not to tell anyone."

"Did it have something to do with Hank?" His knuckles tightened as he grasped his spoon.

Her stepfather. He'd been an ugly part of both their lives. She'd married Trini to escape Hank, but Trini was the reason she'd fled Houston. But since she didn't know how involved Diego was with Trini, she couldn't tell him.

"Yes," she finally admitted. "Hank was a big part of it. And I'm sorry, I can't talk about the rest right now."

"So what else is new?" The sarcasm was back in his voice.

There was no point trying to change his mind, so she decided to take another tack. "What else is new? You asking me here. That's definitely new. Why don't you tell me why I'm here?"

He glanced around, then his gaze came back to her. His irises suddenly seemed huge, his eyes as black as onyx. He leaned across the table and said so softly it was almost a whisper, "I wanted to tell you to be careful. You have no idea what you're getting into and—" He stopped midsentence. "Just…just be careful."

He was concerned about *her.* A tiny bud of hope blossomed. Maybe their relationship was salvageable. "I'm a cop, Diego. I'm trained to be careful."

His eyes penetrated hers. "Your life could be in danger."

"I appreciate the warning. Very much. But, I have a job to do. I can handle whatever comes."

"Your life could be in danger and you're telling me you can handle it?"

"I do it every day."

"This is different."

"Why is that? Do you know something specific? Someone who wants to hurt me?" It wouldn't be the first time that had happened. More than once someone she'd put behind bars had threatened her life. That was part of the job, too.

"You've been asking too many questions in places where people don't like anyone asking questions."

"What people? Marco? Trini? Some gang leader? The Pistoles?"

He slouched against the back of the booth. "The Pistoles take credit for their jobs. They mark their territory and they don't do it with colors."

It definitely sounded as if Diego knew more than he was saying. "Tell me who you're talking about so I can do something about it."

Shaking his head, he said, "All I can say is that you're searching in the wrong place." With that, he finished his chili, gulped down the coffee and stood to leave.

"Wait a sec," Crista said, getting up herself and laying some money on the table to pay the bill. Diego stopped till she caught up with him. "Thanks," she said. "I appreciate your concern. I really do."

He glanced away. "No big deal."

"Yes, it is. And I will be careful."

At that, one side of his mouth quirked up. A hint of a smile, maybe?

"Diego," she added on impulse, "why don't you come over and spend Thanksgiving with me next week?"

The smile disappeared as quickly as it had come. His expression went blank, as if she was a stranger who was getting too personal. But she knew he wasn't as remote as he wanted everyone to believe he was. He cared about her. That's why he'd asked to meet her—warned her.

"Why?"

Crista shifted her weight from one foot to the other. "Because you're my brother." She glanced away, then back to Diego. "We're family."

Diego stared at her for a few seconds, pivoted and headed for the door again. Her heart sank. She'd pushed it. Gotten too familiar too fast. Damn.

But halfway out the door, Diego turned and said, "I'll think about it."

Surprised, but delighted that he'd even think about coming to her place, Crista couldn't hold back a smile. She wanted to say something more to convince him, but then he was gone.

Just as well. She had to be at Alex's for dinner in a few hours. The thought of dinner with Alex and Samantha made her smile again.

Not good. It wasn't a social event. It wasn't a date, even though she felt a little like it was. Having dinner together was meant to make Samantha comfortable before Crista talked to her about the drawing.

She had to remember that.

CHAPTER EIGHT

CRISTA CHANGED from her work suit into a swingy burgundy skirt with a hemline that hovered around her knees. Her pale pink sweater went perfectly with the skirt. Not too dressy, but not jeans-casual, either.

Slipping her feet into black, strappy heels, she thought about the approach she'd take with the child. Nothing direct. Nothing directive. Nothing that would set the child back emotionally. Nothing that would upset Alex.

She had to do things right. She'd been on edge ever since taking the Encanto case and now Englend's edict that she make a collar regardless of the facts had her wondering about her ability to do the job. She'd become a cop to uphold the law, to help people, not do the bidding of a captain who wanted to make his department look good.

The drive-by at her apartment and what Diego had said this afternoon about the Pistoles not marking their territory with colors made her wonder about her objectivity. Was she pursuing the Pistoles angle because of her brother's former involvement with the gang? Did she want them to go down so he wouldn't get involved again? That would be as bad as Englend wanting her to make a collar just to have a suspect in custody. Maybe worse.

But beyond all that was the knowledge that her interest in Alex was becoming personal. Hell, it wasn't becoming personal, it *was* personal. And because of it, her professionalism was seriously at risk.

She had to distance herself. Had to think about the job. Only the job. Her career hinged on what she did with the Encanto case.

An hour later, Alex greeted her at the door and swept her inside, taking her coat and leading her into the family room where Samantha was sitting on the couch watching a children's show.

"Elena tells me dinner won't be ready for about twenty minutes," Alex explained.

"Hi, Samantha," Crista said, sitting beside the child. "What are you watching?"

"Something she shouldn't be watching," Alex answered for Sam. "She's supposed to be helping set the table."

"I was waiting for you," Sam said to Crista, totally ignoring her father. "You can help me set the table if you want to."

"I'd love to help."

Holding Crista's hand, Sam led her to the dining room. "We don't eat in here except when we have company and on special days like Thanksgiving and *Noche Buena.*"

"It's a lovely room," Crista said. Glancing around, she took in a large rectangular table made of some heavy dark wood, eight matching chairs covered in gold and red damask, and a mammoth chandelier in an old world style. Crista felt a little awed. This place was like something from a television show about the homes of the rich and famous.

"You can do the plates while I do the silver." Sam

pointed to a buffet against one wall where everything was laid out.

"But first, let's put on the tablecloth," a woman's voice said in Spanish.

Crista turned and saw the grandmother coming into the room.

"Hello, Miss Santiago. We're happy you can join us tonight."

The woman spoke in her native language and Crista responded in kind. "Thank you, Mrs. Reyes. This is a real treat for me. I don't often get a home-cooked meal."

"Please, call me Elena," she said, and Crista suggested she call her by her first name, too.

"Grandma makes yummy food," Sam interjected.

"I'll bet she does." Crista reached for one end of the gold damask tablecloth Elena held and together they spread it over the long table.

"You can do the napkins, too," Sam said after her grandmother left.

Crista glanced again at the buffet. A stack of cloth napkins sat next to the plates. Gold damask napkins, just like the tablecloth. She felt a twinge of uncertainty. Did the napkins go on the right or the left side? Or on top of the plate?

"Perfect," Alex boomed.

Crista jerked her head up to see Alex ruffling Sam's hair as the child set the silver just so on each side of the plate.

"I made the sharp sides of the knives turn the right way, too," the child said.

Alex smiled proudly. "I see that. Good job."

A tiny feeling of discomfort skittered through Crista—a feeling that hung on through each course of the meal Elena brought in. She was an outsider. She didn't belong here. She didn't belong in Alex and Samantha's world. Except when she was doing her job.

When it came to doing her job, she knew what to do. The thought comforted her, and she was glad when they went back into the family room to talk. She and Alex had discussed when and where Crista should conduct the interview and that Alex would be there, too.

"You want to come to my room? You can see Snuffy," Sam piped up, obviously unaware that her father and Crista had other plans.

The most important thing at the moment was gaining the child's trust, so Crista said, "Sure. I'd love to see Snuffy."

At that, Sam preceded Crista up the stairs and Alex followed.

"See. There's Snuffy. He likes to be on my bed 'cuz it's comfortable."

"It looks very comfortable," Crista agreed.

Sam jumped up on the bed next to Snuffy.

"Here, you can hold him. He might remember you since you gave him back to me."

Crista took the stuffed animal and sat on the bed next to Sam. This would be the perfect time to ask a couple questions. She glanced up to see Alex hovering by the door.

"I wanted to thank you for the lovely picture you drew for me," Crista said. "I brought it along so you could tell me a little more about it."

"Okay," Sam said, taking Snuffy back and placing him on her pillow. "He needs a little rest now."

"That's good. And while he's resting, I'll go downstairs and get the picture."

"I'll get it," Alex said, which surprised Crista since

he'd been so adamant about staying with them while she talked to Sam.

"Thank you. I left it next to my coat."

Alex returned within seconds and handed her the picture. Crista laid it on the bed between her and Sam.

"That's the moon," Sam offered.

"Yes, I can see that. And who are these two people?"

"Two men."

"Real men or people you made up?"

"Real men," Sam said, a little indignantly. "I saw them out the window when I got hurt."

"And what's this?" Crista pointed to the line coming from the box that was supposed to be the car.

"I don't know. A gun I think. Like on TV."

Crista glanced at Alex, knowing he'd never let Sam watch movies with any kind of violence in them. He hadn't told her that, but Crista knew it nonetheless, and she saw the concern in his eyes, too.

"Where'd you see something like that on television?" he asked.

Sam looked down, as if she'd done something wrong. "I don't know."

"It's okay, honey," Alex quickly added. "I just wondered, that's all."

Sam hung her head. "I sneaked up on *abuelita* when she was watching a movie in her room. I shouldn't have done it 'cuz I scared her."

Alex grinned. "I'm sure *abuelita* forgave you for scaring her. She loves you very much."

"I know." Sam smiled happily. "I love her, too."

"So," Alex said. "Maybe you can finish telling us about your picture and then we can have some dessert."

Crista and Alex exchanged glances as if on the same wavelength. If Sam overheard the TV show, she could've overheard Alex and Elena talking about the shooting. She could have drawn the picture because that's what she thought she saw. Alex shifted his stance. He was uncomfortable, Crista realized, and decided to finish this up as soon as possible.

Sam glanced at the drawing still lying on the bed between her and Crista. "That's the grass. That's the car, and that's the moon. This is our house and that's me in the window."

Crista hadn't noticed the dot of a figure in the window before since it was obscured by the coloring Sam had done over it. And from the urgency in Sam's voice, Crista suspected the child was more anxious to get to dessert than explain the drawing. "It's a lovely picture, and I'm so happy you drew it for me. Can you tell me one more thing about it?"

Sam nodded.

"When you were standing in the window, did you see the people in the car?"

Alex's face paled.

Samantha nodded again. "Kind of. But not really 'cuz it was dark."

"I think it's time to go downstairs," Alex stated. His gaze bore into Crista. "We can talk about this some other time. In private."

End of conversation. "Okay," Crista said and stood to go, picking up the picture to take with her. She glanced at Sam, who reached out for Crista to help her jump off the bed. She helped the girl and then stepped away, trying to maintain some distance, but as they descended the stairs, Crista felt a small warm hand nestle inside hers.

Her heart squeezed, and she couldn't stop the sudden rush of emotions that washed over her.

Don't! Don't get involved. But it was far easier to say the words than to do it. Leaving now before she got dragged in any further would be best. She'd done what she came here to do and now it was time to go.

"I'm glad you finally came back," Elena reprimanded when they entered the dining room. "It's time for dessert. Come now." Her words brooked no argument and Crista knew if she were to leave right then, Elena would feel insulted. Her own grandmother had been much the same in that respect. Hispanic culture was chock-full of tradition and unspoken rules.

Sam scooted up onto her chair. "Yummy," she said. "Do you like flan, too?" Her big brown eyes peered up at Crista.

"Uh-huh. It's one of my favorites."

"We're going to have more on Thanksgiving. Can you come and have Thanksgiving with us?"

Silky as the flan was, Crista almost choked on it.

"Great idea," Alex said. "We'd love it if you could join us."

Crista swallowed another spoonful of flan, quickly searching for words to decline the invitation and yet not hurt Sam's feelings. "That's a wonderful invitation, Sam. And I'd love to come, but I've already invited my brother to have Thanksgiving with me at my home."

"He can come, too. Can't he, Daddy?" Sam's big eyes pleaded with her father.

"Of course. We'd love to have both of you. The more people the better."

Easy to say when they didn't know anything about Diego. Would Alex be so magnanimous if he knew where her brother had been for the past ten years?

"Tell me you'll think about it. It's been a while since

we've had a full table and—" his voice softened
"—we'd really like it if you and your brother joined
us."

She nodded, noncommittal, but that seemed to be
enough for Sam—and for Alex. Quickly finishing her
dessert, Crista said, "I think it's time for me to go home."

Sam hopped off her chair, ran over and gave Crista
a hug, and at the same time, Crista heard Elena say, "I
hope you can share in our Thanksgiving. We have
much to be thankful for."

There was a sadness in Elena's voice. She missed
her daughter. Holidays were the worst time for people
who'd lost someone they loved. Crista felt an overwhelming empathy for the woman. She knew the feeling well. She guessed Alex felt the same—only he was
good at not showing his emotions. He was too stoic,
too macho to let anyone see the pain inside.

Alex walked Crista to the door, his hand touching
the small of her back. As light as his touch was, she
could feel his heat. She liked the way it made her feel—
even though she didn't quite know what that feeling
was. Or did she?

Lord, she hoped he didn't broach the Thanksgiving
thing again. That Sam liked her enough to ask her to
join their family at Thanksgiving made her spirits soar.
But professionally, it was a bad idea. Getting personally involved in a case went against everything she'd
learned at the academy. She'd had long discussions
with her friends on the subject, especially after Abby
left the academy to join her lover in North Carolina.

But the years since the academy had taught Crista
that life wasn't always a case of black and white, and
sometimes what you thought was the right thing to do
turned out to be wrong in the end.

Samantha had looked so hopeful when she'd asked Crista to spend Thanksgiving with them, it was difficult to refuse. Elena and Alex seemed so sincere, as if they really wanted her to come. Even to the point of asking her to bring her brother....

But they didn't know about Diego. She had to tell Alex. Tell him why she couldn't make it.

At the door, Alex said, "You caught me off guard back there. I thought you said you had no family."

Surprised that he remembered that, she looked away. "That's not quite correct. I said I had no close family who cared about me. My brother and I have only recently been in contact. He's been away for a long time."

"Ah. An adventurer?"

Not even close. *So tell him. Tell him and get it over with.*

If she told him about Diego, then she wouldn't have to worry about the invitation. After what Sam had been through, there's no way Alex would invite a criminal into his house.

"No, he's far from that. My brother...has been away because he was in jail." She waited a beat to see his reaction and when she didn't see any discernable change, she added, "For ten years." Alex had to know that only someone who'd committed a serious crime would be gone that long.

But Alex's expression was unchanged—as if he hadn't heard a thing. "How long has he been out?"

"A little over a week. He's having a hard time of it."

"I'd like to meet your brother. Maybe I can introduce him to some people who can help him ease the transition."

Well, that wasn't even close to what she'd expected

him to say. "I'm…I'm not sure yet if he'll even come to my place, much less anyone else's. He's a bit of a loner."

"Why don't you extend the invitation and let him decide?"

He had a point. Asking Diego would also take the onus of refusal off her.

What to do? It was just a dinner. A friendly dinner. That's all. And maybe it would be good for Diego to see how others lived. Maybe meeting Alex would spark an interest in Diego to do something different with his life.

"Sam will be super disappointed if you don't come."

Was that the only reason he wanted her there—because he didn't want Sam to be disappointed? Even if it was, it was a good reason—one she could easily understand. The child was so loving, she'd already found a little niche in Crista's heart.

She took a breath. "Okay. I'll ask him."

A smile slowly spread across Alex's face. The midnight color of his eyes seemed to melt into a soft, warm brown. "Great. Maybe it'll feel like a real Thanksgiving again."

AS ALEX WATCHED Crista drive away, a gust of wind rustled the through the giant magnolia trees surrounding his home. Thick, solid trees with fat leathery leaves and fragrant, lemon-scented blossoms in the spring and summer—an intoxicating scent that could almost make a person dizzy.

Marissa had always said the big trees were like sentinels guarding her home and family, keeping them from harm. Just like him, she'd said. When he'd placed his strong arms around her, she'd felt secure and protected.

Marissa had needed him as a buffer from the world, and he'd relished the role. He'd felt necessary. Needed.

But in the end, he hadn't been able to protect Marissa.

He went inside, closed the door and leaned against the smooth wood. Now, the only person who needed him was Samantha, and he'd not been able to protect her, either. Nothing in his world felt safe and secure.

His first instinct after Sam had been hurt was to whisk his little girl away to a place where gangs didn't roam the streets and people didn't shoot each other over nothing.

But he couldn't leave. Not if he wanted to live with himself. Marissa had wanted Samantha raised in her family home. He'd promised Marissa he'd stay. No matter what. He'd made a commitment to her and to the community. He'd vowed long ago not to sit back and let others decide what needed to be done. If he wanted change, then he had to be part of the process to make it happen.

But tonight, he was still reeling from learning that Sam might have witnessed the shooting. He knew Crista had to file a report and tell Captain Englend what Sam had said. Would the captain then want Sam to identify men in a lineup? He couldn't fathom putting Sam through that.

But he also had to consider that if Sam had seen the shooter, they might have seen her—and they might want to make sure she didn't say anything. Nothing had happened to make him think that was the case, and because it had been dark in the room, it wasn't likely they'd seen her. Still, the thought scared the hell out of him, and he wanted to do something to protect Sam. Crista had mentioned a bodyguard. He could hire someone until he knew there was no danger. And he still had to talk to the boys at the center. He couldn't imagine any of them being involved, but someone may have heard something on the street, and if anyone knew anything...

"I hope Ms. Santiago joins us for Thanksgiving."

Elena's voice brought Alex to the moment.

His mother-in-law continued talking as she bustled toward the stairs. "Thanksgiving is for family and friends. It will be nice having people here again. It will be good for Samantha."

"Yes, it would be nice, and good for Sam, too. I'm hoping Crista accepts the invitation. If not, maybe we'll invite some of the boys I work with." As he said the words, he felt an emptiness inside.

He missed being part of a family. Missed family activities on the weekends, breakfast and dinner together, nights in front of the fire watching their favorite shows, though that hadn't happened as often as Marissa had wanted. He'd been too busy with the new job. And since Marissa's death, he'd been so intent on taking up the slack in Sam's life without her mother, he hadn't had time to think about what he'd personally been missing.

He'd put all thoughts of love out of his mind. Not because there weren't plenty of eligible women around, but because the pain of losing Marissa had been unbearable. If he allowed someone else into his life, there was always the chance that it wouldn't work. The chance that something might happen. It was easier not to get involved. Easier to keep the status quo.

But dammit. He couldn't seem to stop thinking about Crista. Despite the all-business facade she presented on the job, he'd seen a vulnerable woman underneath it all. He saw her wistful expression when she talked with Sam, the pain in her eyes when she talked about her brother. When he'd visited her apartment, and even tonight, she seemed a different person. Softer. Sensitive and caring. Vulnerable.

He hadn't imagined there could be another woman besides Marissa who could affect him so deeply.

THE NEXT MORNING, Crista headed to work on a spurt of new energy. After her pleasant dinner with the Del Rio family and a quick workout at the gym last night, she'd felt revitalized. For the first time in two weeks she'd slept like a rock.

Today, she should have the information she'd been waiting for from Ballistics. The results weren't going to solve the case for her, but it was a starting place. If the bullet from the Encanto shooting could be linked to the drive-by at her apartment, she'd have a better idea of what they were looking at.

Diego was also on the list of people she planned to see today. She had to extend the Thanksgiving invitation from Alex, and if he said no, she'd tell him to come to her place and then she'd give Alex her regrets.

And next was Marco. Her earlier plan to talk to him had been derailed, but it was still a good plan. Maybe he could elaborate on what Diego had told her and she'd find out why Diego thought she was searching for evidence in the wrong place. The fact that some people were getting upset by it, told her just the opposite. If she was ruffling feathers by getting too close, then she was looking in the *right* place. And baby, she'd only just begun.

"Good morning," she said cheerily to Hanover on her way by his desk. The spring in her stride reflected her mood and she wasn't going to let anything spoil it. Not even Hanover when he mumbled something unintelligible in response.

Gliding by the other desks, Crista stopped short when she saw Pete in Englend's office. Pete was on vacation. What was he doing here?

She continued to her desk where she attempted to busy herself with two different cases she'd taken on prior to the Encanto case. One involved a double homicide—a man and his girlfriend—and the two prime suspects were the man's wife and his son. But both had alibis. The other case involved a missing teenager whose parents believed he had been murdered. There was blood in the boy's room, evidence that something had happened, but no body and no weapon. No suspects. Both cases had taken a back seat to the Encanto case since the mayor's edict had come down.

But as much as she wanted to focus, she couldn't stop wondering why Pete was here. Had something happened to Sharon? The baby? Pete's hard, angry expression said no, it was something else.

When the phone rang, she snatched it up. "Santiago here."

"I have your information," a woman's small voice said.

"Good information?"

"Why don't you come down and see."

"I'll be right there." But as anxious as she was to hear what Josey had to say, she didn't want to miss talking with Pete. "I'm finishing up something here. I'll be there in a few."

As she hung up, Crista saw Pete leaving Englend's office. He didn't come over but headed for the door. She bolted to her feet and caught up with him in the hall.

"Pete. Wait. What are you doing here? Is everything okay?"

He gave her a thin smile. "Yeah, things are great." His tone held a note of sarcasm.

"Is Sharon okay? The baby?"

He shook his head as if just realizing Crista's concern was about his family. "Oh, yeah, they're fine. This was work related."

"You're still taking the time off, aren't you?"

He nodded. "Sure am."

"Then what was so important that you had to come down and meet with the captain?"

"You don't want to know."

An ominous feeling settled in Crista's bones. "It was about me, wasn't it?" Why she thought that, she didn't know—except that Pete wouldn't normally have any qualms telling her anything if it was about a case.

"Tell me, Pete. I can take it."

At forty-five, Pete still looked like a little boy and, right now, he looked like a kid who'd been caught stealing candy bars from the cupboard.

"C'mon. Spit it out. What did Englend say about me?"

"Nothing about you. He told me I was getting a new partner and asked me if I had any preference."

Crista sputtered. "I—I don't understand. Did you request a change?" She couldn't fathom that Pete would do something like that without telling her first. Pete wasn't the kind to make waves. At his age, he simply wanted to do his time and retire.

He shook his head. "No, I didn't." He moved closer and bent near her ear. "Englend said you're coming off the Encanto case. That they have to get someone who can tie it up fast."

That figured. He'd get someone who'd arrest anyone. Anger grew in her gut. Her blood pressure spiked. It sounded as if Englend wasn't just taking her off the case, he was replacing her. She knew what that meant. A transfer to a back desk deep in the bowels of the building somewhere.

That's what the good old boys did when they wanted to get rid of an officer. Treat him like crap until the officer couldn't take it anymore and resigned. She'd seen it happen more than once. "Was that what you meant when you said I should watch my back?"

Pete shrugged.

Crista couldn't ask Pete what he had said to Englend. He valued his job. Wanted to stay here till retirement. Pete was caught between his loyalty to a partner he'd only had for a couple months and the captain, who held Pete's career in his hands. She felt bad for Pete. He didn't need to be in that position—and he was here because of her.

"Thanks for cluing me in. I appreciate it. And now, I gotta go. Ballistics called."

"They got something good?"

"I hope so."

Crista had started to leave when Pete said, "Now that you got me to spill my guts, don't you want to know what I told him?"

She stopped midstride, but didn't turn. She wanted to know but she was afraid of what she'd hear. She took a breath, turned to face him and braced for the worst. "Sure."

He stepped forward and placed his hands gently on her upper arms. "I told him I have the best partner I've ever had, and I don't want another."

Crista swallowed. "You told him that?"

"Yes. And I meant it."

Tears suddenly welled in Crista's eyes and she couldn't prevent a wobbly smile. She didn't know what to say, but she felt grateful that someone was on her side. She quickly blinked back the uncharacteristic display of emotion. "How did Englend react? What you said isn't going to affect your job, is it?"

He shrugged again. "I don't think so, but if it does, I'll deal with it. Englend seemed to take it in stride. Maybe he respects my judgement."

"And well he should." Crista tried to joke, but the seriousness of her situation flattened her voice and her spirit. And while it felt wonderful to have Pete's support, she could never let him put his job in jeopardy for her. "Promise me you won't do that anymore."

"Do what?"

"Put your career on the line for me."

Pete tilted his head back and laughed flat out. "I wasn't doing it *all* for you, babe. I was doing it for me, too. He wanted to put Eddie Fontanero in your place."

Crista knew Fontanero, not personally, but they'd once worked out of the same precinct. She also knew him by reputation. He was a long time HPD veteran, hired when racial preference points were added to test scores. Rumors abounded that he was on the take, had been for years, but since he had powerful political friends in the minority community and protection from high up on the force, nothing ever came of them.

It was well-known that Fontanero was aggressive and calculating and wasn't above intimidating officers and suspects alike to keep them quiet. His treatment of women on the force was legend. But in all cases, the brotherhood—the silent code of not ratting on a fellow officer, protected him.

Crista knew why Englend wanted Eddie Fontanero. He was the kind of officer who ingratiated himself with those who could do him some good, and if Englend wanted an arrest, Fontanero would make one.

"I see." She really did. While no officer would rat on Eddie, no one who had any integrity wanted to work with the guy, either. "Whoever it was for, thanks for trying to help. Now get home to your wife and that new baby of yours."

Pete left and Crista headed for Josey's office, the conversation still ringing in her ears. Englend had never wanted a woman on his team and it was pretty obvious he would use any excuse to get rid of her. As far as she was concerned, it was a clear case of gender bias. He'd put her on the case to show she couldn't do the job.

Her mind spinning, she nodded absently at a couple officers who passed her in the hall. Her career was in jeopardy and not because of anything she'd done. Worse yet, if Englend took her off the job and the wrong person was arrested, that would leave the real perpetrator on the streets—and Alex would think his family was safe.

CHAPTER NINE

"SEE THIS LINE HERE?" Josey Adams, one of the CSU's ballistics experts, pointed to an enlarged picture of a bullet on her computer screen.

"Yes."

Josey flipped to another screen. "And this one here? The markings are the same on both bullets."

"Which means they came from the same gun." A rush of adrenaline pounded through Crista's veins. She'd known from the empty cartridges at the crime scenes that the weapon used was a .38 caliber semiautomatic handgun. Now she had the evidence to tie the two cases together. Gun markings were like fingerprints and the bullets could be matched to one gun.

"The evidence from the Marigold shooting doesn't match either one."

Okay. That didn't confirm or rule out anything, only that if one shooter had made all three hits, he hadn't used the same gun. That the bullets taken from Alex's home and the ones from her apartment came from the same gun confirmed for her that Alex was the target. She'd suspected as much, but now she had proof.

After Diego's warning that *she* could be in danger, she'd wondered if the bullet at her apartment had been meant for her. She didn't need to wonder anymore.

"Thanks, Josey. Can I get a copy of the report?"

The petite blonde handed Crista a copy she'd already made. "Service with a smile."

Crista felt better than she had since she'd started working the case. This narrowed her search for the gun, which in turn would narrow her search for a suspect.

"I'm running a photo search right now to see if there might be a match with any bullets in other crimes."

"Great. Let me know when you get something." If the results showed the gun had been used before, the crime scene investigation from that case might give her a clue about the owner of the gun.

Crista left the CSU for the parking garage, got in her car and drove out. She made the first turn and headed toward the barrio to see Diego. He'd warned her about coming into the neighborhood and asking questions, but she wouldn't let that keep her away. Aside from her job, rebuilding her relationship with Diego, establishing some semblance of trust between them, was the most important thing in her life.

As she pulled to a stop in front of the house, she saw a tricked-out Harley in the drive. Was Marco here? Trini? Her stomach churned. Trini always rode a Harley.

But that was stupid. Trini had only recently been released from prison, where would he get the money for a bike like that?

She managed to push the past from her mind and eased her way up the steps. Talk to Diego. That's all she was here for. At the door, she listened for voices. Nothing. She knocked once. When no one showed, she knocked again. The door jerked open a crack and her brother peered at her through the slit.

"Hey, Diego," she said.

"What are you doing here?"

"I wanted to talk."

"I can't right now. Someone's here."

The warning in Diego's eyes indicated it was in her best interest not to pursue the matter.

"You don't want to come in," he said under his breath.

Trini was there. That had to be it. And Diego was right. She truly didn't want to go in if her ex was inside.

"Okay, I'll leave. But I have a quick question for you."

His eyes narrowed. "What?"

"I've been asked to have Thanksgiving at…a friend's home. I explained that I'd already asked you to my place, and they invited you to come, too."

"So go."

"I don't want to go alone. I want you to come with me. They're nice people and being with them reminded me of how our family was before Papa died," she said, hoping he remembered and would like to feel that closeness again.

He didn't respond instantly, but his eyes softened. Finally he said, "What friends?"

"Alex Del Rio and his family. I've gotten to know them while working on the case."

His face lit up with interest. "He's the guy running the new center."

"That's right."

He looked down, then asked softly, "Does he know about me?"

She nodded. "I think you'll like him. You'll like the whole family. And if you decide you'd rather not come along, I still want you to have Thanksgiving with me at my place."

Just then Crista heard Trini's scratchy voice. A voice she'd recognize anywhere. "*¿Qué pasa,* Diego?"

"You better go," her brother growled.

"Okay, but get back to me about Thanksgiving as soon as you can. It's only two days away." The words had barely left her lips when Diego shut the door.

As she walked to the car, it was all Crista could do to keep her shoulders from sagging. Diego was keeping bad company and there seemed nothing she could do to stop it.

Diego. Diego. Her heart ached for the innocent boy he'd once been. For the man she wanted him to be. For the man he could be.

Crista slipped into the driver's seat and sped away, her mind reeling. A heavy dread started to settle in her chest, but she shook it off. There might be a point where she'd have to come to grips with the fact that she couldn't help Diego—she drew a deep breath through her teeth—but she wasn't there yet. She would think of something.

In the meantime, she had to focus. There were other things to do. First, she'd go back to the station for a gun search. Man, she hated facing Englend, but if she was lucky, she'd get some names from the database. If she didn't find anything there, she'd head for the gun shops. Pawnshops. Anyplace where someone might purchase a .38 caliber semiautomatic handgun. If she had a name or two, she might be able to convince Englend she was close to an arrest.

As Crista turned the corner, she glanced in her rearview mirror and noticed a black truck behind her. Her skin prickled. She gripped the steering wheel tighter and kept watching behind her all the way to the station. The vehicle was still there. Either she was getting paranoid or she was being followed.

But she was only a couple blocks from headquarters and she doubted whoever it was would follow her into the police garage.

Making a quick right turn and then a left, she pulled into the parking garage and circled up the ramp. Feeling better, and a little foolish at the same time, she glanced over her shoulder just to be sure. Nothing.

One more circle up the ramp to the fourth floor and she pulled into her designated space, gathered her briefcase and pulled the door handle to get out. Glancing up, she froze.

The black truck cruised up the ramp. There was no plate in front. And with dark tinted windows on both her Jeep and the truck, she couldn't see inside. Not even enough to tell if the driver was a man or a woman.

She watched the vehicle take an empty space at the end of the row, and then waited to see who got out. No one did.

She waited. Still nothing. Okay…she was a law enforcement officer and she was in the police parking garage. While she knew all the vehicles on her floor, it could be that one of the detectives simply had a new one. But why then had the truck been behind her all the way from the barrio?

Crista exited the Jeep and started toward the truck. Easy enough to find out who it was. She was halfway across the lot when the truck pulled out, tires screeching in reverse and then forward again as it sped down the ramp. She stood there for a moment, then hurried back to her car, got out her digital camera and went back to take some photos of the tire tracks, smudged as they were. There was nothing to compare the photos to since there were no marks from the other scenes, but she took the photos anyway. Just in case. She didn't get the make of the truck, but it was one of the big models.

Finished, she hurried to the end of the hall straight for the CS unit. She stopped at the desk inside. "Laura, do you have any new vehicles registered for that end space in the garage?"

Laura looked at her with a quizzical expression. "No."

"Any visitors coming in today?"

She shook her head. "Not on my list."

"Thanks." Crista's nerves felt like rubber bands twisted to the max. Well, who wouldn't be edgy after being followed.

At her desk, she put her things away, turned on her computer and punched into NCIC, the national database on criminal activity, and then entered the information on the gun that had been used in both shootings, searching for any local criminal who might have used that type of gun before. If she'd had a license number on the truck, she would've punched that in, too. But she didn't.

The captain wasn't at his desk, so she left him a message about the truck. He'd probably laugh. She had no proof of anything. But a black truck had sped by her apartment when they'd been shot at, Sam had drawn a black truck in her picture, and now today, a black truck had followed her. Were they the same? She didn't know. What she did know was that none of it was her imagination.

After waiting what seemed like an excessively long time, a list of names popped onto the screen. She printed out the list and started the elimination process, ruling out those without any known gang affiliations and those who lived out of the area. Of those that remained, one guy belonged to the Barrio Azteca, another the Latin Kings, and the rest belonged to the Pistoles and Los Locos.

She highlighted the name of a Pistoles gang member. Pedro Castillo, who'd been arrested three years earlier by two of the officers in her unit. Garcia and Munez.

According to the records, the weapon had never been recovered. If she could find out what Castillo had done with the gun she *might* have a lead. It wasn't all that strange to find that a gun used in one crime had been used in another. But if the officers who'd interrogated Castillo couldn't get him to divulge what he'd done with it, she probably couldn't, either.

The chirp of the phone got her attention. She hoped it was Josey. "Santiago."

"What time are we supposed to be at this guy's house for the dinner?"

Crista's spirits lifted. "One o'clock. How about if I pick you up at noon."

"It's better if I come to your place."

"Okay," she said, suddenly a little anxious about the whole thing now that Diego had actually agreed to come along. As a kid, Diego had been utterly charming when he wanted—or downright obnoxious. She wanted to tell him to be on his best behavior, yet if she did, she might scare him off. "I'm glad you're coming," she said, then gave him her address. Hanging up, she felt a sense of satisfaction. She'd made a connection with Diego. Maybe only a small one, but it was there nonetheless.

She picked up the phone again and pressed Alex's number at work, still wondering if spending the holiday with his family was wise. But she realized that even if it wasn't, it was what she wanted to do.

"Alex," she said when he answered. "It's Crista."

"Well, hello. This is a pleasant surprise."

"I thought I'd better let you know that my brother and I will be delighted to spend Thanksgiving with your family."

"Wonderful. Sam will be happy—and I am, too."

Crista's stomach fluttered. She wasn't used to people she worked with getting that close and it felt awkward. "Uh…you said around one o'clock before."

"Right. Will that work for you?"

"Yes. That's fine." It would allow her to get some work done in the morning.

Alex cleared his throat, then said, "I'm concerned about Sam's safety."

"Has something happened?"

"No, but I'm worried that something might."

Crista's muscles tensed. "We're working really hard to find the perpetrator. Aside from that…well, I wish there was more the police could do."

"Yeah. I know. It's not your fault. At any rate, I hired someone to be on watch."

"A bodyguard?"

"He doesn't call himself that, but yes. I've also been thinking it might be a good idea for you to talk with the guys I recruited to work at the center."

Crista's interest was piqued. "Do you think they can help?"

"I don't think so, but you never know. I spoke with them about the drive-by and told you were investigating the case and would like to talk to them."

"What was the response?"

"Not much. But I know they don't like the idea of talking to the police. It sends a message that they're not trustworthy."

When she was still a block away, she spotted Alex's Lincoln Navigator at a stoplight and ran toward him waving her arms. As she got close, he lowered his window.

"Going my way?"

Puffing, not so much from the activity but from worry that she'd miss him and he'd go into the office to find her, she said, "Absolutely."

She hurried around the SUV and hopped in the front seat next to him.

Alex didn't say a word, and when the light changed, he slowly drove ahead.

Crista fumbled with the seat belt, finally securing it in place. "I suppose you're wondering what I was doing?"

He glanced at her, a teasing glint in his eyes. "Kinda."

"It wasn't anything exciting. I went to get some coffee with a friend and I guess I thought I had more time than I did. On the way back, I saw you go by. I didn't want to miss you, so I ran to the light where you'd stopped."

"Oh-kay." The look on his face said he didn't buy it.

"So," she said. "Where's the center located?"

"It's near the shipping channel on Canal Street in an old building that wasn't being used."

"Right. You mentioned you'd had a run-in with the owner." Crista had tried to track Tom Corcoran down for an interview, but so far the man had eluded her.

"It was nothing serious. We worked it out. The building was in bad condition, so we're doing some reconstruction. As I mentioned, some of the work is being done by the neighborhood youths I've recruited to work at the center."

"Are you going to tell me their names, or do I have to guess?"

He cracked a smile. "Right now I have Charlie, an older guy from the neighborhood acting as a supervisor, and there are four guys are doing the main work. Ramon, Daniel, Julio and Richard. Another younger boy, Tommy Ramirez, comes in off and on, but he's too young to work with tools. He likes to hang around and I figure it's better for him to be here than on the street."

She nodded. "You really do think you can change things, don't you."

He looked at her and then back to the road again. "Not overnight. But little by little. Education is key."

Looking at him, Crista realized all she really knew about Alex was what she read in the case file. "Where did you go to school?"

"USC."

"But you grew up in northern California."

"Like most kids, I wanted to be on my own. I wanted to party and have the freedom I didn't have at home."

"And did you party?"

"For a while. When my grades fell, my father refused to pay my expenses, which forced me to go back home and work at the vineyard to earn money to go back to school. When I had to pay my own way, things started to look different. So I did a stint with the military, and after that I went to Wharton and majored in business."

"You have a business degree?"

He nodded. "And an MBA. For all the good it's doing me now." He shrugged. "I should have gone into education." He glanced over again. "How about you? Where'd you go to school?"

Compared to his education, hers was minimal. But

she was proud of what she'd accomplished. She'd done more than anyone ever expected her to do. "I went to a community college and received a two-year degree in criminal justice. I'd like to get a bachelor's degree someday, but there never seems to be enough time."

"Not when you spend all your time on the job or at the gym."

She did tell him that, didn't she. And he had a point.

"Apparently, finishing school isn't as important as the other things you do."

"I guess not." Did he think less of her for not having a bachelor's degree? Not that it mattered. She'd learned long ago that she couldn't live her life for others. She had to be happy with herself.

"What's important is that you like what you do. I learned that the hard way," Alex said.

"I love what I do. I've never thought of doing anything else." Which reminded her that her job was on the line as they spoke. She didn't know what she'd do if Englend brought in Fontanero. Her job was everything to her, even if it was in a unit she didn't exactly love.

"To paraphrase Mark Twain, 'Every job is a good one—unless you hate to do it.'"

She glanced at him. "I'll have to remember that."

"That's how I felt when I was working in the family business. While it was a great place to be, with people I cared about, I didn't want to commit my life to the vineyard. I'd wake up every day hating to go to work. This job has given me something I didn't have before."

"Really? What's that?"

"Passion." His eyes lit. "A feeling that I can make a difference. Without that, it's just going to work every day and bringing home a paycheck at the end of the week."

That was one point where they agreed. There was nothing she'd rather do than law enforcement. By keeping people safe, she felt as if *she* made a difference in the world. But Englend was making it difficult for her to do that job. And her options were limited. She could file a grievance against him, but that was about it.

There were a lot of grievances being filed within the department these days. More in the past two years than the previous ten, it seemed. Look at someone wrong and it's sexual harassment. File a grievance. It seemed the trend, especially with new female recruits. If they only knew how they were screwing themselves and their careers.

The old guard wasn't dead and anyone who believed so was living in a fantasy world. Sure, lots of things had changed for the better, even from when she'd come on board. But to say all cops were equal... No way. If you complained, they'd get you for it. File a grievance against another officer and you were dead meat.

There was a point where you simply had to say no more—only she didn't know if she'd reached that point yet.

"Penny?"

Alex's honeyed voice cut into Crista's thoughts. "Excuse me?"

"Penny for your thoughts? You were deeply involved in something."

She waved a hand. "Not really. I was just thinking about the case. It's a tough one."

"Yeah. Maybe this meeting will help." He pulled into a dirt parking lot next to a two-story building that looked as if it should have a Condemned sign on the front.

"It will. One way or another." She hoped for Alex's sake she'd be able to rule out his boys as possible suspects, and she hoped even more that one of them might have heard something on the street that could help.

Alex parked, they exited and went inside together. The building was a shell, which made all the pounding and sawing echo even louder. A radio blared rap music in the background. The dry scent of sawdust lodged in her nose. Several stacks of two-by-fours rested against the gutted walls and sawdust covered the floor around a boy who was standing by a table saw in the middle of the large room. An older man stood next to him—probably the supervisor. The boy's head came up when they entered the building, then he waved at Alex.

"Hey, Ramon." Alex crossed the room to reach the teen, who appeared to be about sixteen or seventeen, and shook his hand.

Crista wondered why Ramon wasn't in school, why all of the boys weren't in school, but then realized the time. School would be out already.

"Ramon, I want you to meet a friend of mine." Alex turned to Crista. "Detective Santiago."

The teenager's eyes narrowed.

"I'm pleased to meet you, Ramon," Crista said, reaching out to shake his hand. When he didn't reciprocate, she shrugged and said, "I'm here to help Mr. Del Rio."

Ramon turned to Alex for confirmation.

"The drive-by at my place," Alex said. "Remember?"

"I was here working," he said defensively.

"I know," Crista said. "I'm simply looking for more information that might be helpful in solving the case, so Mr. Del Rio and his family can feel safe again."

Ramon had brown puppy-dog eyes, eyes that said they'd seen too much in his short life. His hair was a light caramel color and he wore faded jeans and a long T-shirt, both about two sizes too big. When he reached for a piece of wood, she noticed the *cholo* tattoo on his right forearm. *Cholo* meant "gangster" and the tattoo, a man with a hat, mustache and goatee, meant the boy had been transitioned away from his family into the American street-gang culture.

"I haven't been on the street since I agreed to help you, Mr. D. I don't know nuthin'."

"I'm just covering all bases, Ramon," Crista said in Spanish, thinking it might make the boy more comfortable. "I thought someone on the block knows the ropes and might have heard something."

He stood a little taller, but shook his head. "I don't know nuthin'."

Crista's conversation with the other guys went the same way. The only kid she didn't talk to was Tommy because he wasn't there.

"That wasn't too productive," Crista said to Alex on their way out of the building. "But it was nice to see that your boys are committed to doing a good job here at the center."

"Yeah, which is why I didn't want to take the chance that they'd resent the intrusion. But when I realized Sam could be in danger I couldn't leave any bases uncovered."

"I appreciate it. I'd still like to talk with the other boy, though."

"I'll tell him the next time I see him. If I see him."

"You think he'll be back?"

Alex opened the car door for Crista. "I don't know. He hasn't been here for a week."

Crista's interest piqued. "Really? Do you know what day that was?"

"Before the shooting."

When Alex climbed in on the other side, she said, "Maybe you can give me his home address."

"If I knew it, I would."

That the boy hadn't been here since the shooting raised a flag for Crista. "Did he come around a lot before?"

Alex held up a hand. "I know what you're thinking. But don't. I heard from one of the other boys that Tommy has a lot of family problems."

"And you think that's why he hasn't been here?"

Alex started the SUV. "I don't know. The last time we talked, I told him if he wanted to hang out he had to show me he was doing a good job in school. That's a condition for all the boys. As far as I know he's not involved in any gang activity yet, and I hope he comes back."

Okay, so Alex didn't know all that much about the boy. It didn't matter. She had his name. She'd ask around. She'd check the school.

"Where to now? Do you have time for a bite to eat before going home?"

She'd love to. She hated eating alone. "I better not."

He reached out and placed his right hand over hers. "You have to eat someplace."

His hand was warm and reassuring. She felt acceptance in his touch. Acceptance and respect. Something she hadn't felt much of from the men in her life, and the knowledge sent a shiver of excitement through her.

His sincerity disarmed her, and she fought an urge to pull him close, to feel his body against hers and maybe discover what she'd been missing all her life. He squeezed her hand softly, his thumb tracing circles on her palm. Desire curled low in her belly.

"I'll grab something later. Right now I have some work to finish at the station," she lied. She was about to come undone if he didn't stop that right now. And considering her sexual deprivation for the past couple of years, the man could be in serious trouble if she accepted his offer. "But thanks anyway."

He released her hand and tightened his grip on the steering wheel. She saw the sting of rejection in his eyes. "Rain check?"

She could think of nothing she'd like more—and nothing that was more wrong. If Englend found out, she'd not only be off the case, she'd no longer have a job.

"Maybe."

He turned to look at her, his mouth tipped up slightly as if pleased with her answer. "Okay. So I guess that means I take you to your car."

Yes. Her car—which she'd parked a half mile from the station. "Great. You can just let me off in front of headquarters. I have a couple things to do before I go home."

CHAPTER TEN

ALEX DROPPED CRISTA off at the Travis Street entrance of the HPD, and she got the distinct feeling that he wanted to lecture her about taking time to have a little fun instead of working so much. But he kept his opinions to himself. Good boy.

As soon as he drove off, she tucked her chin and hurried the six blocks to her Jeep hoping none of her colleagues drove by and saw her.

The walk was invigorating and it gave her time to process some of the information from the boys who worked for Alex, spare as it was. She felt a couple of them knew more than they had said. And now that she'd been there, she might be able to go back and talk to them again—without Alex. While Alex thought they'd be more comfortable with him there, she knew the reverse could be true.

The boys revered and respected Alex, and if any of them had information, they might not say so in front of him because he might think less of them.

The ride home seemed longer than ever and she felt a sense of relief when she pulled into the parking lot. It had been a long day, and she was both mentally and physically exhausted. She hadn't felt that way for years.

She went inside and trudged up the stairs, each step an effort. Almost to the third floor, she noticed the hallway light was out. Her pulse accelerated. She glanced around, her gaze circling, scanning. The shadowy halls were eerily quiet, but nothing seemed out of place. When she was tired, she sometimes overreacted.

As she continued toward her apartment, she fished in her purse for her key. At the door, her breath caught. It was open a fraction of an inch.

Without flinching, Crista drew her gun and flattened her back against the wall, listening. Nothing. She glanced at the lock and the door frame. No evidence of a break-in. Inching the door open with her toe, she reached inside and switched on the light. Waiting, she heard nothing but the hum of the fluorescent light. She kicked open the door, making as much racket as possible—a police tactic used to intimidate and scare the hell out of anyone who didn't expect it. Gun raised, she edged inside.

Her gaze shot first to the right and then to the left. Nothing. Had the caretaker come in for something and forgotten to close the door when he left? What reason would he have for coming inside? She eased her way from the living room into the kitchen. Nothing out of place there, either. Still skirting the wall, she crept down the hall toward her bedroom, stood out of range beside the door and shouted, "Don't move or you're a dead man!"

Still nothing. Slowly, cautiously, she placed one foot in front of the other and entered the room, gun poised for action.

Everything was exactly as she'd left it. Weird. Just plain weird. She went back to the living room, double-locked the door and stood with her back against the wall. She let out a sigh of relief, and then went to Calvin's cage and lifted the cover.

What the—! Calvin was gone. The cage door—closed. How could he get out? Had someone taken him? Maybe Calvin was making a lot of racket and someone complained so the caretaker came up and removed him? No, that didn't make sense. Calvin didn't make noise when he was covered.

"Calvin. Calvin, are you here?" She dashed around searching everywhere for the bird.

Oh, God. The apartment door had been open. If he'd somehow gotten outside, he couldn't survive.

Fear for Calvin filled her with dread. She hadn't realized how much the silly bird meant to her till this very moment. She looked in the closet, on the bookcase, under the table in the kitchen, atop the cabinets. Her heart sank. He wasn't anywhere.

"Awk!" a faint squawk sounded.

"Calvin. Calvin, where are you?" She heard thumping coming from somewhere near the bathroom. She bolted down the hall and still calling his name, she burst into the bathroom. She didn't see him anywhere and ripped back the shower curtain.

Her mouth fell open. Calvin was thumping around in the bathtub, covered with something black and greasy—like oil. "Oh, Calvin. Poor Calvin."

On her knees, she picked up the bird in her hands and cradled him to her chest. Tears fell on her cheeks. "Who would do such a thing to you?" What kind of sick mind would hurt a helpless bird? She stroked his wings and the back of his head. "You're a mess," she sniveled. But he was here—and he was alive.

Still holding the bird, she called the police to report the incident. When they came, they took the information and said that since there was no evidence of a break-in, there wasn't much they could do. She knew that before they arrived; she'd done the same many times. Take the information, talk to the neighbors, file a report. Do nothing. Because there was nothing to do without a lead of some kind.

While the officers did their thing, Crista called a twenty-four-hour lock service, and then sat Calvin in the kitchen sink and washed his feathers with a soft sponge and a gentle detergent. She remembered hearing on the news that after one of the big oil spills they'd used dish detergent to clean the seagulls.

When Calvin was as clean as she could get him without removing all his feathers, she dried him off, put him back in his cage, gave him some fresh water and food and prayed he'd be okay—that he wouldn't suffer any permanent problems.

"Better get those locks replaced," one of the officers said on his way out.

"I already called someone," she responded, then double-locked the door behind him. Weary, she flopped onto the couch to wait for the locksmith. Animal cruelty. She couldn't fathom it. Had vandals broken in and was this some sick person's distorted idea of fun? Or was it something more serious?

A warning maybe? If she put this incident together with the truck she'd thought was following her, she might conclude she had a stalker. Trini was her first thought. Diego's warning could have been about Trini and had nothing to do with her asking questions in the wrong places.

But the pattern didn't fit Trini's M.O. His method was to let her know he was there, watching her, stalking her. That way she'd never feel safe. In addition, that scenario didn't answer the truck question. So far, a black vehicle had been involved in the Encanto shoot-

ing, the one at her place and today, a black truck had
been following her. But the Encanto shooting had happened *before* she'd had the run-in with Trini. He hadn't
even known she was back.

Which meant, even if he was at her apartment, he
wasn't the person in the truck. What she didn't know
was if there was a connection between the shootings
and the assault on Calvin.

Someone who thought she was getting too close, as
Diego said.

Another thought assailed her. If Englend learned of
tonight's incident, he'd have more ammunition to take
her off the case. If she was being threatened, the captain might think she couldn't do her job properly. Hell,
he already thought that. Her head hurt. Her body was
riddled with fatigue and her eyes felt as if she'd rubbed
them with sandpaper.

She glanced at Calvin again. How could anyone…
How could they! Her fatigue quickly morphed into
anger. Anger at whoever had done this. Anger at the
shooters who'd hurt Samantha and with herself that she
hadn't been able to solve the case—that she'd allowed
herself to get in such a precarious position.

Well, dammit. She wasn't going to sit idly by and
watch her career go down the tubes just because Englend wanted an arrest. She wasn't going to let some
stalker intimidate her and she wasn't going to allow
Alex and Sam to live in fear.

How she was going to fix all that, was the million-
dollar question.

MORNING BROUGHT Crista's problems into a clearer
light. Lying in bed, she took a few minutes to stretch
and sit up. As she did, she decided there were things

she could do something about and things she couldn't. As an officer of the law, she knew if someone was stalking her, the police couldn't do anything without proof. If she could prove it was Trini, she'd get a restraining order.

The only thing she could do on the Encanto case was keep working on it, get the evidence and make an arrest. And if Englend was going to cut her legs from under her, she wouldn't stand for it.

With Englend, she had two options. File a grievance against him for gender bias or keep her mouth shut. She flopped back on the pillow. She needed to talk to someone. She needed advice. But who?

Her friend Risa knew all about being in a position where your job is on the line. But that was a different situation. Risa had been accused of shooting her partner and was found innocent. Gender bias hadn't played a part. And what made her think Risa would want to give Crista advice now that their positions were reversed?

Crista's stomach knotted with regret that she'd abandoned Risa because she'd been worried about her own job.

Lucy, Abby, Mei, Crista and Catherine—they'd all had reasons for distancing themselves, and Crista wasn't all that sure anymore what those reasons were. Except for her bitter disagreement with Lucy. Lucy had all but said flat out that she thought Risa was guilty, and then she'd suggested they "trust the system" to make the right decision. Crista knew from experience that trusting the system was a crock.

Bitter memories lay rock-hard in Crista's gut. She'd been a patrol officer for five years and, for half that time, she'd been assigned some of the worst shifts and some of the worst beats. She'd taken the bad with the good and never complained. She got the job done. Eventually, she'd been accepted by her team, and while she hadn't become "one of the guys," she'd believed her teammates respected her.

But when she'd stood up for Risa at the beginning of the investigation, all their so-called respect vanished like snow on a summer sidewalk. Her faith in the "system" had been shaken to the core.

Crista had understood that Catherine might still be reeling from her husband's death six months ago, and the promotion to chief of police put her at a disadvantage when it came to offering support for her friends. Cathy couldn't do anything that might give the appearance of favoritism. But in Risa's case, Crista believed their new chief had gone too far in the opposite direction. The IA investigation seemed more intensive than any other cop would've received, and Catherine hadn't won any points with Crista on that one.

The only member of the group who'd remained somewhat neutral was Abby. But even she had backed away. Maybe it was because Abby was on her second chance with the department already. She'd left the academy for love and moved to North Carolina with the Delta Force officer she'd fallen for. When the relationship failed, Abby returned to Houston and finished her academy training in a different class, determined to show her friends that she could stick it out this time.

No, Abby wasn't the person to call. Abby still viewed the world through rose-colored glasses, and any advice she might give would reflect her innate belief that people were good at heart. While Crista held that belief most of the time, she was also realistic. There were mean people out there. People out for their own gain.

With question after question playing havoc in her head, Crista decided to get up and go to the gym. In the back of her mind, she hoped she'd run into Mei. They'd always been able to talk about most anything.

The decision energized Crista and she bounded from the bed, threw on her sweats and, for later, took along a rust-colored pantsuit and a soft white turtleneck sweater. According to the weather channel last night, a cold front had come in and the temp was going down to freezing. She grabbed her black leather coat, but on her way through the living room the scent of motor oil made her stop. Calvin. What was she going to do with Calvin? Despite having the locks changed, she didn't feel comfortable leaving him alone.

Quickly she went to the next apartment and knocked on Mrs. McGinty's door. The elderly woman occasionally looked in on Calvin when Crista had to be gone for a day or two.

"Crista, how nice to see you," the woman's crackly voice echoed in the hall. A grandmotherly type, she was a little hard of hearing and she tended to speak louder because of it.

"Hi, Mrs. McGinty. I have a big favor to ask. Can you peek in on Calvin from time to time during the day? He's not feeling that great and I want to make sure he's okay."

"Of course. I'd love to," the woman said. "I have a better idea. Why don't you bring Calvin here? He can keep me company."

Perfect. Crista went back to her apartment, placed Calvin in the smaller cage and carried him to Mrs. McGinty's. She gave the older woman her cell phone number in case anything came up.

When Crista pulled into the Shao-Lin Studio's parking lot fifteen minutes later and saw Mei's car, she felt a mixture of relief and apprehension. She parked in front and dashed in, hoping Mei would have time to talk, even if it was only for a few minutes.

Mei was working with one of the instructors. The length of a match usually depended on the routine, so Crista engaged one of the other instructors in a shorter match so she'd be finished about the time Mei was.

While Crista stretched to ready herself, she saw Mei move into position. One quick strike from her opponent put Mei on the defensive. *Always strike first, Mei.* Apparently she'd forgotten the mantra Crista had taught her: Be First, Be Fast, Be Ferocious.

Even so, Mei came back quickly, using the linear style of straight-on movements. Attack, head-on block, in and out. Mei had improved since they'd last worked out together, and Crista was impressed.

Wing Chun was based on a clear understanding of fighting concepts and strategies expressed through a minimal number of techniques. Simplicity, directness and efficiency were key. When Crista was ready, she positioned on the mat and went directly on the offensive, mixing circular blocks with her linear attacks. When finished, she bowed to her instructor and in her peripheral vision, saw Mei and her instructor were also done. Perfect timing.

Mei looked up, saw Crista and a wide smile formed on her expressive face. She immediately came over. "Hi."

"Hi," Crista answered.

"I was going to call you to ask if you wanted to work out some time, but now that you're here, I can ask in person."

"Sure. Anytime," Crista said, the warmth of their old

friendship rushing back, almost as if it had never been interrupted. As they walked to the locker room together, Mei said, "How about if I call you after the holidays?"

Crista knew Mei usually worked extra hours over the holidays so other people could have the time off. "Great. I'll look forward to it."

They both showered and then sat on a bench, towel drying their hair together, just as they'd done in the past. "I heard you're being considered for lieutenant," Crista said. "People are saying good things about you."

Mei glanced away. She'd never handled compliments well and always downplayed her own skills and expertise.

"If I'm lucky, it might happen," Mei said.

"Right. Only you're forgetting something. I know how hard you worked to get where you are, so you can't play coy with me. Luck has nothing to do with it." They laughed together at Crista's observation.

"How is the new job going for you?" Mei asked. "I was surprised to hear about your transfer to the Chicano Squad. I thought your dream was to work in Special Ops, but I guess you changed your mind."

Crista shook her head. "No, I didn't. But it's a long story. Suffice it to say, it wasn't my choice."

Mei put down her towel and looked at Crista. "What's going on?"

They'd been close for too long and even the break in their relationship hadn't changed the intuitiveness they felt with each other. "I wish I knew," Crista said.

"Then what do you *think* is going on?" Mei refused to let Crista off the hook.

"Too many things," Crista said on a sigh. "I've been assigned a high-profile case and the captain is on my back about getting it done ASAP. The evidence is minimal and I'm sure the victims, a man and his daughter, are in danger. And as much as I want to, I can't do anything about it except stay close to them."

One of Mei's thin, dark eyebrows arched knowingly. "Sounds like personal involvement to me."

Crista closed her eyes and nodded. "I'm afraid so." She knew what Mei's response would be to that. For Mei, the job was primary. Crista had the same philosophy, so there was no point even getting into a discussion.

Mei's gaze narrowed. "So what else? I've never known you to be easily shaken, especially over a case, no matter how tough it is."

Crista pressed her lips together, finding it unusually hard to say the words. She'd never been one to complain. Never took the easy way out. But this was so different. And her job was on the line because of it. "Discrimination. Gender bias."

There was no surprise in Mei's eyes.

"I know. I know. We've all had to deal with lots of things because we're women in a guy's world. I expected that. But this is…different. Very different."

As they dressed, Crista explained in detail everything that had happened with Captain Englend. "From the beginning, I never expected the job to be a cakewalk, but I truly thought once I proved myself, things would change. Only I haven't been able to do anything in this unit, and now the one opportunity I've been given looks like a setup."

Mei shook her head. "I've faced problems with discrimination from individuals, but nothing that blatant."

"In my position, what would you do?"

Crista's friend thought for a moment. "You've always made a decision, then went ahead full-steam. On something like this, I might think about it before I leaped."

A feeling of hopelessness was growing inside Crista. "You're right. I want to take a stand so bad I can taste it, but I know from experience what that means. Basically, I'm damned if I do—" she managed a sarcastic laugh "—and hell, I'm damned if I don't."

"Call Catherine," Mei said. "She's always been someone we could count on for good advice."

"I thought about that. But with the media stirring up all kinds of dirt about the department, she has enough to worry about. My situation is nothing compared to what she has to deal with on an hourly basis."

Nodding, Mei agreed. "But on the other hand, she might welcome a friendly voice right now, and it would give her someone else's problem to focus on." Mei waited a second, then added, "Besides, it's her job to give advice."

Crista smiled. Even if Mei didn't have the answer, it felt good to get another opinion. And beyond that, it felt good to talk to Mei again.

Despite her despair about the job, Crista saw a ray of hope—hope that one day they could restore their friendship. "You're right, of course. I will call Catherine."

ON HER WAY to headquarters, Crista phoned Mrs. McGinty to make sure Calvin was okay. After that, her goal was to get to the station, check in and check out—avoid Englend so he couldn't take her off the case. Tomorrow was Thanksgiving and her schedule gave her the rest of the weekend off.

Apparently others had time off, too, because the

place was almost empty when she arrived. Englend wasn't even there.

She picked up the phone and connected with Laura. "Where is everyone?"

"We had an 11-99 a half hour ago. Didn't you hear it?"

Officer needs help. "No. No, I didn't. Who was it?"

"The call-out went so fast, I didn't hear."

And neither had she. Crista set the phone down and immediately checked her mike. It was on. If there was a call-out, she should have heard it, no matter where she was. She closed her eyes. Nausea assailed her. This couldn't be happening. Not again.

Inhaling deeply, she fished her cell phone from a pocket and punched in Catherine's number.

"Detective Santiago to speak with Chief Tanner, please."

"I'm sorry, she's unavailable. Can I take a message?"

"Please ask her to call me as soon as she can on my cell phone." She gave the assistant the number.

"I'll tell her. But she's really busy."

Yeah, Crista knew that. "Please give her the message." She clicked off and pocketed her phone. Okay. What now? She quickly gathered the information she needed to work in the field, but she couldn't shake the sickening feeling she had over not having heard the dispatch on the call-out. She knew what it meant. It was a not-so-subtle way of showing an officer she didn't belong. And if the call was important enough for the captain to go out, he wasn't going to be happy she didn't show.

What she didn't know was who was behind it. Someone wanted her on the captain's blacklist. Some-

one who knew she was on thready ground as it was—
and this could be the clincher for the captain.

Just as she was packing up, Crista's cell phone rang.
"Santiago here."

"Crista, it's Catherine."

"Thanks for returning my call." Now that the chief
had called back, Crista felt a little funny about saying
anything. She hoisted the briefcase strap over her
shoulder and headed for the parking garage, talking as
she went. "I know you're terribly busy, maybe I should
call back some other time."

"I have time right now. What's up?"

Crista bit her lip. "I need some advice. That's all."

"As the chief or as a friend?"

"Both."

"You got it."

Crista climbed into the Jeep so she could talk more
comfortably. Within moments, she'd told Catherine
everything she'd told Mei, leaving out her feelings for
Alex, whatever those were.

When Crista finished, she asked Catherine, "Any
thoughts?"

"It's a tough call. You know what to expect if you
file a grievance. Are you ready to take the heat?"

Crista sighed. "I honestly don't know. But I do know
I can't ignore it, either. It's gone too far."

"Do you have proof? I know the captain doesn't like
change, but he always seemed a fair man to me."

"He wants to bring Eddie Fontanero in on the case."

There was a long pause on Catherine's end. Fontanero's reputation must've reached upper management.
But Crista knew the chief would keep her feelings
about Fontanero to herself.

"It's Englend's job to get things done the best way he

can. I don't see bringing in another officer as gender bias."

Catherine played the devil's advocate well. Just talking to her told Crista what she'd be up against if she filed a grievance. She didn't have any actual proof that Englend was planning to get rid of her because he didn't want a woman on his team. She didn't know a single person who'd testify on her behalf. Pete, maybe, but she wasn't going to have him put his job on the line for her, either.

"Think hard about it, Crista. Once you file a grievance, there's no going back."

Crista knew the drill. You don't rat on fellow officers and you don't complain. You never admit weakness in yourself or in other cops. File a grievance and you're headed for a paperwork job in the basement.

"It could mean giving up your career—or your career as you've planned it."

Hell, what she was doing now wasn't what she'd planned, either. "What do you suggest?"

"If it were me, I'd work with it. Keep proving I can do the job. But I'd document everything. If things didn't change, and I had documentation to prove my case, I'd do what I felt necessary. But that's me. Only you can decide what's best for you." She cleared her throat. "Just remember, there's no turning back. Once you make that decision you're committed. You have to follow through. Believe me, I know what I'm talking about."

Crista knew Cathy was talking about the media frenzy and rumors of corruption on her watch. But the chief forged ahead, doing her job as it should be done. Crista realized then that she shouldn't have called. The chief had enough to deal with and Crista's problems were insignificant in comparison. "Can I do something to help?"

"I wish. But I'm afraid any support from my friends might do more harm than good. I can handle it."

"Well, thanks for the advice. Just talking about it has given me a different perspective."

They closed the conversation on a businesslike note. But Catherine's mention about support from her friends left Crista with a warm feeling. If Catherine could suck it up, so could she.

CHAPTER ELEVEN

ALEX PARKED his SUV and headed inside the center, still wondering if he'd done the right thing by bringing Crista here yesterday. The boys had seemed to take her questions in stride. But the thing that bothered him was that he hadn't realized Tommy's absence coincided with the date of the shooting. Not that it meant anything, but it bothered him that he hadn't connected the dots.

The noise from the table saw, the hammering and the music blaring from a boom box in the corner nearly raised the roof. Alex went over to where Ramon was working. Ramon was the obvious leader in this group and the other boys looked to him for direction. Ramon stopped sawing when Alex came over.

"How're we doing?" Alex asked.

"Right on schedule. Charlie's got a couple more guys coming in to help."

"Great. When will they be here?"

Ramon shrugged and looked at the supervisor. Like many things in the boys's lives, time wasn't important.

"Maybe tomorrow," Charlie said from a few feet away.

"Tomorrow's Thanksgiving. I don't want anyone working on Thanksgiving."

"No big deal." Ramon shrugged again.

"It is to me. I don't want anyone here tomorrow."

"Okay." Ramon picked up another board and was about to start sawing again.

"If you're not already going somewhere, why don't you come to my place tomorrow? We have a turkey so big, we can't possibly eat it all."

Ramon's eyes lit, but just briefly.

Alex turned down the boom box and said to all the boys, "You're all invited to my place for Thanksgiving tomorrow. One o'clock. Here's the address." He pulled out a business card and wrote the street number on the back.

"I don't know, Mr. D.," Ramon started with an excuse, but Alex cut him off.

"Here." He handed him the card. "If any of you can make it, fine. If you can't, no big deal."

The boy nodded.

"I'd like to get in touch with Tommy to invite him, too. Do you know how I can reach him?"

The blank look he got said he might as well have asked Ramon if he knew the theory of relativity. "Well, if you happen to see him, would you please tell him to get in touch?"

"Sure, Mr. D."

Alex left the building feeling as if he hadn't accomplished a thing. He wished he had some inside track on how to deal with these kids.

Just as he was getting into the vehicle, David came outside. Alex stopped and stood at the car door. At sixteen, David was a small guy who carried his anger at the world right up front where everyone could see it. Alex knew little about any of the youths' backgrounds and he wasn't sure he wanted to know. The relationship he had with his crew started the day they came to the center. Anything that had happened before wasn't important. Their future depended on what they did now.

Glancing around, David walked over to Alex. "You want to know where to find Tommy?"

Alex nodded.

"He hangs with the Pistoles."

The news caught Alex by surprise. Tommy couldn't be more than twelve, but then Alex knew most gangs allowed younger boys, the gang wannabes, to hang around so when they're ready they'd know the drill. "And where do I find the Pistoles?"

David shrugged. "Talk to a guy named Marco."

The name sounded familiar. Then he remembered that Crista had asked if he knew a Marco Torres—or had heard anything about him. Now that he knew there was a connection between Marco and Tommy, it was important to find out. "Do you know where I can find him?"

The boy shrugged again. "He lives in the hood."

Alex knew he wasn't going to get specifics, but he was happy he had the tie-in. "Thanks, David. I appreciate it. Hope to see you tomorrow."

"Can't. I've got other plans," David said, then turned and sauntered back inside.

Alex doubted the boy had other plans. He knew the kid wasn't about to be beholden to anyone, and if he shared a dinner with Alex, he'd feel as if he owed Alex something. Boys like David didn't want to owe anyone anything. Sad.

He started his SUV and drove away, wondering what to do with the information he'd just been given. He really needed to talk to Tommy before he mentioned anything to Crista. But he had no idea how to get in touch with the guy named Marco.

CRISTA PACED the floor, checked her watch and then went to the window. Diego should have been there by now. They were supposed to be at Alex's in twenty minutes and she hated to be late. It would be just like Diego to change his mind and not let her know.

Five more minutes. She'd give him that, and if he didn't show, she was out of here.

Glancing around to make sure she hadn't forgotten anything, she remembered the flowers she'd bought and went to the kitchen to retrieve them from the refrigerator. Calvin was safe at Mrs. McGinty's for the afternoon, and Crista was relieved that the woman liked the bird enough to take him in. After what had happened to Calvin, she didn't want to leave him alone. If it was Trini trying to get even with her, or some gang member who didn't like her asking so many questions, new locks wouldn't stop them.

But who was she bothering and why? If she had that information, she might also have a suspect in the shootings.

She glanced at her watch again. Diego's five minutes were up. Late already, she gathered her things, locked the door behind her and flew down the stairs. As she reached the front of the building, a loud squeal of tires sounded outside.

She jumped back, remembering the last time she'd heard the screech of rubber. Her adrenaline pumping, she cautiously opened the door and saw Diego getting out of a beat-up van. He'd made it. Relief swept through her—until she saw Marco at the wheel.

"Hey, *chica*," Diego said when he reached her.

He seemed to be in a good mood. Too good. Almost

as if he'd had one drink too many or was high on something. "C'mon, let's go or we'll be late," she said.

Marco waved and smiled as he drove off. Crista's stomach knotted. If she'd had any doubt that Diego was involved with the Pistoles again, she didn't anymore. Why else would he be hanging around with Marco? But she wasn't going to get into that right now and spoil what she hoped would be a wonderful day.

They walked to the parking lot in back of the building. Getting into her Jeep, Diego said, "Nice ride."

"It's ten years old." Her apprehension about sharing Thanksgiving with Alex's family and bringing Diego along left her patience paper thin. She turned the key in the ignition, shifted into gear and pulled out and into the street.

"Yeah, but you gotta admit, a ten-year-old set of wheels is a whole lot better than no wheels."

"Okay, you got me there." She grinned, relaxing a little. She liked when Diego joked around.

"So are you and this Del Rio guy getting it on?"

"Diego!" Crista swerved and nearly drove up on the curb. "I'm working with him. Trying to solve a case."

He nodded. "Uh-huh. You have Thanksgiving dinner with many people on your cases?"

"He's very traditional. Having lots of people around makes him happy."

"Does he make you happy?"

He was teasing her, but still, her nerves skittered under her skin. When she was around Alex, she felt happier than she did most of the time. But how would Diego know that, or even suspect?

"It's business, Diego. But since he invited me…us…I thought it would be fun to do something different. It's better than being alone."

Diego's eyes seemed to soften. She guessed he knew all about being alone. Even in prison with hundreds of people, it had to be very lonely.

"So. You're going to be your most charming self today. Right?"

He looked over at her. "You want little brother to make a good impression?"

"That would be nice. But mostly, I don't want them to regret inviting us."

They arrived exactly five minutes late and as they drove up to the house, Crista noted a gray sedan parked close by and a man sitting inside. The security guard Alex had hired. He'd told her what kind of car the man drove so she wouldn't think it was someone else.

Alex and Sam greeted them at the door, and inside, the scent of turkey and stuffing and all the delicious foods that went with Thanksgiving filled the air.

Crista introduced Diego to both Alex and Sam. Alex hung up the coats while Sam led them into the living room. "We gots more people here today," Sam said, her excitement evident as she skipped from the foyer.

Entering the living room, Crista was surprised to see Ramon, Julio and Richard. She shouldn't have been. Big extended families joining in holiday festivities was part of the Hispanic culture.

Alex introduced Diego to the others, after which Crista said, "I think I'll go into the kitchen to see if I can do something to help."

"I'm sure Elena will appreciate it," Alex said and winked at Crista.

She felt her stomach flutter like a teenager. Heat rose in her cheeks. Embarrassed by her reaction, which she was sure everyone in the room noticed, she was relieved when Sam said, "I'm going to help, too." She took Crista's hand and led her from the room.

The kitchen counters were filled with plates of food, squash blossom quesadillas, sugared fritters, pumpkin and pecan pies. Crista was swept back in time to when her own grandmother had fixed holiday meals for their family. They might have been poor, but on holidays, they always celebrated. At some point, she'd blotted those memories from her mind. It did no good to pine.

"Bienvenido a nuestro hogar," Elena said, welcoming Crista to the Del Rio home, and then she gave Crista a big hug.

"This will be the best Thanksgiving ever." Sam danced around the center island. "I set the table before. Do you want to see?"

"Of course," Crista said. "And then I'd like to do something to help your grandmother."

"Here," Elena said in Spanish, handing Sam some napkins. "You can put these on the table."

Crista and Sam rolled the napkins and placed them inside napkin holders decorated with turkeys. "I picked these out," Sam said proudly, her dark eyes shining.

"And you did a fine job." The child's self-confidence was delightful, and she had to give Alex a world of credit for making his daughter feel so secure. They went back into the kitchen where Elena already had the turkey out of the oven and was scooping stuffing from the bird into a bowl.

"Here, let me help with that," Crista said in Spanish, and while the two women worked, Sam left the room to join the others.

"We're happy you could come today," Elena said. "It's good to have the house filled again. Alejandro spends too much time alone."

"From what I can tell, he works very hard."

"He works too much. He needs to enjoy life while he's able. He needs to socialize more, maybe find a good woman who will take care of him and the little girl like Marissa did."

"Marissa was your daughter." Crista knew that from the information she'd gathered on the family when investigating the case.

Elena nodded. "She was a good daughter. A good wife and mother."

It sounded as if Elena was warning Crista that if she were interested in Alex, she'd have a whole lot to live up to. "I'm sure she was."

"She stayed at home to care for her family."

Oh, yes. A confirmation of what Crista had already thought to be true. Alex held traditional values and beliefs, and she was sure any woman he married would have to feel the same. "I admire people who can do that. Unfortunately, I'm not one of them."

Elena went about her work and without looking at Crista, she said, "A woman should be married and have a family. You just haven't found the right man yet."

That last part was true. She hadn't. But even if she found the right man, got married and had a family, she doubted she'd give up everything she'd worked for. "You're right, Elena. I haven't found the right man and I don't think I ever will."

Elena glanced at Crista out of the corner of an eye. "Some people don't recognize what's right in front of them. They're too busy going in other directions and they ignore the obvious."

And sometimes the obvious is all wrong.

"A person must be open to many things. Otherwise the heart goes unfulfilled."

This was getting much too deep for Crista, and she had a sudden urge to bolt.

As if Elena understood what was going through Crista's head, she changed the subject. "We can put the food on the table now and Alex will carve the turkey."

Crista's father had always carved the *guajolate*, she remembered. Why had she forgotten that? Had the horror of her mother's remarriage wiped out everything that was good in her life? She was pleased that she'd come, glad to be reminded that there had been happy times in her past.

As they passed dishes around the table and stuck forkfuls of food into their mouths, the boys laughed, verbally sparred with each other and talked sports with Alex and Diego. Diego teased Sam, who seemed intrigued by him. Crista gazed across the table at the odd mixture of people sitting with her. How different they all were—separated by age, education and background. But listening to all the talk and laughter, the differences seemed to disappear. Their common link was that they all wanted to share the holiday with someone, to feel a sense of family. Alex had given them that.

When they finished dinner, Elena banished them all to the enclosed garden to wait for dessert. Ramon, Julio and Richard declined, saying they had to leave, so Elena sent dessert home with them. Diego, who'd been talking to Sam about her drawings, went to a separate table so he and Sam could draw together.

Sitting at the round tea table with Crista surrounded by a plethora of plants, Alex nodded toward Diego. "He likes kids."

Crista's heart warmed watching them. "He does. He's always been good with children. But he's been away for so long, I wasn't sure what to expect."

"Why?"

"We didn't see each other when he was in prison. He didn't want me to see him there, I guess."

He nodded his understanding. "He really seems interested in art."

"He's an excellent artist. His paintings are beautiful. I'd like to see him do something with his talent, but I'm afraid he'll never leave the barrio and never be able to put his talent to use."

"He doesn't have to leave the neighborhood to put his talent to use," Alex said. "He could do something right there and help himself as well as others."

"You mean something like what you're doing."

"Absolutely. I have an art program that could use a teacher."

"You'd take someone who's been convicted of a felony?"

"I see the whole person. I look at the future, not the past."

A wonderful philosophy, if the person wanted to change. If he didn't— "I can't answer for Diego. But he's very proud and because you know me, he'd probably feel as if his sister was pulling strings for him." What she really wanted was for Diego to leave the barrio altogether. There was too much temptation for some people.

"Does he sell his paintings?"

"Not that I know of, but he could. I wish he would."

"Maybe I can look at them. Hanging paintings by a local artist at the center when it's finished would be wonderful. We couldn't afford to pay much though."

"Again, I can't answer for Diego."

As they were talking, Elena came to see if they wanted coffee or tea, so Crista went back to the kitchen with her to help. She didn't know how she was going to eat any more, but when she saw the pies and even some rice pudding, Crista decided she'd manage.

Crista and Alex spent the rest of the evening in comfortable conversation, laughing and joking. Alex had a great sense of humor, Crista discovered. Diego spent most of the time drawing with Sam, who seemed to adore him. And before Crista knew it, it was eight o'clock and Sam's bedtime.

As Crista was getting ready to leave, Alex took Diego aside. She assumed it was to talk about Diego's paintings. When they finished and Diego had stepped out the door and gone to the Jeep, Alex stopped Crista. "I learned something interesting yesterday, and I'd like to talk to you about it." He leaned closer. "But I'd prefer to talk privately. It's about the case."

"When?"

"I can come by in an hour, if that's okay."

She looked at her watch. "Sure. I'll be waiting."

CRISTA DROPPED Diego off at a neighborhood bar, and tried not to be judgmental about him hanging with the wrong people. "I really enjoyed the day," she said, wanting to give him a hug, but knowing it was too soon.

"Me, too," he said, and then he was gone.

Picking up Calvin was next on the list. At Mrs. McGinty's, she knocked on the door and waited. Remembering the woman was a little hard of hearing, Crista knocked harder.

"Come in. It's open."

Going inside, Crista found Mrs. McGinty hovering over Calvin, cackling and cooing and making strange noises that she apparently thought parrots made.

"He hasn't uttered a word," Mrs. McGinty said, then poked at the bird between the bars. "What's wrong with him?"

"He's a moody bird. He only talks when he has something to say," Crista joked.

"Well, that's okay. I get moody, too, sometimes." Mrs. McGinty shuffled across the room and lowered herself into a battered recliner in front of her television.

Crista picked up Calvin's cage and walked toward the door. "Thank you so much, Mrs. McGinty. I really appreciate this."

The woman waved a gnarly hand. "I like that bird." She coughed and settled into the chair. "Oh, there was a phone call for you, too," she added absently.

Crista stopped half in and half out of the door. "A phone call? Here at your place?"

Mrs. McGinty nodded. "A man. He said something about giving you a message."

How would anyone know to call Mrs. McGinty to leave Crista a message? How would anyone even get the number? And why wouldn't they just leave a message on her machine?

"What did he say?"

"That was the odd part. He said you'd know."

Crista felt a sudden chill. Whoever this sick person was, he knew she'd brought Calvin to Mrs. McGinty's. Which meant he was watching her—and probably knew her every move.

"Thank you," Crista managed and then rushed back to her apartment. Inside, she double-locked the door, gently lifted Calvin out of the small cage and put him into the larger one that was his home. Her thoughts churning, she closed the cage door and then noticed the message light flashing on her phone.

Filled with apprehension, she forced herself to go over and push the button. A strangely distorted voice said, "Hi, sweetheart. Sorry you're not home, but don't worry. I'll call back."

Her whole body tensed. No name, no message. Just a voice that sounded like Donald Duck on oxygen. She didn't think it was Trini. He'd never bothered to disguise his voice in the past. He'd always wanted her to know it was him. To scare her to death. But if not Trini, then who? A knock on the door caused her to nearly jump out of her skin.

Then she remembered that Alex was coming over, and relief swept through her. But she peeked through the security hole just to be sure before she opened the door.

"Hi." Alex stood with one arm against the door frame and, wearing a black leather jacket over a white dress shirt and black jeans, he looked sexier than any man had a right to.

"Hi. C'mon in," she said, trying to maintain her composure. "I just barely arrived myself. I had to pick up Calvin from the lady down the hall who was watching him."

He came in and sauntered toward the couch. "I thought birds were fairly self-sufficient. Give them food and water and they're fine for days."

She shrugged. "I don't know about other birds. But Calvin…he likes company." She didn't feel the need to tell Alex why she'd really taken Calvin to Mrs. McGinty's. It had nothing to do with her investigation of his case. And if she told him as a friend, then she'd have to tell him that it might be her ex-husband. She didn't want Alex to know all the ugly details of her life.

There were reasons to think it was Trini and also reason not to think it was him. Trini would know that

if she suspected it was him, she'd slap him with a restraining order faster than he could say the words. She
doubted Trini was stupid enough to do something
that could get him thrown back in the slammer. But
on the other hand, he was a vengeful sort. He'd want
to make her pay for humiliating him in front of his
friends.

"Please, sit," Crista said.

Alex dropped onto the couch and she sat opposite
him in the pumpkin chair again, just as she had the first
time he'd been here. "So…you said you'd learned
something that's pertinent to the case."

"It might be. Or it might not. I just thought you
should know."

"If it involves the case, I definitely should know."

"The boy we talked about earlier, Tommy Ramirez.
He hangs out with the Pistoles."

"Where did you hear that?"

"One of the boys at the center."

"You think Tommy is a gang member? He's awfully
young."

"I don't think anything. Sometimes the gangs let
younger boys hang around so that they'll know the
ropes when they're ready to join. And apparently
Tommy's older brother was a member of the gang before he was sent to prison, so it's possible the boy
wants to follow in his brother's footsteps."

"Do you know his brother's name?"

"No."

"Okay. Thanks for telling me. I think we might have
something to work with. And it's more than we had before." She could talk to Marco Torres and find out more
about Tommy.

Alex smiled. "Good."

Still a little disturbed by the phone message, Crista wasn't ready for Alex to leave quite yet. "I was about to get a drink. Would you like one, too?"

"Sounds good."

"I have beer and wine, water, milk, coffee and tea. What's your preference?"

He leaned against the back of the couch, one arm over the top, a sultry, seductive look in his eyes. A look that said his preference wasn't a drink.

Her stomach did a flip. Feeling suddenly self-conscious, she launched to her feet and headed toward the kitchen. "I'm having a beer."

"Make that two."

Though she wasn't looking at him, she heard the smile in his voice. He knew she was flustered.

Crista brought in two Coronas and a couple of Pilsner glasses. She set the bottles on the table and handed a glass to Alex.

"You take it," Alex said. "I'll drink from the bottle."

Surprised, she handed him a beer. He'd been raised in a wealthy family, knew all about the finest wines and here he was drinking beer from the bottle. Adaptable. She liked that.

One beer led to another and soon they were laughing and joking and Crista felt completely at ease. It had been a long time since she'd just let go. A long time since she'd enjoyed someone's company so much.

"So," Alex said, "we never did find out who was the most expert in martial arts."

Crista's interest was piqued. "That's right. So you tell me your experience and I'll tell you mine. Then we'll know."

Alex wrinkled his brow. "Actually I was thinking more of a physical test."

"Such as?"

His gaze turned soft and thoughtful. "I don't know." He reached up and gently brushed a lock of hair away from her face, touching her cheek in the process. "Maybe I better rethink that idea."

Crista's breath hitched. His eyes locked with hers, intimate and compelling, drawing her in.

"Come to think of it," he said, his voice low and husky. "We never finished what we started on the steps last week." And almost before he finished the sentence, his lips met hers.

Warm mouth. Soft lips. Just as she remembered. Even though they'd had an abrupt end to their first kiss, she remembered every second. Dreamed about it, again and again. Nothing had felt as good in a long time and remembering that, she wanted more. As much as she could get. She melted against him, suddenly not caring if this was right or wrong or what the ramifications might be. It was right for right now. That's all that mattered.

Within seconds they were prone on the couch, the length of his body on top of hers. He pressed against her and she pressed back, wanting to ease the growing ache of desire.

Mouth to mouth and body against body, her skin felt as if it was on fire. Blood pumped through her veins like hot lava, and her heart hammered so hard, she was sure it was going to implode.

It had been so long since she'd been intimate with a man…so long that she'd felt anything so physically pleasurable.

Yes, she wanted more. She wanted all of him. He was practically a stranger and she wanted to make love with him. Right here. Right now.

His strong hands caressed her breasts, then slid

downward to her bottom and came around to slip between her thighs.

"Crista. You're so beautiful," he murmured between kisses.

He was gentle, yet forceful, passionate and caring, and at that moment he seemed everything she wanted. Her breathing came in short, quick gasps and she wanted to give herself to him as she'd never given herself before.

His fingers went to the buttons on her blouse and in seconds her pink lace bra was exposed.

Quickly, she unbuttoned the front of his shirt, exposing his muscular chest. She leaned forward to kiss his neck and saw a small silver cross on a chain. She pushed back, stopping what she was doing to look at it. She tamped down a quick burst of Catholic guilt that threatened to ruin the moment. She hadn't gone to church in years. She didn't do guilt anymore. Still, a warning went off in her head.

If she did this, it would be like having a one-night stand with a stranger. Because, she realized, Alex *was* a stranger. He didn't really know her. They didn't really know each other. Not enough to make love.

Her body warred with her common sense. And common sense finally got the better of her. She gently pushed herself away.

"What?" Alex asked. "Am I hurting you?"

She shook her head. "No. I just…it's too soon. We hardly know each other."

His expression switched from lust to complete surprise. "You're joking. Right?"

She shook her head again. "No, I mean it. We don't know each other all that well."

He sat back, incredulity on his face. "You know more about me from investigating the case than almost anyone. You've just spent Thanksgiving with me and my family. How can you say we're strangers?" His dark eyes filled with the sting of rejection. She should have expected that. Alex wasn't the kind of man to take rejection lightly.

"I know *about* you, Alex. I don't really know you. I don't think you know me very well, either."

"I think I know you very well."

"What's my favorite color?"

He kept his gaze locked with hers. "I might not know that, but I think I know you. I know who you are in here." He touched the fingertips of one hand to her chest. "I know you're caring and gentle, I know you have a passion for life, strong values and an incredible sense of justice. I've seen your gentleness with Sam and your empathy and concern for your brother. I've seen how you considered the feelings of the boys I'm working with and the respect you gave them. Even if I don't know the details, I know you very well, Crista. In the most important ways."

A lump lodged in her throat. She didn't know what to say.

"I think you know me, too," he added.

That was the problem, she realized. She knew him enough to know she wasn't the woman for him.

"But, regardless of what I think, if you believe we need more time to get to know each other, I respect your feelings."

Crista sat up and reached to button her shirt. "Thank you. I appreciate that."

Alex reached over to button her top buttons, his large hands not very adept, but she let him do it anyway.

Studying her, his eyes suddenly lit. "I have a great

idea. You mentioned that you have this weekend off, and since I do, too, why don't we use that time to get to know each other better."

Even though she wasn't going to the station, Crista had planned on working on the case. "I don't thin—"

He placed a finger to her lips to shush her. "Don't say no yet—not until you hear my suggestion. Okay?"

She nodded, hesitant.

"I promised Sam when she was in the hospital that I'd take her to the beach in Galveston for a couple days, and we made plans to go tomorrow night. Why don't you come along with us?"

Spend a weekend with Alex in Galveston? She'd have to be crazy. If she spent any more time this close to him, she wasn't sure she could be held responsible for her actions.

"It would be perfect. You could room with Sam, and get to know us both a little better."

A weekend in Galveston sounded wonderful. White sand beaches and the clear aqua water of the Gulf, in the company of her two favorite people. How could that be bad? Especially if she was rooming with Sam.

"It'll be a diversion," Alex continued, running long fingers through his dark hair. "For the past two weeks, nearly all I've thought about is the shooting. I even dream about it happening again. I want to take Sam away and forget this for a while."

Crista swung her hair behind her shoulders. "That's understandable. I feel that way myself." Only she had a job to do. It was her number-one priority.

Alex's eyes darkened, a frown creased his brow. "As much as I hate to admit it, even with someone guarding the house, I don't feel very safe anymore. I want to protect Sam, but I don't know how to do it except to take her away. Even if it's only for a few days."

She worried about that very thing herself and if she, as a cop, felt helpless to do anything about it, how must Alex feel? If she could just find the shooter....

He reached out and gently placed a hand over hers. "Don't answer now. Think about it," he said. "I'll call tomorrow morning and we'll talk. Okay?"

Ambivalence coursed through Crista. It would be so nice to get away. She couldn't remember the last time she'd done that. She wanted to go—but she shouldn't. Couldn't.

"We'll have a great time." Alex's eyes were bright with excitement. "I promise I'll be on my best behavior. And most importantly, Sam will be tickled pink if you come."

She'd be tickled pink to spend time with Sam, too. It was spending time with Alex that worried her. Still, he looked so hopeful…like a kid waiting to hear if he was going to Disneyland.

"Okay," she said even though it was against her better judgement.

"Okay, you'll think about it? Or okay, you'll come along?"

"Okay, I'll think about it."

CHAPTER TWELVE

MORNING SWOOPED DOWN on Crista like a hawk. The night hadn't been long enough—not long enough to make a decision that might affect other people's lives. Though she'd spent most of it going back and forth about spending the weekend with Alex and Sam, she still hadn't decided. That was totally unlike her, she'd never been wishy-washy before. She usually made a decision and went dead ahead.

But how could she decide when she didn't know what Alex wanted from her. She didn't know what she wanted from him. All she knew was that when she was around Alex, she felt like a different person.

When she was with Alex, all her senses seemed intensified. The sky seemed bluer, the flowers brighter. Little things seemed more important. A smile. A touch. When she was around Alex, her stomach fluttered, her hands got clammy and heat rose to her cheeks, not to mention some other parts of her body. She hadn't had those feeling since… She couldn't remember when.

She admired Alex, she respected him. She cared about him. Too much. She cared about Sam and dammit, she wanted to spend time with them.

But Alex's life was contrary to everything she'd planned for herself. She could never be the kind of person he would want in a serious relationship. And he wasn't the kind of person who'd settle for a relationship that was less than his strong values and beliefs would allow. She knew that about him as well as she knew herself.

Or thought she knew herself. Lately, she'd even begun to wonder about that. Maybe she'd just convinced herself of what she wanted because she didn't believe anything else was an option.

Was she selling herself short by not opening up and waiting to see what might develop? Could a relationship with Alex ever work? Could she ever change and be the kind of person he wanted? She didn't believe so. She was who she was.

Could Alex ever change and accept her as she was? She doubted it. Alex had a daughter who needed someone who could give her what she lost when her mother died. Why then did Alex even contemplate getting involved with her? He, more than anyone, had to know it could never work.

That settled it. She couldn't spend the weekend with Alex and Sam, no matter how much she wanted to.

The decision made, Crista rose, brewed a latte and then went to the kitchen table to draft a plan of action for the day. The same gun had been used in two drive-bys, and the same gun had been used in another crime a few years ago. In all three cases, the weapon had never been found. Pedro Castillo had been a member of the Pistoles, but he was in jail. That eliminated him as a suspect. However, if she could find out what Pedro had done with the gun…she might be closer to an answer.

Since she wasn't going to the station today, she'd have to get her information directly from the source. She decided to start by contacting Marco. He and Pedro had been members of the gang at about the same time, and Marco might know something. If that didn't work, she'd go to the prison and talk to Pedro.

She headed for the shower, turned on the water and let it run hot. Just then the phone rang.

Her stomach did a funny roll. *Alex. It had to be Alex.* And she had to tell him no, she couldn't go with them. She went into the bedroom and answered on the extension. "Crista here."

"Hi," he said, his voice filled with exuberance. "It's Alex."

"I recognized your hi."

"Good. I like that. You must know me very well to recognize my voice," he joked.

She laughed—only she didn't like that she recognized his voice. It meant that he was important enough to remember. It meant that he affected her.

"I hope you've decided that joining me and Sam in Galveston for a couple of days will be fun."

"I'm sure it would be, but—"

"It isn't a life commitment or anything. Just a weekend away."

His upbeat manner and comment made her think again. It wasn't a life commitment. And it could be fun.

"If you find you really can't make it, we could reschedule. Sam might be disappointed but she'd understand."

Did he mean that if she said no, he wasn't going to go? He needed to take Sam away, not just for fun but for safety reasons. She didn't want to be responsible for him postponing the trip. If something happened she'd never forgive herself. In fact, if she had her way, Alex would stay out of town until they nailed the shooter.

"No strings. Just a relaxing weekend away from Houston. I have a feeling you might need that as much as Sam and I do."

She sighed. He was so right. She did need it. "You're very convincing. And that's bad."

"Is that the good bad, or the bad bad?"

"I'm not telling." She sighed again. If they didn't leave until later in the day, she could get some work done before they left.

"So are we on?"

Still reluctant, she had to clarify the circumstance. "Okay. We're on. But only because I feel it's good for Sam." She wanted to say they'd be safer away from Houston, but wasn't going to dwell on it. He was worried enough about his family as it was.

"Whatever the reason, I'm glad you're coming. Sam will be over the moon when I tell her. I'll pick you up at six. And bring a jacket. It might be chilly at the beach."

CRISTA HAD FORGOTTEN to shut the shower off while on the phone with Alex, and going into the room she felt as if she were in a steam bath.

Standing under the showerhead, she angled her face into the hot spray. After a moment, she adjusted the nozzle for more pressure, turned and let the water massage the back of her neck where the tension always settled.

She still couldn't believe she'd agreed to go to Galveston when moments before she'd decided just the opposite. Had Alex been all that convincing, or had she turned into a marshmallow?

The only way she could justify going with Alex and Sam was because she felt both of them would be safer away from Houston, and because he'd threatened not to go if she didn't come.

A little voice inside said that maybe he'd played the threat card because he knew it would get her to agree to come along.

It was a cynical thought and probably not deserved. But working the streets had a tendency to make a person cynical. She didn't like that about the job, but that's the way it was. If you didn't disengage, you couldn't do a good job. If you didn't make jokes over some of the tragedies, you'd go stark raving loco.

Still, she felt bad that she'd questioned Alex's motives. He was a good man. His intentions honorable. He just wasn't right for her.

She finished in the shower, wrapped her head in a fluffy white terry towel and then patted herself dry with another. Preoccupied with her thoughts, she heard a noise. Like a door opening or closing. She froze, her senses on red alert.

Holding her breath, she tucked the towel around her body then flattened herself against the wall behind the bathroom door. She heard another faint sound—like the movement of fabric. Like the sound clothes make when you walk.

Someone's in the apartment.

And her gun was in the bedroom.

Unwilling to wait until whoever it was reached her, Crista grabbed a small hand mirror off the sink and held it just outside the door so she could see down the hallway. The coast was clear.

Her pulse beating erratically, she sprinted down the hall as quietly as she could. She stopped at the bedroom door, flashed the mirror to make sure no one was in the room, and then ducked inside.

Still holding the towel around her, Crista reached for her gun. As she did, the towel covering her hair fell off and landed on the floor with a dull thud, the sound subtle, but loud enough for someone to pick up if they were listening.

She slipped behind the bedroom door and flipped the safety on her gun. She heard a click, like a door shutting.

Breathing heavily, she waited a couple minutes and when she didn't hear anything more, she crept down the hall toward the living room, gun at the ready. She glanced at Calvin's cage. The bird appeared fine. She saw nothing out of place.

After checking the rest of the apartment, she began to wonder if she'd simply imagined hearing something.

Then she glanced at the door. It wasn't locked.

She checked the door. No evidence of a break-in. Whoever had opened it was a professional. Then she saw that the window near the fire escape was open. The intruder hadn't come through the front door—but he went out that way. Or vice versa. And whoever it was got out of here when he heard she was home.

She checked the window. No evidence of forced entry there, either. Had she left it open? She couldn't remember. Damn. She hated that she was second-guessing herself. She had to report this. It would be backup evidence in case something else came up in the future. Still, she felt stupid reporting it. An unlocked door didn't make for a break-in and neither did an open window. Nothing was out of place, and she knew from experience the police could do nothing with it—except take the information.

Still shaky, she called it in anyway just to have it on record. A couple of cops came out, guys she didn't know, thankfully, who took the information and apologized on their way out that they couldn't do anything. She assured them it was okay. She knew the drill.

She'd called a locksmith while they were still there and within the hour, she had another new set of locks on her door and on her window. That made her feel a bit safer, but not secure, and she was glad she'd decided to go to Galveston with Alex and Sam.

But before she left town, she had some things to clean up. Dressed inconspicuously in jeans, a fuzzy blue cowl-neck sweater and one of her older jackets, she hit the road with a list of addresses and people to interview.

Marco was first. He lived in the East End but in a different section than Diego. It was a part of the neighborhood she hadn't been to before, and she quickly discovered the streets crisscrossed and deadended, with no rhyme or reason to how they were laid out. And none of the streets matched the map spread out on the seat next to her. Several bad turns and a lot of blue words later, she managed to find Galena Street, which ended at St. Mary's Church. According to the map Crista had printed out from a Web site, Marco's place was two blocks behind the church and three streets over.

Finding Jacinto Avenue and the house number, she pulled into a parking spot in front. There wasn't much activity on the street because it was still early, and she was glad for that. Any time a police officer went into the hood, there was potential for trouble. Or if trouble broke out, she couldn't ignore it, even though she was off duty.

The house looked more like a shed, and the yard like a used car junkyard. Rusted-out vehicle parts were practically stacked on end, and near the pile was a For

Sale sign. Was that how Marco supported himself? There was nothing in his record that gave any indication he worked at anything, which was sometimes the sign of a drug dealer. But if he was, he wasn't very good at it, or he wouldn't be living in such a ramshackle place.

Picking her way through the tires and hubcaps, she reached the door and knocked. She wasn't nervous because Marco was her brother's friend, and he would respect that. But she was always careful, and always prepared.

The door swung open. Marco stood there shirtless and shoeless, clad only in black boxer shorts. His hair was disheveled and he smelled of alcohol. He squinted against the brightness of the early morning sun.

"Beunos días," she said.

"Bueno." He seemed confused at seeing her there. "Is Diego okay?"

She guessed he thought the only reason she'd come to his place was if something had happened to Diego. "Diego's fine. Can I come in?"

He shrugged. "It's not clean."

She stepped inside. He was right about that. Beer cans and pizza boxes littered the room and the bitter scent of stale alcohol was overwhelming. No sweet scent of drugs however. The one-room shack had a mattress in one corner and a table with a hot plate in another. She couldn't imagine living like this but was all too aware that many people did.

"I'm not here for an inspection. I just want to talk to you for a few minutes."

"About Diego?" he asked again.

"Sort of," she said, realizing that was the best way to start.

Marco mumbled something and then stumbled over himself, trying to find a clean spot for her to sit. He pulled out a wooden chair from a tiny table, brushed it off, and indicated she should sit. He went into the bathroom and came out wearing a pair of ratty jeans, pulled up a stool and then sat next to her.

"*¿Qué pasa?*"

Lord. Where to start. "Nothing is going on with Diego, and that's the problem. I want to help him get on his feet, but he refuses to let me do anything. I thought maybe you might help me convince him it's not a bad thing to get help if he needs it."

He frowned.

"He's your friend, Marco. Don't let him get involved with the Pistoles again."

Marco gave an indignant *humph*. "I don't do gangs anymore. I got a good thing going here with a legitimate scrap business. I asked Diego if he wanted to work with me, but he said no." He shrugged. "Diego is his own man. I can't make him do anything."

Surprised to hear Marco say he wasn't with the gang anymore, she hesitated. Usually gang members were members for life. Even if they didn't participate when they were older. But he seemed sincere about it and about his business, too. "I understand. Maybe you can help me with some other information."

His eyes narrowed. He pulled out a cigarette and offered her one.

She shook her head. "No, *gracias.*"

"What kind of information?"

"I'm looking for a boy named Tommy Ramirez. I heard you might know where he lives."

He dragged on his cigarette. "What's he done?"

"Nothing. He's been hanging around the new cen-

ter being developed in Paloverde, and the director
thought he might want to join one of the programs," she
lied. Well, it wasn't entirely a lie. Alex would let him
participate if the boy was doing okay in school. "But
Tommy hasn't been in school or around the center for
a week or two and the director is worried about him."

Marco gave a snort of a laugh. "Tomás can take
care of himself."

She had no doubt that was true. Most kids in the barrio learned how to survive early on. "Do you know
where I can find him? I heard he hangs with the Pistoles."

He frowned, then stood up. "He's too young to be
a Pistole. If he hangs around, he hangs around." He
paced a couple steps, then, as if suddenly angry, he
came toward her and shook his finger in her face like
a parent reprimanding a child. "You know, you
shouldn't be down here asking questions. You could get
yourself in big trouble."

His concern surprised her. "Yes, I know that. But
I'm here with you. I'm not out there." She tipped her
head toward the door. "Do you know where Tommy
lives? It's important."

He turned, and with his back to her, said under his
breath, "Tommy hangs out near Gulfgate and sometimes by the Pierce Elevated."

He swung around. "But you didn't hear that from
me."

She knew what he meant. "It's between you and
me."

"Good. Now I have to go someplace."

Buoyed by the information she'd just received,
Crista said thank-you and headed straight for her car.
The mall was a hangout for teens, some known gang

members. But why he'd be hanging out at the Pierce Elevated, she didn't know. The area underneath the freeway was a port for the homeless. As far as she knew, Tommy wasn't homeless, though Alex had said the boy had family problems.

She climbed into her Jeep, locked the door and fastened her seat belt. It was still quiet in the neighborhood and she doubted that anyone had seen her. Feeling good about what she'd accomplished, she glanced in the side mirror to pull out.

The reflection of a black truck appeared in the small square of glass. She gasped. Fear and anger knotted inside her. *Okay. That's it!* She checked her gun, ready to find out once and for all who was stalking her. If it was Trini, his ass was grass.

She had her hand on the door handle when she heard a motor roar to life and... Oh, God! The truck was accelerating straight at her. Her heart slammed against her ribs. She gripped the gun tighter and turned sideways, ready to use it, but the truck sideswiped her Jeep. She jolted forward into the steering wheel like a rag doll, her head hitting the window. Her vision blurred. She tried to get a fix on the license plate. There wasn't one. Within seconds, the truck careened around the corner and out of sight.

Gripping the wheel with one hand, she turned the key in the ignition with the other, hoping to catch the truck. The motor made a grinding sound. She slumped back. Dammit. The side mirror was gone and the door bashed in. Her emotions seesawed between rage and more rage. Pain pounded in her head.

She glanced in the rearview mirror to see the damage. Blood spurted from a small cut on her forehead. She grabbed a tissue and put pressure on it to stop the bleeding. If Trini was stalking her again, she was going to take him down. She called for an APB on the truck, but couldn't give a license number or make on it, and she didn't know the direction the vehicle was headed. It was a futile call, and she felt foolish for making it.

Her adrenaline still pounding, she turned the key again. This time the Jeep sputtered to life. She pulled out and jammed her foot on the gas, hoping she might still be able to catch a glimpse of the truck. But after turning the next corner and winding around a couple streets, she realized it was hopeless. The truck was gone.

Okay. What next? Now was not the time to find Tommy. She decided to go home and regroup—watching her back all the way there. By the time she pulled into her parking space, she'd regained some semblance of control. But the incident had unnerved her, more than she could ever imagine.

Getting out of town for a couple days was looking better and better.

CRISTA WATCHED Houston disappear as they cruised down I-45 in Alex's plush Lincoln Navigator. Soft music played from a CD Alex had inserted a few minutes before, and Sam slept in back, securely fastened in her car seat. Crista touched her head where the cut was hidden under her hair. She hadn't told Alex about the truck because she needed to talk to Englend about it first. As much as she hated a confrontation with the captain, she had to tell him what evidence she'd collected. As far as she was concerned, the truck incident was confirmation that she was getting too close to finding her suspect. A warning maybe—telling her to back off.

Despite what had happened this morning, she felt good about the trip. She hadn't told anyone she was going to Galveston with Alex. Not even Diego.

After the phone call Mrs. McGinty had received, Crista hadn't been comfortable leaving Calvin there any longer. When she told Alex she didn't have anyone to watch the bird, he'd suggested she leave him with Elena, who was delighted to have the company.

Her head against the back of the seat, Crista hummed along with a Sarah McLachlan song. Galveston was only an hour from Houston, but Crista felt as if she were going to an exotic island. She'd only been to the beach town once before as she passed through on her way to find another life. Fourteen years ago.

At the time, even in her terrified state of mind, she knew it was a place she wanted to return to. And now she was back—with Alex and Sam.

Maybe spending a weekend with Alex wasn't the best decision of her life, but all things considered, it wasn't the worst, either. "I love how the scenery changes from city to bayou," she said.

Alex glanced at Crista and then back to the road. "When I first moved to Houston, I was surprised to learn the city had been built on a swamp."

"They don't call it the Bayou City for nothing," Crista joked. "Most newcomers are surprised. They think New Orleans and Florida are the only places with swamps."

Alex laughed. "Before I moved here, I thought Texas was all cattle ranches and cowboys."

"I thought California was the place where all the fruits and nuts went to live."

"Just goes to show how wrong assumptions can be."

"I'm not totally convinced I was wrong."

"Yet." Alex winked at Crista. "I guarantee you'll think differently after this weekend."

"Are we there, yet?" a small voice came from the back.

"Just about, Samita," Alex said.

Crista liked Alex's easy way with Sam. She liked that he wasn't afraid to show his affection. A child needed to know she was loved. Crista couldn't think of anything more important.

"How much longer? I need to go potty."

"About fifteen minutes."

"How long is that?"

"Not long."

"About as long as a cartoon," Crista chimed in.

"Do you want me to stop now?" Alex asked.

"No, I think I can wait."

"How about if we play a game?" Crista said.

"What kind of game?"

"A car game. I'm not sure what it's called, though. One of us thinks of something we can see and the others have to ask questions and guess the answer."

"I know that game," Sam said with excitement. "I spy with my little eye."

"That's right."

"Are you going to play, too, Daddy?"

Alex glanced at Crista and shrugged. "Sure."

"Can I go first?" Sam asked, her voice singing with excitement.

They had time for only three questions before Alex pulled into the Royal Gardens Hotel. "I picked this place especially for you, Sam. There's an aquarium, a paddle-wheel boat and a rain forest where you can see jungle animals and exotic birds."

"Will I see a parrot like Calvin?"

"I think so. And there's lots of other stuff to do, too."

Alex pulled up to the entry, which was surrounded by tropical trees and brightly colored flowers, and gave the keys to the valet to park the SUV. A bellhop loaded their luggage onto a cart and led them into the marble-floored lobby where Alex stopped at the registration desk. As they waited for him, Sam slipped her small hand into Crista's, as if it was the most normal thing in the world. Crista's heart swelled.

Twelve floors later, they walked into their suite. Crista had never stayed in such an opulent hotel and, glancing around, she felt a little out of place. Or maybe she realized just how many worlds apart she and Alex were.

As a teen she'd desperately wanted to fit in and had practiced her English over and over, learning how to speak without any accent at all. At the community college, she'd taken classes in art history and even one in etiquette, but nothing changed the way she felt about herself until she'd mastered the mental enlightenment of Wing Chun. When she learned she was in control of her life, she felt confident in most any situation.

While she couldn't change the things that had happened to her, or what might happen in the future, she had control over how she responded to them. She could wallow in self-pity and feel worthless, or she could embrace life and all its vagaries. She'd chosen the latter. But for some reason her insecurities seemed to be resurfacing. When she was with Alex, she didn't feel in control at all.

"I like this place," Sam said. "It's pretty."

"It is beautiful," Crista agreed, glancing around the living room. Two white couches with puffy pillows faced one another with a monster-size coffee table of glass and mahogany between them.

The bellman pulled open the window coverings. "And you have a beautiful view of the beach," he said with a wide smile.

The setting sun splayed magenta and purple across the horizon like an oil painting. It glinted off the clear water and tinted the fine, white sand a pale pink. The winter breeze that ruffled the palm fronds seemed to also carry away Crista's worries.

It was more than beautiful. It was magnificent. Magical. She felt as if they'd landed on a fantasy island.

"There are two bathrooms, one right over here." The bellman pointed to a powder room near the entry. "And another in the bedroom."

Crista turned to Alex.

"My room adjoins yours," Alex said, and motioned toward a door on the other side.

As Alex tipped the man, Sam yanked on Crista's hand and said, "If we get scared at night, Daddy is here to protect us."

Crista glanced at Sam, then knelt down to the child's height. "There's nothing to be afraid of, sweetie. But it's good your daddy is here, just in case."

"And remember," Alex piped up after shutting the door and locking it, "Crista is a police officer. She's good at protecting people. That's her job."

Crista was surprised at Alex's response. It was almost as if he approved. Had his opinion about women in law enforcement changed? Or was he simply making Sam feel better?

Sam's eyes widened. "But policemen get hurt, too. I don't want you to get hurt."

"I'm not going to get hurt, sweetie. I have lots of training."

"Do you have a gun?"

Alex glanced at Crista aghast.

"I have one. But I don't have it with me. I only carry it when I'm working." That was partially true. While she carried most of the time, even when she was off duty, she hadn't brought the weapon on the trip.

Relief settled in Alex's dark eyes.

What had he thought? That she'd take her gun along when a four year old would be sharing a room with her?

CHAPTER THIRTEEN

THE NEXT DAY after breakfast at the Rainforest Café, and a ride on the paddleboat, Crista stretched out on a beach blanket watching Alex and Sam play near the water. Sam skipped toward the shore and when the water lapped closer, dashed back to Alex again. The water was too cold to swim in, but the sun was warm and it felt almost like a summer day. She smiled as she glanced at their shoes, all lined up together at the edge of the blanket. Alex's, Crista's and Sam's tiny sandals. So far, the weekend had gone better than Crista could have imagined.

She felt content. Happy.

Last night after dinner in the hotel restaurant, they'd stayed up late watching a Disney movie on pay-per-view TV and munched popcorn and peanuts out of the minifridge. When Alex said good-night and left, Sam hadn't wanted to sleep in her big bed all alone, so she'd climbed in with Crista, handed her a book to read and then snuggled in next to her.

Somewhere between *The Cat in the Hat*'s arrival and *Thing One and Thing Two,* Sam had fallen asleep—and with the fresh scent of baby shampoo and this sweet little girl clinging to her, Crista felt an ache of longing.

This is what it would have been like with her own

daughter. She'd wanted to give her child all the love she had to give—the love Crista never had. She'd wanted her little girl to feel safe and secure—that her mother would always be there to protect her. She'd glanced at the dark curls and pink cheeks of the child nestled in her arms and knew Sam didn't have to worry about any of those things.

Even with her mother gone, Sam felt secure and loved. Alex would never let anyone harm his little girl. And somewhere deep inside, Crista wished that Alex felt that way about her.

Leaning back on her elbows, Crista pulled up her white capri pants and wiggled her toes. She tipped her head back and closed her eyes, letting the sun warm her face. Savoring the salty scent of the sea and the slight breeze fanning over her, she didn't know what could be more perfect. She couldn't remember the last time she felt so at peace with herself. No need to rush to the gym or get back to work immediately. It was enough to be here with Alex and Sam—and to know they were safe.

Yes, she still had a case to solve, but all in due time. Taking time off had been a balm for her mental well-being.

Hearing a swish of movement in the sand near her, Crista opened her eyes. Sam was still playing by the shore, but Alex had come back. He looked quite continental in his rolled up, lightweight cotton pants, and baggy, pale blue French terry sweatshirt. The color complimented his bronzed skin and made his hair and eyes appear even blacker.

"Tired?" he asked.

She squinted up at him. "No, not at all. I was just enjoying how peaceful it is here. It's revitalizing."

He dropped down beside her, his sandy feet next to hers. The contrast was like the two of them. Her skin was a lighter mocha color, where Alex's skin was a dark bronze. Masculine and feminine. She'd even painted her toenails bright red for the occasion.

"I thought maybe Sam had kept you up all night with girl-talk after I left." He leaned over and flicked some sand off the shoulder of her red T-shirt.

"No, but I would have enjoyed it if she had. She didn't want to sleep alone, so she climbed in with me. We read a story and Sam fell asleep. She didn't wake once."

"Good. I was a little worried, being in a strange place and all. Since the shooting, I worry about how she's going to react to different things."

"Has she had some problems?"

"No. But now she asks questions all the time."

Crista frowned. "What kind of questions?"

He looked down and pressing one hand against the other, cracked his knuckles. "She's asked if the police have caught the men who hurt her."

"Oh, wow. She's obviously more aware than you thought."

"Seems that way. But she doesn't appear upset by it. She asks about you all the time, too. I wonder if she feels safer with you around?"

Crista raised an eyebrow. "It's possible she just likes me."

Alex nodded. "That's true. And that makes two of us." He winked, his smile languid, the kind that made no secret of what he was thinking.

Crista glanced away, not wanting to read more into his words than he meant. They were friends, that was all. "Sam is a beautiful child. You've done a wonderful job raising her."

A wistful smile crossed his face. "I've had a lot of help. Marissa was…a good mother. And Elena has been a godsend. I don't know what I would've done without her."

Crista knew what it felt like to lose someone. Her father. Her mother. Her child. The pain might fade, but it never disappeared altogether. It was obvious Alex had loved his wife very much. Still did. "Life isn't kind sometimes."

"Yeah, isn't that the truth." He glanced to the beach where Samantha was still playing. "But I have Sam. She brings me a joy that's indescribable."

"It can't be easy trying to be both mother and father."

He nodded. "It's a humbling experience. I never realized how much I didn't know until I had to take care of Sam on my own." He gave a wry laugh. "I've discovered I'm a lousy mother."

"You're doing a great job."

The light returned to his eyes as he reached to take Crista's hand in his.

His hands were warm and gentle and she felt his heat flow through her like warm honey. As Alex's gaze met hers, she saw no pretense in his eyes—only desire. He wanted her as much as she wanted him. Arousal simmered deep within her. The ache of desire between her legs intensified. She needed him. And because she needed him she felt vulnerable in a way she'd never felt before.

"Daddy, Crista, see what I found," Sam's voice broke the spell. She ran toward them, holding out her hand for them to see what she had in it. "It's a seashell with a decoration on it."

"It's a sand dollar," Crista said, regrouping.

"Can you help me get some more?" Sam pleaded with Crista.

"Of course. I'd love to look for shells." But getting away from Alex was even more important. She knew exactly where they were headed. And even though she'd could think of nothing she'd like more than making love with Alex, she knew no good could come of it.

CRISTA GLANCED out the car window, sorry to say good-bye to a place that gave her such contentment. Two long warm days at the beach with her two favorite people had her fantasizing about what it might be like to live like this all the time. Just being with Alex and Sam had made her feel a part of something important. *She* felt important. Needed.

But the nights had been hard. Knowing Alex was off-limits, knowing she couldn't touch him or let him know how she felt only heightened her desire. Her awareness of him in the next room was pure torture, and when it was time to go home, it wasn't too soon.

They dropped Sam off with Elena and then Alex drove Crista and Calvin home. Riding quietly, Crista examined Alex in profile as he drove. She liked his looks. Yes, he was handsome, but what she really liked was his strong jaw and the sensuous curve to his lower lip that made her want to lean over and kiss it. She liked the shape of his ears and the way his hair curled down in the front. His eyelashes were dark and so full, most women would give their firstborn to have lashes like that. So lost in him, she didn't notice when they pulled into her parking lot.

"I'll carry the cage," Alex said.

"Oh…" She glanced around and saw they were

parked. "Great. Thank you." She'd only brought one small weekend bag with wheels, and she could handle that with ease.

He parked next to her Jeep and opening the door to get out, he said, "Oh, man. It looks like someone rammed into you."

"Yes, that happened the other day when I was parked."

"Did you get a name and insurance information?"

She shook her head. "The person was long gone and he didn't leave a phone number. Normally I could do a trace with the DMV, but not without a license number. My insurance will cover it though, all except the deductible."

"I can't believe how some people can destroy other people's property without batting an eye. It's beyond me."

Crista knew Alex was talking about more than her car, and she couldn't blame him. It was normal to be reminded of what had happened, and it was healthy to get angry about it. "I see it all the time in my job."

He opened the back door on the Navigator and reached for Calvin's cage. "I'm sure you do."

She knew that if he had his way, women wouldn't work in a dangerous profession. He'd made that perfectly clear. She let the subject drop, picked up her suitcase and headed for the apartment.

At the door, she did a quick inventory as she always did these days. Nothing seemed out of place. They went in and Alex helped her switch Calvin from the small cage into the larger one that filled one corner of the living room.

"There. Are you glad to be home, Calvin?"

Calvin tipped his head at Crista. *"Dios te salve*

María," the bird said, then squawked and flapped his wings.

"Oh, boy," Alex said with a smile. "After a few days with Elena, he probably knows the whole Rosary by now."

Crista chuckled. "Maybe that'll cut down on some of the cuss words he learned from his previous owners."

An awkward silence fell between them. His gaze caught hers and he held it.

"Would you like…something?" She didn't want him to leave just yet.

"Something?" he said with a teasing grin. Then as if he thought he might've embarrassed her, he said, "Sure. A glass of wine. A beer. Whatever."

Crista put down her purse and hurried to the kitchen where he couldn't see her. Her heart was racing and she could actually feel her pulse pounding at the base of her throat. They were making small talk to put off what they both wanted. She knew it. He knew it.

She poured two glasses of Chardonnay and brought them back into the living room where he was now lounging on the couch, looking as relaxed as if he'd already had the wine. She was as nervous as a skittish cat and he was as cool as…anything.

"Thanks," he said taking the glass she handed him, and with his other hand, he pulled her down next to him. He was so sure of himself. So confident.

"I didn't get a chance to tell you how much I enjoyed the weekend," he said.

"It was wonderful, wasn't it. I haven't felt so relaxed in a very long time." Hell, she couldn't remember when she'd enjoyed something as much as this weekend.

"It was the company that made it special for me."

Alex raised his glass and clinked it against hers. "Here's to more of the same."

Crista felt a silly smile on her face and clinked her glass against his. "To more of the same."

He eased back against the pillows, his gaze thoughtful. "I never did tell you that when I first met you I was totally blown away."

"No, but I got the general idea. You expected a detective to be a man."

"That, too. But what I meant is that I saw you as a woman, a beautiful woman." He set his glass down, reached for hers and set it on the coffee table, as well.

He slipped his hands over hers and said, "I hadn't looked at a woman with that kind of desire for two years, and suddenly, I felt liberated."

Crista had to smile. She'd been aware of the sexual attraction between them from the get-go.

"And it wasn't long before I realized that it wasn't just my body you affected." His smile grew softer, his eyes gentler, and he leaned to kiss her.

The softness of his kiss took her breath away and as he pulled her closer, she leaned into him, exploring his lips and his mouth with the tip of her tongue.

As Alex's kisses went from soft and sensual to harder, hotter, stronger, Crista felt her world tilt. It wasn't the wine, it was the heady elixir of desire. Passion. Arousal. She kissed him back harder, hotter, stronger. If this was a mistake, she didn't care.

"Crista, Crista," he said, pulling back a little, his voice a ragged whisper. "If you want me to stop, it has to be now."

Her breathing came in quick bursts. He was giving her an out, but she didn't want an out. She looked into his eyes and saw not only his passion, but also his gentle heart, his ability to love so easily. Everything she saw in those eyes told her what she wanted to know. He cared about her. This wasn't just a one-night stand for him. Knowing that, she should send him away— but she couldn't. It made her want him even more.

"I don't want you to stop." And she kissed him again.

He swept his tongue fiercely into her mouth and then his hands were in her hair and on her face, her throat, her breasts. His hands were everywhere, as if he didn't know where to touch first. It had been two years he'd said, and it had been that long for her, too. She pressed hard against him and he kissed her deeper. She felt his hand on her leg, on her bottom and between her legs.

She felt swollen with arousal and pressed harder against him, moving to ease the ache of desire that was building and building inside her. He was still kissing her when she felt his hand slip down inside her pants to touch her in just the right place. His fingers were warm and large and she wanted them inside her. She wanted him inside her.

As she ripped at the buttons on his white shirt, he suddenly sat up and tore it off, and then he reached for her top and pulled it over her head exposing her white lace bra. She hoped he liked lacy underwear. But he paid scant attention and within the blink of an eye, her bra was on the floor and so were her jogging pants. All they were left with was her barely there lace panties— and his black jockey shorts, his arousal clearly visible.

She reached out to him to come back, but he whispered, "Wait. Let me look at you. You're so beautiful."

She waited, feeling beautiful because he'd said so.

After a moment, he reached out to her. "C'mon," he whispered.

She clasped his hand and in one swift movement, he pulled her up against him, and standing in the middle of her living room, he kissed her breasts. "I've been dying to touch you all weekend," he said between kisses. "You can't imagine how much."

A smile formed on her lips as she felt the rasp of his tongue against her nipples. "Yes, I can." Her voice sounded hoarse and far away. "I couldn't stand knowing you were right there in the next room."

He knelt down, his kisses trailing from her breasts to her stomach and even lower where she felt his hot mouth right through her panties. If he didn't stop she was going to combust. And just when she couldn't stand it—thought she might climax right then and there—he placed both arms around her bottom and, lifting her with him, he stood and carried her to the bedroom.

Alex laid Crista gently on the bed and settled himself next to her. He was so ready, more than ready, but he didn't want to hurry and not give her the pleasure she deserved. He prided himself on his lovemaking. He took his time, made his partner feel special and in doing so, gained more than just sexual gratification. Though there were times when that was okay, too. But only with the woman he loved.

He was old-fashioned when it came to love. The thought surprised him. He loved Crista. And his heart felt so full with love, his passion seemed small in comparison. But only in comparison, because right now, his need for her was overwhelming. He leaned in to kiss her, his fingers caressing her neck. She turned and started to put her arms around him, but he held her back.

"Let me give you pleasure first. You don't have to do anything but enjoy."

She closed her eyes, giving her consent. He trailed his fingers from her neck to her stomach, his lips following the same path. Her skin was smooth, her stomach was flat and hard and he wondered if all her exercise would make her climax harder. He'd heard exercise was an aphrodisiac of sorts. But who needed that? All he needed was her. *She* was his aphrodisiac.

Feeling his warm mouth on her breasts and on her stomach was enough to send Crista over the top, but when his fingers touched her again right there and he slipped a finger inside and stroked her, she was sure of it. She moaned and bore down on his hand writhing with desire. And just when she thought she might come, he stopped. Sitting up, he moved down between her legs and then gently pulled them apart.

And then his lips found her, his tongue touching everywhere but the right place and just when she couldn't stand it, he placed his mouth exactly there. As he pressed hard against her, touching her most sensitive area with the tip of his tongue, her world exploded. And exploded. Again and again, and she thought the orgasm was going to go on forever.

When she came back to earth, he was watching her, a silly grin on his face. Maybe she should've felt embarrassed, but she didn't. Not at all. She realized then that at some point he'd put on a condom and she felt a flicker of surprise that he'd come prepared. But it was a good thing. She wanted him, and she wanted him now. Apparently he could read her mind, because just then he settled his body between her legs, and holding himself with one arm on either side of her, he entered her slowly. As he did, he leaned in to kiss her. Her scent was on his lips and while she used to think that would've turned her off, she moved with him, kissed him deeper.

He was big and harder than she could have imagined and her loins ached with wanting. She pressed into him taking him deeper and deeper inside, and matching his rhythm with hers, she felt his body go rigid. Another thrust and another and she heard him moan while his body shuddered in release.

After a moment, Alex moved to the side. "Sorry if I squished you," he said.

She grinned. "I didn't notice."

He raised himself on one elbow and pushed back a lock of hair from her face. "That was fantastic."

Fantastic couldn't begin to describe the experience. She'd never been so physically involved in her whole life. Granted her list of lovers was short, but she'd had a couple after Trini.

"When you care about someone it's always fantastic," he whispered.

A warning went off in Crista's head. She cared about Alex. Too much.

Crista decided it was the afterglow of sex that made Alex so effusive. He was a passionate, expressive man and didn't mind letting people know what he thought of them. Yes, she believed he cared about her, but she'd be foolish to think it was anything more. She hoped he didn't think he had to assure her, or make some kind of commitment just because they'd made love.

She'd received as much enjoyment from the experience as Alex had, and that was that.

CHAPTER FOURTEEN

ALEX'S WORLD had come alive. He'd never imagined he'd feel such closeness with anyone again, and with Crista, the feeling had been more intense than ever. He'd never been so physically and emotionally engaged. He loved her. He knew that much.

He reached over and stroked Crista's cheek. "You're beautiful," he whispered. "In every way."

He watched her stretch like a lazy cat. "Even though you don't know me in every way, I'll take the compliment." She smiled with contentment. "And no matter what I look like, I feel wonderful."

"Me, too. I feel better than ever." Alex stretched out on the bed, rolling over, half on top of Crista again, his mouth close to hers. "I could get used to this."

"Used to what?"

"You. Having you around. I like the idea."

A frown creased her smooth forehead. "Some ideas sound better than they actually are." Her tone of voice teased, but her expression seemed serious. She held his gaze, traced his lips with her fingertips. "Hey," she said. "I don't want you to think you have to reassure me that it was anything more than sharing a wonderful night together." She pulled to a sitting position and hugged her knees.

Alex sat up next to her, feeling the sting behind her

words. He drew his head back. "Are you saying this was just a night of physical pleasure and we should leave it at that?"

"I'm saying it was a wonderful night. We don't need to think about anything more than that."

He gritted his teeth. "Someone must have hurt you badly," he said. "So much, you have to convince yourself that our being together was just a fun night."

Her eyes darkened. "If it was anything more, I'd know it."

He'd seen the wariness in her eyes the second he started getting close. But he'd thought he'd gotten beyond that wall, if even just a little. "Okay. I guess we'll just have to have different views on that then."

"What do you mean?"

"It was more than just sex to me. You can tell yourself it wasn't, but that doesn't change my belief. I care about you. And I wouldn't be here in this bed if I thought it was nothing more than a physical encounter. I wouldn't have asked you to join me and Sam for the weekend if I didn't think there was potential for a serious relationship between us."

She drew her gaze from his and lowered her chin, fiddling with a thread on the quilt. "I...have feelings for you, too, Alex. But I'm also a realist. I know it would never work between us. We're too different. We want different things."

His nerves bunched. "I think we want the same things, but you're afraid to admit it."

Her brows came together in a puzzled expression. "I'm not afraid to admit anything if it were true. But the fact is, you don't know me as well as you think you do."

Crista *was* afraid, but not for the reasons he thought.

She was afraid of making the wrong decision. Afraid of opening herself up to a world of hurt. It was easier not to fall in love than it was to deal with the aftermath when love turned bad. And it was preordained that this would.

She drew a deep breath. *Easier not to fall in love.* Wasn't that ridiculous? It was too late for that. She was already in love with Alex. But the worst thing for her to do would be to act on her shaky emotions.

Alex moved from the bed, picked up his hastily discarded clothes and started dressing. "I've got to get Sam off to school in a couple hours. Why don't we talk about this later. Tomorrow night, maybe." He glanced at his watch and gave a lopsided grin. "I guess that's tonight since it's already after midnight."

As much as Crista wanted to see him, she knew it was the wrong decision. God knew, she wanted a relationship with him, wanted it more than anything, but wanting something that badly could only destroy them both. "I'm sorry. I have to work."

"Then tomorrow night?"

Her throat felt dry and scratchy and it was hard to get out the words. "I can't. I need to put all my energy into solving the case. And if I don't do it soon, I probably won't have a job to worry about."

Alex buttoned his shirt and then tucked the tails into his jeans. "Why do you say that?"

"Because." She turned to sit on the edge of the bed facing the wall. "The captain has told me if I don't have something concrete soon, he's going to take me off the case. It would be a black mark on my record."

She couldn't tell him the rest, that she thought getting rid of her had been the captain's plan all along. She couldn't tell him that she was thinking of filing a grievance for gender bias, because she knew Alex would never understand.

"That doesn't seem right. Some cases take longer to solve than others. Right?"

"Yes, but since the mayor has made it a priority, the captain is under the gun. He thinks I'm not doing enough and he has someone in mind to take over from me."

Alex's face hardened. "That's ridiculous. Are you sure?"

His reaction surprised her. "Of course I'm sure. He told me as much."

"Okay, I'll talk to the mayor and see if he'll get the captain to let up."

Crista's stomach knotted. She prided herself on doing her job well without others running interference for her. The idea that Alex thought he could simply take care of things for her was another example of how different they were. She bolted from the bed, holding the sheet around her like a sarong. "Thanks, but no thanks."

He frowned. "Why not?"

Because if she accepted Alex's help, she'd be proving the captain right, and she'd be showing not only the captain, but everyone else in the unit that she couldn't handle the job on her own. "It's important that I do this myself."

"That's silly."

"Excuse me?" Crista was astonished. "Are you saying that having pride in my work and wanting to prove I can do the job is silly?"

"No, I'm saying that not accepting help when you can use it is silly. Being self-sufficient is admirable, but it can work against you sometimes."

"Maybe. But in this case, taking your help would

undermine everything I've worked for. It would undermine who I am."

Alex pressed his lips together tightly. He slipped his jacket on and walked over to where she stood still holding the sheet. Placing his hands on her bare arms he said, "Why don't you get some rest. Things will look differently in the morning."

If only they would. But she knew better.

ALEX DROVE HOME feeling as if he'd done something wrong, but he wasn't sure what. It seemed as if all the good feelings they'd shared over the weekend disappeared once he'd mentioned talking to the mayor. Or was it when he'd said he could get used to having her around? How could that be wrong? How could helping her be wrong? Maybe she was right when she'd said they were too different.

When he'd asked her to join them for the weekend, he'd hoped their friendship might become more than that. And he'd thought it had. Entertaining the idea of a relationship with Crista or with anyone meant he had to think about whether there was a future with that person. He wasn't going to allow his daughter to get attached to someone who was just a passing fancy. He'd assumed any woman he'd fall in love with would want a home and family and that would be enough. But he was wrong. He'd fallen in love with Crista—and Crista talked as if her job was a lifetime career.

Reaching home, Marissa's home that had become his when she died, he pulled into the garage and quietly went inside, careful not to make any noise. Since the shooting, he'd been sleeping with one ear open and he figured Elena probably did the same.

If he went to bed now, he could get a couple hours

of sleep before Sam got up. But an hour later he was still thinking. Random thoughts. Thoughts about Marissa and Crista and the future. Marissa never had any qualms about accepting his help and he'd always thought her a strong woman. She liked having someone take care of her, and she'd liked taking care of their home and family. She shared his values and beliefs and those were the things that had first drawn them to each other.

But that was Marissa's personality, he realized. It wasn't Crista's. He'd realized the first day he met her that Crista was unlike any woman he'd ever known. He'd been intrigued by her self-sufficiency and candor, her ability to make him laugh. Yet he'd sensed a wariness behind the bravado—a private pain that tugged at all his protective instincts.

She *was* different, and those differences were what had drawn him to her. He liked everything about her, including that she was protective of the people who were important to her.

He'd seen her vulnerable side, too. The side that said she wasn't going to let herself feel too much. The side that said she couldn't trust her own feelings, and because of that, she'd closed the door to the possibility of love. And marriage.

But who was he to talk? He wasn't sure he could trust his own feelings, much less hers. He'd fallen in love with Crista without thinking of anyone but himself and his own needs. He'd simply assumed Crista would feel the same. What an ass he was.

Crista deserved an apology. He should have respected how important her job was to her. Instead, he'd been upset because she hadn't responded in the way *he'd* expected.

He picked up the phone and dialed her number. After five rings, the message machine clicked on and he remembered she'd turned off the ringer so they wouldn't be disturbed. "Crista, this is Alex," he said. He hated to leave a message, but wanted her to know right away what an idiot he was. "I'm calling to apologize for being such an ass. When I suggested helping you, I was only thinking of what I could do for you. I didn't think about how you might feel about it. I'm sorry. Please accept my apology."

LYING IN BED listening to the tenderness in his voice, Crista felt as if her heart might crack in two. Alex was a prideful man, one who believed his way was the right way. She knew his intentions were honorable, but she'd reacted on instinct because she'd felt threatened. How stupid was that?

And when she thought of how much it must have taken for him to call and apologize, she wanted to crawl in a hole and stay there.

She still remembered what Alex had told her not long after they met—that if he were ever to marry again, Sam would be the most important consideration.

He wanted a traditional wife, a stay-at-home mother for Sam. She wasn't that person.

Early the next morning, Crista drove to the Pierce Elevated. She'd spent far too much time worrying about personal issues and not enough time trying to solve the case. Her goal today was to find Tommy.

Driving off the freeway and onto the service road underneath, Crista found a spot, parked her Jeep and stepped out. She glanced at a man sleeping on the ground a couple yards away. He was covered with newspapers for warmth, and she wondered why when there were shelters available, some people refused to take advantage of them. Walking farther down under the bridge, she saw a ragtag group of people huddled around a large barrel with a bonfire inside, tossing in whatever they could find to keep the fire going. Their clothes were tattered and dirty, and some had strips of fabric tied around their hands to keep them warm through Houston's uncharacteristically cold winter.

Her gaze darted, searching for an eleven-year-old boy.

"No, no, no!" a woman's voice rang out. Crista spun around. Near the column on the other side of the bridge, she saw a scuffle, the flash of a uniform and someone attacking a police officer. Crista ran to help, drawing her gun as she went. As she came closer, she saw that the officer was a woman, and it seemed that instead of subduing the person, the officer was warding off the blows. Crista leveled her gun. "Stop or I'll shoot!" she yelled. But the person kept swinging…and, ohmygod…the officer was Abby. Abby Carlton.

In an instant, Crista was on them. She pulled the attacker away from Abby and threw him to the ground, knocking her friend backward in the process. Abby stumbled and fell. Using her own body weight, Crista held the person down and wrenched both of his arms back. It was only when she was cuffing him that she realized Abby's attacker was a woman.

"Abby. Are you okay?" Crista shouted. Keeping her weight on the woman, she glanced over to where Abby had fallen.

"I'm okay. Don't hurt her." Abby scrambled toward Crista. "She doesn't know what she's doing."

Crista stared incredulously at her friend. Abby had scratches on her face and she was visibly shaken. "I'm sorry," Crista said. "It looked to me like she knew exactly what she was doing. And seeing her attacking an officer, she's lucky I didn't take her out."

Abby knelt next to Crista. Reaching out and brushing the woman's cheek, she said softly, "It's okay, Janie. No one is going to hurt you." Abby turned to Crista. "She's off her meds."

Suddenly the woman snarled like a wild animal and her head lunged forward as if she was going to take a bite of Abby's hand. Abby jerked back, her dark eyes round with surprise.

"I'd say she doesn't want your help." Crista stood, then held out a hand to assist Abby.

"I know what it looks like, but she's not in any condition to decide what she wants."

Crista hadn't talked to Abby since Risa's investigation and seeing her today sent an enormous wave of regret through her. How could she have let all her friendships go? The longing to have her friends back suddenly felt overwhelming. But if she wanted things to change, Crista knew it was she who had to take the first step.

"Are you taking her in?" Crista asked. "I'll help you get her to your car."

Abby knelt down again. "Are you okay, Janie? I can help you if you'll let me." Janie didn't answer.

"Nothing's changed, I see."

Abby glanced up at Crista. "What do you mean?"

Petite Abby Carlton looked like the all-American girl. The cheerleader in high school. The homecoming queen. But Crista knew different. Abby hadn't had it easy at all.

"You're still trying to save the world." Crista hoped Abby would take the comment as lightly as it was intended. She handed Abby the keys to the handcuffs.

Shoving a lock of brown hair from her eyes, Abby inadvertently smeared dirt across her scratched cheek. She smiled uncertainly. "Yes, I am. One person at a time."

While Abby calmed the woman, Crista realized how much she admired Abby's strong beliefs, the strength of her convictions. Though Crista and their other friends thought Abby had been crazy to give up everything she'd worked for when she left the academy, Abby had done what she believed in. She'd been brave enough to leave the academy for love and she hadn't been too proud to come back when it didn't work out. Crista wondered if the experience was worth it.

Maybe she'd do well to take a lesson from Abby. Open herself to the possibilities of love and see what might happen. It wasn't the end of the world if it didn't turn out, was it? Abby had come out of it just fine, maybe she was even stronger.

It only took a few minutes for Abby to calm Janie, and together Abby and Crista helped the woman up, one on each side, and walked her to Abby's squad car.

"I'm going to remove the handcuffs, Janie, but before I do, I want you to give me your word that you'll be good."

The woman's chin dropped to her chest, as if she was now ashamed of what she'd done.

"Okay?" Abby prompted.

The woman nodded. "Okay. I'll be good."

With that, Abby settled Janie into the back seat of her car, took Crista's keys, removed the cuffs and closed the door.

"Thanks, Crista. We'll be fine now. I'm going to take her to the shelter, get her cleaned up and see if I can do something about her meds."

"Does she have a case worker? They usually handle those things, don't they?" Law enforcement encountered problems with the mentally ill all the time, and a good percentage of the homeless had some kind of mental disability. If the person received medical assistance from the state, a case worker usually helped with medications and life skills.

"So," Abby said, ignoring the question, "I'm surprised to see you here. What's up?"

"A lead on a homicide. A drive-by."

"Maybe I can help. I'm down here a lot."

"I'm trying to find a boy named Tommy Ramirez."

Abby shook her head. "Haven't heard the name. And there aren't many youngsters here. Maybe you should check a family shelter."

"Maybe. But I'll ask around here anyway. Someone may know him."

"Over there." Abby pointed to a man sitting on a wooden box near the fire. "That's Horatio, and he knows everyone. Tell him I suggested you talk to him. He knows me."

Janie suddenly started banging on the window. "I— I need to go," Abby said and opened the driver's door. Halfway inside, she stopped, looked wistfully at Crista and said, "It was really nice seeing you, Crista. I wish…" She hesitated for a second and then said, "I wish things were different."

Crista didn't know what to say. If Abby wanted things to be different, why had she been so remote? Nothing would happen if they all sat back and waited for the other person to make the first move. "Me, too." Crista said with a smile. "So let's do something about it."

An uncomfortable silence ensued, as if neither knew where to go from there.

Janie started making more racket, and Abby said, "I really do have to go."

"Sure," Crista said. "I understand."

Crista felt a lump in her throat as she watched Abby drive away, and her longing for her friends kicked up another notch. Just then, a ruckus broke out near the fire and two men started yelling at each other. Crista hurried over and flashed her shield. "What's going on guys? Someone got a problem?"

Both men stared at her, then backed away as if she were the devil himself.

Crista looked at the man named Horatio. "Hello," she said, showing her badge again. "I'm Detective Santiago."

The man had a scraggly gray beard and motley long hair. His skin was leathery and his ragged layers of clothing reeked of body odor and urine. He appeared to be in his late sixties, but she suspected hard living made him look older than he was.

"I'm pleased to meet you, Miss. My name is Horatio Algier," the man announced in a booming orator's voice.

"Officer Carlton told me you might be able to answer a couple questions for me."

His eyes lit at the mention of Abby's name.

"I'm trying to find a boy named Tommy Ramirez."

"Ah, Tomás. He isn't in any trouble, is he?"

"No. I just need to ask him a few questions. Do you know where I might find him?"

"He's a good boy," Algier said. "You might find him at the new center they're putting up…ah, I forget the name."

"La Frontera. I've been there. He hasn't been around for a couple weeks."

The man gazed off into space and Crista wondered if she'd lost him. Then he said, "He goes to see his brother sometimes."

"And where does his brother live?"

"Tomás lived with his brother until the older boy got into some trouble a while back. He goes to the prison to see him."

"Do you know his brother's name?"

"Pedro," the man said. "Pedro Castillo, I think. Different fathers."

Pedro. Pedro Castillo was Tommy's brother! Crista felt as if she'd hit the mother lode. Tommy would have had access to Pedro's gun, and he'd gone missing right after the Encanto shooting.

The good feeling faded as fast as it came. The thought of a boy as young as Tommy being in a gang made her sick. And when he heard, Alex would be devastated. But maybe Tommy wasn't involved? Maybe he'd given the gun to someone else…or sold it?

CHAPTER FIFTEEN

CRISTA'S FINGERS clenched the steering wheel, her nerves tingling as if they were on the outside of her skin. The mixture of anticipation and apprehension made her edgy.

She had a good solid lead and it was only a matter of time before she had a suspect. Englend should be pleased about that. But still she grew more anxious the closer she got to the station. Even with a new lead, she dreaded a confrontation with Englend. She didn't trust him.

Driving into the parking garage, her senses went on red alert. She glanced at the stall where the truck had been earlier. Empty.

She went inside and headed directly to Englend's office. He was sitting at his desk, reading the paper and drinking coffee.

"Excuse me, Captain."

Glancing up, his eyebrows rose in question. "Yes."

"I just wanted to update you on the Encanto case."

He waved a hand. "You're too late, Santiago. I put Fontanero on it last Friday, and this morning we have a suspect in custody. You can give Fontanero any information you have."

Crista looked up and saw Eddie Fontanero sitting at Pete's desk. How could Englend do that to her? She clenched her hands into fists and gritted her teeth. Either Fontanero had inside information, or he'd made an arrest to appease the powers that be.

"He'll be here till Pete returns."

Her anger abated a little. At least he hadn't replaced her. "Who's the suspect?"

The captain picked up a file on his desk. "A punk named Marco Torres."

Marco? She'd just spoken to Marco Friday morning. And she hadn't found any evidence to implicate him in the crimes. He wasn't even a gang member anymore. Where was Fontanero getting his information? "What's the evidence?"

"The gun. The slime had it in his possession."

Stunned, Crista held on to the back of the chair. How could that be? According to NCIC, the gun used in the Encanto case was the same gun used by Pedro Castillo in a crime three years ago. And according to records, that gun had never been found. Since she'd talked to Horatio, she'd been going on the assumption that Tommy might know where his brother stashed the weapon, and had either used it, given it away or sold it to someone else.

She'd thought if she could trace the gun, she'd have her suspect. But she never expected the perp to be Marco. Yes, he'd been friends with Pedro and both of them had been members of the Pistoles. Had Pedro or Tommy given Marco the gun? Had Marco used it against Alex?

"What's the motive?"

"Pistoles' turf war."

"That doesn't make sense. Not when Del Rio was at the scene of two shootings. That makes him a target in my mind."

"You have evidence to support that theory?"

She didn't have squat. "No, I don't."

"Then the case is closed as far as you're concerned. Fontanero will handle it from here."

Yeah. Marco would be convicted and that would be it. Except that if Marco wasn't the right suspect, Alex and Sam might still be in danger. Her mind spinning, she stormed from Englend's office, went to her desk and gathered everything she needed. Fontanero stared at her, as if waiting for her to say something, but she simply nodded. She was going to finish what she started whether Englend wanted her to or not.

An hour later, she was at the Huntsville prison. Another hour later, after all the paperwork had been completed, she entered the visitor's room. Castillo was sitting on the other side of the glass, and his gaze raked over her like she was something delectable he wanted to have for breakfast. Why not? He had no idea who she was or why she was here.

"Good morning. I'm Detective Santiago," she said, getting right to the point.

The lust in his eyes switched off. "Too bad for you."

"I'm investigating a case and I'm looking for information—information I think you might have."

Pedro was a swarthy young man with well-developed biceps and several tattoos running the length of both arms. One tattoo was of Our Lady of Guadalupe and another was the praying hands, which supposedly asked forgiveness for crimes committed. She never understood that. Did criminals really think asking for forgiveness absolved them?

The man's gaze turned lecherous again. "What's in it for me?"

"The case I'm working on involves your brother Tommy."

She saw him flinch. "Is Tommy in trouble?"

"Maybe. I don't know, which is why I'm here."

He didn't respond, so she went on, telling him what she could about the shootings and that Tommy had been hanging around La Frontera, but had gone missing about the same time as the shootings. "The gun you used in the robbery three years ago is the same gun used in the drive-bys. And since yours was never found, that leads us to believe that Tommy might be involved and was using your gun."

He stared at her incredulously, so she added, "If you gave your gun to someone else, a friend, maybe, tell me now and your brother won't be picked up."

Pedro gave a wicked laugh. "I don't know where you're getting your information, *chica,* but my gun couldn't have been used in those shootings."

"And why is that?"

"Because the police took it."

Crista blinked. "The gun you used was impounded?"

"If that's what you call it—yeah. They impounded it."

She tried to remember what she'd read in Castillo's file. An eyewitness, she remembered that. He'd been convicted on eyewitness testimony. So why would he think they'd impounded the gun when they hadn't?

"So," Pedro said. "Tommy can't be in any trouble." He shook his head. "I think you cops ought to get your shit together."

Crista was still trying to get her mind around what he'd just told her.

"Y'know, *querida*, I'm getting paroled in a few

weeks and I could take care of a pretty woman like you really good."

Crista came to attention. "Not likely." *You sleaze-bag.* She stood and, still reeling from what he'd told her, turned to leave.

"I haven't seen Tommy in a while. Do you know if he's okay?"

Pedro's question stopped her at the door. Maybe the sleazebag actually cared about his little brother. "I don't know. He's been hanging out at La Frontera, but the director won't let him participate unless he gets back in school. And he hasn't been around since the shootings."

"Dammit! He knows he's got to stay in school." Anger flared in Pedro's dark eyes. "I'm gonna beat the crap outta him when I blow this place."

Frowning, Crista said, "Probably not the best way to get him back in school, but I'll tell you what, you keep our conversation quiet and I'll find him and see what I can do."

Pedro nodded. "Tommy's smart," he said. "He's got a future. I don't want him ending up like me."

Crista knew what he meant. Her brother had a future, too, and she didn't want him back in jail again. And like Pedro, she didn't know how to help him.

She left the prison even more determined. She had to talk to Diego about Marco. To see if he knew anything that further implicated Marco in the crimes. And she had to get another look at Castillo's file. Talk to the arresting officer.

On the way to her car, her cell phone rang. She glanced at the number and recognized it as Alex's. She'd been avoiding his calls for two days and she really didn't want to talk to him now. After the fifth ring, he left a message. Hearing his smooth voice, she felt queasy.

"Crista, it's Alex. I have to talk to you. Please, call me."

She closed her eyes. She couldn't do it. If she saw him, talked to him, she ran the risk of convincing herself she could be something she wasn't.

"It's about the case," Alex finished. "It's important."

Oh, man. A jolt of awareness hit her. She'd been letting her personal life, her feelings for Alex, interfere with her job. If anyone else had called about a case, she'd be right on it. She punched the call return button. No answer, so she left her own message that she'd meet him in an hour and a half at her place if he could.

ALEX DROVE around the block three times waiting for Crista to arrive. He longed to see her, but dreaded what he had to tell her. He didn't want to believe it, but she was Diego's sister. She had a right to know.

Finally, he parked on the street in front of her apartment where he could see her pull in when she arrived. As he waited, he noticed an older black pickup truck pull in a few cars behind him. Nobody got out. Odd. Probably someone waiting like him.

When he saw Crista's Jeep rounding the corner, he got out of his SUV and hurried to where she'd just parked.

"Hi. I'm sorry I didn't return your other calls. I was at the prison and it would have been too difficult to talk there."

"No problem."

As they walked to the building, Alex saw the same black truck that had parked behind him pull into the parking lot. It idled for a second, backed up and drove away. "You know anyone who drives a black Ranger?"

Her head jerked up. "Why?"

He shrugged. "One pulled in a couple cars behind me while I was waiting for you, but no one got out. And just now, the same truck pulled into the drive back there and then left. I thought it might be someone you know. An old boyfriend," he joked.

She shook her head, but her expression told him she wasn't being truthful. Maybe it wasn't an old boyfriend. Maybe it was someone else—someone she'd started dating recently. His jaw clenched at the thought.

At the door, she stopped to glance around. "Something wrong?"

"No, everything is fine."

Except it wouldn't be in a few minutes.

"C'mon in," she said as she opened the door. "I'm anxious to hear. Something about the case, you said."

He stood behind her as she put her briefcase on the table and then motioned for him to sit. No formalities, no "Would you like something to drink?" For her, this was pure business.

"Sort of," he said, taking a seat on the couch. He waited till she sat, too, but she chose to stand, far from him. He cleared his throat. "Word on the street…" Damn. How could he say this without hurting her. Seeing the anticipation in her eyes he knew that wasn't possible. She'd be hurt no matter how he said it.

"I recently learned that Diego has been seen on several occasions with the boss of Syndicato Tejano."

Shock registered on Crista's face.

"It doesn't necessarily mean anything, but I thought you should know."

When she caught her breath, she said, "Yeah, I should know. I should definitely know." Anger hardened her voice. "The Texas Syndicate is one of the most notorious jail gangs in Texas."

That was true. The TS was known as the most dangerous and far reaching of all the jail gangs, using former prisoners to carry out their business outside prison. Some gang leaders ran multimillion dollar enterprises from behind bars.

Crista couldn't believe what she was hearing. "So who saw Diego? And who was the person he was seen with?"

"I don't want to say who saw him. I'd be breaking a confidence."

She whirled around. "For God's sake, Alex. This is my brother. I have a right to know what's going on, especially if he's in trouble. And from the sounds of it, it could be deep trouble."

Alex shot to his feet and started to pace.

"Who was he seen with? You can tell me that much, can't you?"

"All I know is that the guy's name is Trini."

Trini. A member of the Syndicato? The leader? She swallowed a huge gulp of air.

Yes, she could see it. But Diego, she couldn't. The TS was known for its ruthlessness. Diego wasn't ruthless, no matter what mistakes he'd made.

"You're right. Even if Diego has been seen with someone from the Syndicate, that doesn't mean he's involved with them."

But no matter what she told herself, she had a sickening feeling about it. "I'm going to talk to Diego. He'll tell me the truth." She saw Alex flinch.

"If your brother is hanging out with the TS, it's not safe for you to go there. No matter how well trained you think you are."

Crista usually balked at being coddled, but for some reason Alex's protectiveness felt right. Still, she had to go. "If Diego is there, I'll be safe."

"Then let me go with you. For moral support if nothing else."

Without hesitation, she shook her head. "No. You can't do that."

"Why not?"

"Because you're a civilian and I can't put you in danger. Besides, Diego wouldn't talk to me if someone else is there." And she'd be mortified for Alex to see where she grew up. "I need to talk to him alone."

"If not me, then take someone else along. Your partner. A friend. I'd feel better about it if you did."

Crista's heart went out to Alex. She knew what it felt like when someone you cared about might be in harm's way. She knew all too well. "I'm not on duty. I can't ask Pete to come with me." Then, to appease him, she said, "But okay. I'll call someone to go with me. A friend."

"Good." He came over, pulled her into his embrace and held her without saying a word. Crista closed her eyes and tried to draw some of his strength. After a few moments, she pulled away. "Thanks, Alex. I know this was hard for you."

"Not as hard as it is for you," he said. "I'm here if you need me. Anytime. Anywhere."

From her window a few minutes later, she watched Alex climb into his SUV and drive off. She double-checked her gun under her jacket and was out the door—heading straight for the barrio.

CHAPTER SIXTEEN

IT WAS DARK by the time she hit Guadalupe Street. Dim yellow streetlights lit her way past parked cars on both sides. Rock music blared from open doors and loud voices and laughter carried on the cool night air. A gang of boys huddled on one corner, their body language asking for trouble. Another group of teens sauntered toward them on the other side of the street. They looked as if they were ready to oblige.

Not her problem tonight. She was here to talk to Diego and find out what the hell was going on. She'd planned to talk to him earlier about Marco's arrest and find out if he knew that Marco had the gun used in the shootings. Now her mission was twofold.

She turned the corner and for the first time since she'd come back, she noticed how well kept some of the houses looked. She could see the owners took pride in their homes, and she wondered if the Martinez family still lived in the one she'd just passed. They were nice people. Big family. Always willing to help. Always pleasant.

Approaching Diego's, she saw the house was dark. He wasn't home. Fine, she had a key, she'd go in and wait. But the streets were jammed, leaving no place for her to park, so she drove around the corner, parked there and hurried back to the house.

The possibility that Diego was involved with the TS gave her a determination stronger than anything she'd ever felt before. She didn't know what she could do to prevent him from ruining his life, but she knew she wasn't going to let it happen. No matter what.

Reaching the door, she knocked a couple of times to make sure she wasn't barging in on something. When there wasn't any answer, she used her key. It was dark inside and the scent of stale tobacco hung in the air. With the streetlight next to the house on the side, enough light shone through the window that she could find her way around. She decided not to turn on the inside lights, because if Diego knew she was here, he might not come in.

She parked herself in the only chair in the room and waited. A half hour passed with no sign of Diego. Then another half hour. Okay. She had all night if that's what it took. She wasn't leaving until she had this out with him.

Angling her head from side to side to ease the tension in her neck, she heard a sound on the porch. Footsteps. Then a knock. It wasn't Diego. He wouldn't knock.

Leaping to her feet, she drew her gun and stole toward the door, careful to stay away from the windows. She flattened her back against the wall, then heard a voice. A voice she'd recognize anywhere. "Crista, open up. I know you're here. I saw your Jeep down the—"

Crista jerked open the door and pulled him inside, quickly closing the door behind them. Holstering her gun, she drew him into the kitchen away from any windows and standing with her feet apart and her arms crossed, she demanded, "What the hell are you doing here, Alex?"

"What does it look like? I followed you. I knew

you'd do something stupid like this. And when you didn't come out, I got worried."

"It's not stupid. And I sure as hell don't need a baby-sitter."

"You don't know how dangerous it is to be here."

Crista almost laughed. This was the perfect opportunity to tell him she knew the dangers better than he did since she'd spent seventeen years of her life in this hellhole. But before she had a chance to get the words out, she heard voices and shouting and then a gunshot right outside the front door. Drawing her weapon again, she motioned Alex to get back. "Stay out of sight," she whispered and then she crept around the corner to the bedroom and flattened herself against the wall.

The front door burst open and through the crack between the door and the jamb, she saw two men come in. Diego. And Trini behind him. But as they came farther inside, she saw Trini had a gun jammed against Diego's neck.

Oh, God! Crista tightened the grip on her weapon. She didn't know what was going down, but she knew she had to wait for the right moment to do something or Diego was a dead man. She prayed Alex didn't make a sound.

Still holding the gun on Diego, Trini shoved her brother into the chair. "It's blood in, blood out. You know that!"

Crista's chest constricted as she saw the large TS tattoo on Trini's forearm. Alex had been right. Diego was involved with the jail gang. Blood in, blood out meant the only way into the gang was to maim or kill someone. And the only way out was to die.

Trini bounced from one foot to another, his hand twitching on the butt of the gun. "You want out, that's the only way it can go down," Trini said. He paused, waving his weapon in Diego's face. "This ain't easy for me, *mi amigo*. I'm cutting you a break. You take out Del Rio, and I'll turn my back while you go."

"You're cutting me a break? You're a lying sack, Trini."

"We're amigos. Why don't you trust me?"

Diego scoffed. "For one, I asked you to lay off Crista, and you agreed. Only now I find out you've been stalking her."

Trini shrugged. "I gotta do what I gotta do, man."

Stunned, Crista held her breath. Trini wanted Diego to kill Alex? Was all this because Trini wanted to get back at her? But that couldn't be it. Alex had been a target before she came on the scene.

"What's it going to be?" Trini stood with his feet apart, twitching and waving his gun at Diego.

One wrong twitch and his gun could go off.

Suddenly Trini glanced toward the kitchen as if he'd heard something.

Oh, God. Alex. Alex had heard everything.

"I can't do it," Diego said.

Trini drew his gaze back to Diego. His eyes narrowed and, with his hand still on the gun, he spat out, "I'm giving you a chance, and you're throwing it in my face. The Syndicate finds out I let you go without blood, we're both dead."

"Not if we get protection."

Trini let out a cackle of crazy laughter. "You're loco, man. The Syndicate is deep in the blue. That's why everything works so well."

Diego looked up, his eyes on the bedroom door. Crista stood perfectly still.

Trini let out a sigh of resignation, as if he wasn't sure what to do now.

She had to make a move.

"With Del Rio out of the way, the Syndicate moves one of our men inside and everyone looks the other way. Business gets even better."

Trini stepped closer to Diego, bent over and waved the gun in Diego's face. "We took care of you in prison, *mi amigo*. It's payback time."

Diego's lips thinned.

Trini straightened and pulled out a cigarette, offering one to her brother.

Crista aimed her gun. *Now!* Suddenly, Alex appeared behind Trini, directly in her line of fire. She couldn't risk shooting Alex. Taking the only action she could, her gun still aimed at Trini's head, she stepped into the room. "Drop it!"

Trini turned. His mouth fell open.

"Drop it or you're dead!"

Still holding his own weapon, Trini's gaze raked over Crista, his confidence seemingly unshaken. "*Querida.* You can't shoot me."

"I said drop it!"

He gave a smarmy smile. "You couldn't shoot a man who gave you so much pleasure, could you? A man who knows how to satisfy you."

Crista didn't flinch. "Try me. I'll start with the *co-jones.*"

As the words left Crista's lips she saw Alex lunge for Trini's gun and in a sudden flurry of motion, Crista kicked Trini's legs from under him. Trini went down, his weapon crashing to the floor. Crista dropped a knee on Trini's back and shoved the barrel of her Glock at his temple.

"Bring your hands around behind you, above my knee," she ordered, and then jammed her gun harder

against Trini's head. "Diego, get the cuffs from my purse."
When he did, both Diego and Alex held Trini down while
she cuffed him. After Trini was secured, they stood, chests
heaving. No one said a word, each apparently trying to
make their own sense of what had just happened.

Crista glanced at Diego and then Alex. Alex turned
away, as if he couldn't look at her.

Hauling in a lungful of air, Crista pulled out her cell
phone and called for backup.

Within minutes, the sirens sounded outside and
Crista went to the door.

The first patrol car on the scene was Captain Englend's.

AFTER GETTING the basic information from Diego about
the assault, the captain directed one of the other officers to take Trini into custody. Alex drove himself to
the station and Diego rode with Crista. Before they left
the house, Crista advised both Alex and Diego not to
say anything about Trini's accusations. If there was
corruption in the system, they didn't know who they
could trust.

Crista and Diego rode in silence, as if talking about
the incident might make it worse. Finally, Crista
couldn't take it any longer and said, "Can you tell me
what was happening back there? I only got the gist of
what Trini was saying."

She expected him to say no, but then he said, "What
do you want to know?"

What *didn't* she want to know. "Are you a member
of the Texas Syndicate?"

Diego's expression hardened. "It's not what you
think."

"Okay. Clue me in."

He hesitated, then cleared his throat, as if this was difficult for him to talk about. "When I got to Huntsville, I learned the only way to survive was to join one of the jail gangs. The Texas Syndicate tried to recruit me, but I held back. I knew how ruthless they were."

Crista held her breath. Blood in—blood out. She couldn't imagine Diego hurting anyone.

"I was attacked one night and I fought the guy off. He cut me twice, but I wrestled the shiv away from him and…" He stopped, unable to finish.

Crista's hands tightened on the wheel till her knuckles went white. "You…killed someone?"

He closed his eyes and nodded. "It was self-defense. He attacked me and would have killed me if I hadn't gotten him first. The guards saw it all. No charges were filed."

She'd fired on criminals before, but she'd never killed anyone. She couldn't imagine how that would feel—no matter what the situation. A human life was a human life.

"The Syndicate saw that fight as my initiation. From that point on, I had protection from the TS." His face held no expression, almost as if he was talking about someone else.

"It was the only way to survive in there. Trini was a member of the TS when he was in Gatesville and the Syndicate expects their guys to recruit on the outside once they leave. Since Trini and I were barrio brothers, they had him contact me before I was released. I told him I wanted out."

She glanced at him. Was he telling the truth?

"Both of us knew there was only one way out. But he had a job for me, and he figured if I carried it out, that would cover me. Only I couldn't do it. He got crazy. He figured he was helping me and I was screwing him over."

"Why couldn't you do it?" Had meeting Alex and his family been a turning point?

He turned to her, his expression incredulous. "I'm not a killer," he said. By the inflection in his voice, he thought she should know that. "Then you showed up. I thought if you could turn your life around, maybe I could, too."

He sank back against the seat. "I was wrong. It's not possible. Not for me."

"But it is," Crista said quickly. It was what she'd always wanted for him. "What's to stop you now?"

"If I testify against Trini, I'm a dead man."

"I'll get you protection."

He scoffed. "From who? The Houston Police?"

"Yes."

"You're wearing blinders, *m'ija*. The police are as corrupt as the Syndicate. Who do you think ordered the hit on your friend?"

She turned so quickly to look at him, her neck cramped. Her foot jammed hard on the gas. "Are you saying someone in the department ordered the hit on Alex?"

He nodded.

"You have proof?"

Diego rubbed his eyes with his thumb and forefinger. His mouth turned down at the corners. "Trini does. Ask him before the police let him go."

"He's not going anywhere. He has a list of charges against him as long as my arm. Including assaulting an officer."

"Doesn't matter. The Syndicato won't let either of us testify."

She frowned, her mind scrambling for a solution. "Well…maybe we won't need your testimony. Alex was there. I was there. We know what happened and I think we have enough evidence to put Trini away for a long time."

Diego gave her a look that said she was naive. "You think that will help? There'll always be someone else to take his place."

She couldn't blame him for being cynical. "You might be right, but taking Trini off the streets is a start. If we can show kids that joining a gang isn't all that great…" She stopped herself. Now she was sounding like Alex. She gripped the wheel tighter. "Did you know they arrested Marco for the Encanto shootings?"

"Marco? That's ridiculous. With what evidence?"

"The gun."

"He doesn't own a gun. It had to be a plant."

Something she'd already thought of. They needed a body and Marco was as good as any. But a plant meant there was a dirty cop in her unit. Someone who had access to Pedro's gun. Was it Fontanero? He was the logical pick since he'd made the collar.

But she couldn't let her dislike for the man color her thinking. She needed to see the file. See who'd been with Fontanero on the arrest. If what Diego said was true, if someone in the department had ordered the hit on Alex, it happened before Fontanero came on board, and if the dirty cop wasn't Fontanero, who could she confide in?

Turning the corner, she saw several squad cars returning to the parking garage. Her call had generated more backup than she'd seen in a long time. Then she saw Alex's Lincoln sandwiched between two squad cars.

Alex. What could he possibly think after all this? What would he think of her now that he knew she'd been with Trini? Her throat closed. If ever she'd thought they might have had a future…. Hell, who was she kidding? She knew it was a fantasy when she first met Alex. She knew it now. Making love—falling in love—didn't change that.

She parked the Jeep and started to get out, but Diego didn't move. "You need to come inside with me. They may have more questions for you."

"Where's Trini?"

"He's with the captain. He'll be in a separate room. You won't even see him."

Diego fidgeted. He looked as if he was ready to bolt, and she couldn't blame him. His experience with cops had always been bad. But this time he was the victim. "I'll be there for you, Diego. I promise."

The first thing Crista did when she went inside was to take Trini's gun to Josey in CSU. "Top priority," Crista said. "I need the information ASAP."

After that, she asked Diego to sit at her desk and wait. No one knew he was her brother, but that was going to come out very soon. Alex was in with the captain.

She pulled out the papers to start her report, but the phone rang.

"Can you come in here, please," the captain's voice boomed.

"I have to go for a few minutes, Diego. If someone comes to question you, don't say anything except what you already said."

She passed Alex leaving the captain's office as she went in. His jaw looked as if it were wired shut and his expression could've been chipped from granite.

"If you're looking for my report, I'll have it done within the hour," she said to Englend after Alex left.

Englend's gaze bored into her. "I'm going to lay it on the table, Detective. It's come to my attention that you and Mr. Del Rio are romantically involved."

"Who told you that?"

"It doesn't matter how I know, only that I do. You've broken department policy and it's going to cost you."

Trini. He was going to get even with her, one way or another. "You took me off the case. Remember? How is that breaking policy?"

He ignored her question. "And your screwups almost lost us the Encanto case."

"Screwups? What are you talking about?"

He didn't answer. "There'll be an IA investigation. And until we get the results of that, you're on administrative leave."

Crista couldn't believe what she was hearing.

"I want your gun and your badge."

Her stomach knotted. "You're going to need my testimony to wrap up both cases."

"Forget it." His voice was cold. "The Encanto case is solid. We're done with it."

She didn't think so. The fact that the gun used in the shootings and the gun Pedro used were the same changed everything. Pedro's gun had been confiscated by the police. So how could it possibly show up in Marco's possession? She had a pretty good idea, but she couldn't tell Englend. Not until she made sure. Not until she knew who the dirty cop was.

Not until she knew who ordered the hit on Alex.

She set her gun and her badge on his desk, then went back and sat by Diego.

The captain quickly came over. "You can go, Santiago."

"I'm here on my brother's behalf, Captain. Captain Englend, I'd like you to meet my brother, Diego. If you're done with him, we'll be happy to leave."

Diego stood and extended his hand.

The captain sputtered and without acknowledging Diego, he stormed back to his office. Just then her phone rang and she picked it up.

"You're not going to believe this," Josey said.

"Josey, I don't have time for guessing games."

"There were two sets of prints on Navarro's gun, his and another. The other print matches one I found on the gun used in the Encanto crime."

"You check AFIS?" If the print was in the Automated Fingerprint Identification System, they had a suspect.

"I did. There's nothing on the second print. The only match was Navarro's."

If the other print belonged to the cop who planted the gun on Marco, it wouldn't be in the criminal system, but it might be in the state system. All cops had to be fingerprinted.

"Can you run it through the state's database, and call me on my cell phone with the results?"

"Uh, sure," Josey said. "This is getting more interesting all the time."

Crista sighed. "Let's not say anything until we get some results. Okay?"

"Sure thing. Confidential all the way."

"Thanks," she said, then hung up and turned to Diego. "I need to go again, but I'll be back soon. When they interview you, don't offer anything. Just answer their questions. The only thing these guys have the right to do is ask questions and take the information from you to file charges against Trini. Once you're finished, go to my car. If I'm not there yet, get inside and wait for me." She pulled open her desk drawer and gave him her duplicate key.

Fontanero was gone. Good. She did a quick check to make sure no one was watching and then pulled the Encanto case from his desk, shoved it into her briefcase and headed to Closed Cases before anyone could find out she'd had to relinquish her badge. The clerk at the screening desk recognized Crista and let her go directly inside without checking her status. Finding Pedro Castillo's case file, Crista riffled through it again just to be sure. Nothing. Nowhere did it say the gun had been impounded. Either Pedro was lying or there was a cover-up.

ANGER CHURNED in Alex's gut as he drove home from the police station. If he hadn't been working on the task force, none of this would've happened. His daughter had been injured because of him and it could've been worse.

Had Crista been right when she'd said nothing would change in the barrios? God, he hoped that wasn't true. He couldn't think that way or everything he believed in wouldn't mean a thing.

He'd already seen progress. All the boys working for him had been in gangs, or on the verge of joining. Now they were spending more and more time at the center, and a couple of them actually talked about improving their grades and maybe going on to college.

But if it meant putting his family in harm's way…could he justify it?

Deciding against going home, he turned and drove directly to the center. It was late, after ten o'clock, and no one would be there. The perfect place to think about what the hell he was doing. Someone wanted to take him out. The Syndicate wanted to get their guys inside and according to Navarro, someone in the police department was behind it. Did Navarro's arrest mean his family was safe? Alex didn't think so.

Navarro's words kept repeating in his head. *"You couldn't shoot a man who knows how to satisfy you."*

In shock, he'd been unable to talk to Crista after that. And every time he thought about it, he felt like he might puke. She'd told him she'd been married once and it hadn't worked out. She'd told him about her brother and her job, but that was it. She'd never mentioned being involved with a ruthless hood. What other dark secrets was she hiding?

He'd thought he knew her. He'd been certain there was a future for them. But she was right. He didn't know her at all, and this new revelation made him shake with anger. He felt stupid. Betrayed. She'd been with him, with Samantha, and never said a word about her past.

If his judgment was that impaired, how could he make a sound decision when it came to doing right by his daughter?

He pulled in next to the center, got out, unlocked the door and went inside the cavernous room. In the darkness he kicked a box in his way and the noise echoed off the twenty-foot ceilings. He was about to flip on the portable lamp when he saw a light coming from one of the back rooms.

What the...

Holding his breath, he crept down the hall, picked up a two-by-four on the way, and stopped near the door to listen. Not a sound came from the room. If some teenagers had come in looking for a place to party, he'd hear them. Maybe one of the boys had left a lamp on after finishing work. Cautiously, he peered around the door.

Somebody was lying in the corner of the room underneath an old army blanket. A homeless person, maybe. He didn't know if he had the heart to disturb him. But he couldn't house the homeless when there was a shelter just a couple blocks away.

He walked over and tapped the guy's shoulder with his toe. "Excuse me." He reached down and pulled the blanket lower revealing a head of dark hair.

"Tomás? What the devil are you doing here?"

"Go away," the boy groused and pulled the blanket up over his head, obviously not quite awake. "I'm sleeping, leave me alone."

"Yeah. I can see that. But why are you here?"

A small delicate boy, Tommy lifted his head, prying his eyes open as he did. Surprise registered on his face when he saw Alex. "Mr. D. I—I didn't know it was you," he said sleepily. "I thought you were one of the guys." He rubbed his eyes with his fists. "I don't have no place to go."

"Where are your parents?"

"I don't know. I lived with my brother, but then he went to jail. I stayed at his place till they kicked me out."

"And where have you been staying since then?"

He shrugged. "With friends sometimes. Wherever."

Wherever meant the streets. Damn. And that was probably the reason the boy hadn't been going to school.

"You ain't gonna put those welfare workers on me are you? I'm not going to one of those foster homes."

Alex didn't know what to do. There had to be a shelter for kids, but it was too late tonight to find one.

"I guess you'll have to come home with me. We'll figure something out in the morning."

Tommy stood and pulled his blankets together. It was cold in the building and the boy was shaking, his expression anxious, like he might run. "It's okay. I'm not going to call anyone. We'll get you a shower, something to eat and then a good night's sleep."

The boy's eyes lit up. "Okay. As long as you don't call those welfare people. My brother's getting out in a couple weeks and we're going to find a place."

"It's a deal." Alex held out his hand to shake on it.

Later, after Tommy was settled in at Alex's place and sleeping soundly, Alex went into the library and poured a drink. A double. Standing at the bar, he downed the whiskey in one swallow and poured another. Tonight he'd heard that someone wanted to kill him. Navarro was just the hired gun. If someone inside the police department was involved as Navarro had said, who could Alex even talk to about it?

Crista had heard everything. He could talk to her. And maybe he'd also find out how she'd gotten mixed up with that creep. Maybe he'd misunderstood and it wasn't what it seemed?

His phone rang and he went to pick it up. Who'd be calling at this time of the night? "Hell—"

"Alex, it's Crista. I need to talk to you."

His nerves tensed.

"I'm sitting in my car outside."

"Do you want me to come out there, or would you like to come inside? It's warmer in here and everyone is asleep."

"Okay."

They hung up and he went to the door. She was standing on the steps, looking as if she hadn't slept in days. Dark smudges under her eyes and worry lines around her mouth confirmed she was strung out. He had the crazy urge to pull her close and comfort her. Instead he said, "C'mon in."

He led her into the library. "I'm having a drink. Would you like one?"

She nodded. "I could use something strong right now."

He poured her a shot of cognac, handed her the glass and motioned for her to sit. He brought his own drink over and dropped into the leather chair next to her. He felt as weary as she looked. "I'm sorry about your brother's involvement with the Syndicate. That must have hurt you."

"Well, the good thing is that he was trying to get out of the gang. But it's not easy to leave." She glanced away. "I guess you know all that."

"So what happens now?"

"If Diego testifies against Navarro, we can put the creep away for a long time."

Alex winced at the mention of Navarro's name. "But that's not going to solve anything. Navarro said someone inside the department had given the orders. That's pretty frightening. And if Navarro goes to jail without revealing who it is, nothing has changed."

Her head tipped back as if in resignation. "I know. Believe me, I know."

"So what happens now?"

After a moment she sat up and squared her shoulders. "I need to find out who's behind it. And in the meantime, we need to ensure your safety. Sam's safety. Whoever's pulling the strings inside the department is going to be lying low. I doubt they'd try anything now and risk exposure. But I still recommend being cautious."

He nodded. She was still worrying about them. But he felt as if he were talking to a stranger. She was all business, as if they'd never been close. Never been intimate. "I still have security on payroll, and he's good. I'll hire more if necessary."

She nodded.

"What about Diego?"

"I need to make sure he's safe, too, but it's tough when I don't know who I can talk to in the department. And Diego is being stupid about the whole thing. He refuses to go into hiding."

"Where is Diego now?"

"I wanted him to stay at my place, but he wouldn't. He's at home."

"Didn't you tell me the chief of police was a friend of yours from the academy? Can you contact her for help?"

"I could, and I probably will—but first I need some solid evidence."

"Can't someone get Navarro to talk?"

"He's a gangster, a convicted felon. His word isn't going to count for much, and right now he's not going to give up anything. I'm sure he believes his connections will have him released by morning. I need to get some other evidence to support what he said at Diego's."

"Can you do that?"

"I have a pretty good lead."

All the talk about Navarro grated on Alex's nerves. How could Crista have been with such a lowlife?

She stared into her glass and swished the amber liquid around.

Dammit, he couldn't sit here and talk about everything but that. "Crista."

Her gaze caught his.

"I can't pretend I didn't hear what Navarro said."

"I didn't expect you would."

He wanted an explanation, dammit.

She held herself very still, her chin high. "I'm sorry about what you heard, Alex. Maybe I should have told you all the gory details of my past, but none of it is relevant to who I am now. So I chose not to say anything."

The air left his lungs. He felt as if he'd been suckerpunched in the gut. He loved her and she didn't feel the need to be honest with him.

"I never thought we'd get as involved as we did, and when it happened…" Her voice cracked with emotion and she stopped talking. She inhaled deeply, then exhaled, regained her poise. "Well," she said, her voice a soft whisper. "I don't think any of that matters now."

CHAPTER SEVENTEEN

CRISTA FELT as black and as empty as the night. As she drove home, tears ran down her cheeks. For a girl who never cried, she was doing a spectacular job of it.

How could her past matter when there was no future for the two of them? They lived in two different worlds. As much as she loved Alex and Sam, she couldn't be the kind of wife he wanted. She couldn't be the kind of mother Sam needed.

More than once she'd fantasized that if they truly loved each other, they could make it work. But tonight had ended those fantasies.

How could she explain her past to Alex when there was no explanation? She couldn't erase it and she couldn't excuse it. She was who she was.

Finally home, she went into her apartment and lifted Calvin from his cage. She held him against her chest and felt his heartbeat thumping wildly. Still holding him close, she sat on the couch and stroked his back feathers, feeling terrible that because of her he'd been a victim of Trini's rage. "You're a good bird, Calvin. I'm so sorry you were hurt, but you're safe now."

What she'd told Alex was true. She didn't feel anyone would try something now, and with Trini in jail, she felt enormous relief. The police had impounded his truck and in it they'd discovered several cans of oil and,

on the right front fender, red paint that matched her
Jeep. Trini admitted stalking Crista, but wouldn't admit
to anything else. Which left more than one question un-
answered. If Trini wanted Diego to carry out the hit on
Alex and Diego had refused, who was the shooter on
the two drive-bys?

It could be Trini, but it could have been anyone.
Maybe even Marco. She hoped that the CSU would
find enough trace evidence in Trini's vehicle to prove
he was involved in the shootings. Even without that,
the D.A. thought they had enough to convict him on
stalking and attempted murder.

There would be a hearing and a trial and everything
about her past would come out. Everyone would know.
Her co-workers, Alex, Elena, Risa, Lucy, Abby, Mei
Lu, Catherine—everyone. Her friends knew more
about her than most people, but they didn't know all
of it. She couldn't imagine what they'd think of her.

She leaned back against the couch pillows, exhausted. She'd thought her past was behind her, that her
life had new direction. But it was obvious now that she
could never escape. The past was always there, like a
latent virus waiting to attack when your defenses were
down.

But thinking like that wasn't going to help with anything. If people were going to judge her for past indis-
cretions, let them.

She wrestled her thoughts away from her personal
problems and directed them to where they should be.
She might be on leave pending investigation, but she
had to find out how Castillo's gun got into Marco's
hands. If she didn't, an innocent man would be convicted and a murderer would be allowed to remain on
the streets to commit more crimes.

Settling Calvin back into his cage, she pulled the large Encanto file out of her briefcase. She went to sit at the kitchen table and flipped through the pages. Nothing in the documentation indicated anything was amiss. While Fontanera had made the arrest, there'd been other officers on scene. Garcia, Hanover and Munez. Garcia and Munez, she remembered had been on scene when Castillo was arrested.

Just then her cell phone rang. She didn't feel like talking to anyone, but was relieved to see on the caller ID that it was Josey. "Hey, Josey."

"Sorry for calling so late."

"No problem. I was up. Are you still at work?"

"No, I'm at home. I thought it best to call from here. I didn't want this to get to anyone but you."

"What's up? Did you get a match on the print?" Crista's hope mushroomed.

"I did. You won't believe whose it is."

EARLY IN THE MORNING, Crista called Catherine and asked to meet her. After an hour together, Catherine shook her head and laughed. "The newspapers are going to have a field day with this one. One more thing for the media to latch on to and give credence to the rumors of corruption under my administration."

"But if corruption is there and you clean it up, that ought to give the press a different perspective, don't you think?"

Catherine, sitting model-straight, blond hair perfectly coiffed and clothes impeccable, steepled her long fingers. "I'll reserve an opinion on that one." She smiled and then her pale blue eyes fired up with determination. "We need a plan. Getting IA involved won't work. And we can't just go in and make an arrest based on a fingerprint that might be explained away."

"I have a plan," Crista said. "But implementing it will be difficult. I'm going to need to talk to Navarro and Marco Torres, but given my situation, I don't have authority to—"

"I'll make it happen."

Her adrenaline coursing, Crista left Catherine's office and took the stairs down to the CSU so she wouldn't run into anyone. Like a small town, gossip in the department spread faster than the speed of a bullet. By now everyone knew she was on administrative leave, and everyone knew about her relationship with Trini—and with Alex.

After getting the records she needed from Josey and meeting with Marco and then Trini, she made one last stop. Captain Englend's office.

"You're not allowed here, Santiago."

"I'm a citizen. I'm allowed." She entered his office and stood, arms akimbo, in front of his desk. "I believe I have some information that might interest you."

"I don't have time for this. I'm due in a meeting."

"I just spoke with Navarro and I think you'll want to make time to hear what he had to say."

His eyes narrowed. "What're you talking about?"

"Mr. Navarro seems to think someone in the department is hooked up with the Texas Syndicate and has a nice little side business going."

Englend bolted to his feet, rounded his desk and closed the door. He stepped forward, in her face. His usual mode of intimidation. Towering over her, he said, "He's scum. A convicted felon. He'll say anything to save his ass. But I guess you would know that better than anyone."

"You won't get any argument from me there. But the fact remains, there's a dirty cop in this unit."

"You're crazy, Santiago. I know my men. They're above reproach."

"There's evidence to back up Navarro's testimony."

His eyes turned dark. "If there was evidence, I'd know about it."

"The gun evidence. Apparently the gun used in the two recent drive-bys is the same one from a case three years ago. The gun was impounded, so it seems strange that it would turn up again."

"Are you saying someone lifted impound evidence?"

"Let me back up a little, Captain. Since this case also affects me and my job, I want to mention something else first."

"I don't have time for long, sad stories, Santiago. I have a meeting."

"This involves you."

"Everything in this office involves me. And I don't give a rat's ass about you or your job." He barreled past her and headed down the hall toward the parking garage.

Undaunted, Crista followed, talking while they walked. "When I was assigned lead on the Encanto case, I was pleased. Even when I found out the case was urgent, I was still pleased. I thought the assignment showed your confidence in my abilities."

At his car, he rounded on her, his mouth a grimace.

"By the way, nice ride you have there. Not quite as nice as the Mercedes roadster you have at home, though. I hear the SL600 goes for over a hundred grand. I didn't realize a captain's salary was big enough to cover those kinds of luxuries."

His jaw clenched and he reached for the door.

"Wait. You really do want to hear the rest of this. If not, I might think you don't care that you have a dirty cop in your unit and I'll have to go somewhere else with the information."

He stopped cold.

"Anyway, when I realized you had no intention of letting me solve the case, I thought it was because you didn't want a woman on your team. But then I discovered you didn't *want* the case solved. When the mayor got on you about the case, you gave him a warm body. Marco Torres."

As if what she'd said didn't faze him, Englend said, "You're full of crap, Santiago. The gun was in his possession."

"Exactly. The same gun used in the Castillo robbery three years ago. Hanover made the collar."

Surprise lit his eyes as she went on. "You had Hanover write the report as if the gun was never found."

His laugh was terse. "And if you could prove any of this garbage, you wouldn't be standing here right now."

"Hanover was with Fontanero when Torres was arrested. Hanover was backup on the Castillo arrest."

"Speculation isn't evidence."

"Evidence? You mean like your fingerprints on the gun used in both drive-by shootings? Oddly, your prints are also on Navarro's gun. A gun which was impounded from another crime and which mysteriously appeared again—in Navarro's possession."

Englend's face twisted into an angry knot. "You're going to regret this, Santiago."

"Is that a threat, Captain?"

"Damn right it is! You don't know what you're getting into."

"Why? Because you have a deal going with the Texas Syndicate and get a nice cut by ignoring the Syndicate's activities? Extortion and drugs pull in big bucks. Enough to pay for that expensive car you have at home. Enough for you to want Alex Del Rio gone so you could put your own man in his place and keep the business running smoothly."

Almost before she spit out the last word, Englend pulled his gun.

"What are you going to do? Shoot me? I'm not the only one with this information."

Englend reached for her throat.

Big mistake. Crista kicked Englend's knee, throwing him off balance. At the same time she grabbed his arm, turned her body and threw him over her back.

His weapon flew. He landed on the floor, grabbed her leg and pulled her down. She hit the floor with a thud and her head cracked against the concrete. Stars burst in front of her eyes. Her vision blurred and doubled and she thought she saw Englend scramble for his weapon. The next thing she knew he was standing over her with a gun barrel directed between her eyes.

She did the only thing she could. One swift kick in the groin. He went down, holding his crotch. At the same time, a swarm of officers, including the chief of police, poured into the garage, all guns on Englend.

While cuffing the captain, the arresting officer said, "William Englend, you're under arrest. You have the right to remain silent…"

Crista pushed to her feet and removed the wire she'd been wearing. When the officer finished reading Englend his Miranda rights, Crista added, "And there's a whole long list of other charges to go along with that one. Hanover has a great singing voice."

"So how's the gang slayer?" Pete winked at Crista as he folded himself into the chair across from her.

It was Pete's first day back and to say she was delighted to see him was an understatement. "You *know* how I am. All you have to do is read the paper or listen to the six o'clock news."

"You're famous."

"Infamous is more like it. Don't remind me."

"I hear you're getting a commendation."

She sighed. "Y'know, I wish they wouldn't bother with all that stuff. I was just doing my job."

"Sharon and I plan on being there."

"Thanks. Bring the baby, too."

"Maybe, if the colic's over by then." He flipped on his computer. "So how'd it go with your new partner? Fontanero?"

"I don't know. He's been the invisible man since Englend's arrest." It had only been a week since the big bust, but everything in the office seemed back to normal. Actually, it was better than normal. They had a new captain, Hector Salazar, a guy she'd worked with a few years ago, Pete was back and with both Englend and Hanover gone, it was a pleasant working environment.

Pete ran a big hand through his blond hair, then leaned forward to whisper, "I heard something else. I heard that you might get that transfer to Special Ops."

Crista jerked to attention. "Where did you hear that?"

"Can't say."

Pete had been with the department for years and had many sources. God, she hoped he was right, but she didn't want to get her hopes up and have them come crashing down. "I can't imagine that happening just because I solved a case."

"I can't believe you," he said, his voice rising. "You didn't just solve a case. You took down the most notorious jail gang in Texas *and* uncovered police corruption. Give yourself some credit, woman."

Crista glanced away, a tad self-conscious at the compliment. "Okay," she said. "Now I have to get back to work." She pulled out a new case that had come in two days ago.

It felt so good to talk to Pete. She needed a friend.

Though she'd told him most of what had happened while he was gone, she hadn't told him about her relationship with Alex. He'd more than likely heard via the grapevine, but they didn't talk about it.

While she'd been busy the past week, she missed Alex. She missed Sam. Every time she thought about never seeing them again, a profound grief settled on her.

She grieved over the loss of their relationship. The loss of hope. Somewhere in her unconscious, she realized, she *had* hoped she and Alex could work things out. Other people worked out their differences, why couldn't they?

But she'd seen the piercing hurt and disappointment in Alex's eyes when he'd learned about her relationship with Trini. She knew it was impossible.

She'd wanted to explain to Alex, tell him that Trini was another lifetime ago. That she was a different person then, a person who'd felt unworthy, a person who'd had to fight for every scrap of affection she'd ever received.

She wanted to tell him she wasn't that person anymore. She was strong and confident. She believed in herself.

And in realizing that, she also realized the irony.

All her adult life she'd been running from her past, pretending it didn't exist, when, in reality, it was her past that had shaped her life, made her who she was today.

Alex had given Crista something that would be with her for the rest of her life, something she couldn't have found on her own. A new appreciation for her heritage. For so long, all she remembered were the reasons she'd wanted to leave it all behind. But with Alex, she'd discovered that what she'd hated was also what she loved the most.

Though tired and emotionally drained, Crista went directly to the gym after work. The workout and a double espresso revived her. Between the exercise and the caffeine, her energy level was over the top. She didn't feel like going home, so she drove downtown again.

Maybe a little Christmas shopping would get her into the spirit of things. She had to buy presents for Diego, for Pete and Sharon and something for the new baby. And she planned on getting something for Sam, whether Alex let her see the child again or not.

She parked in the closest empty spot and started walking, not sure where she'd go first. The crisp air was scented with pine and evergreen brought in for the season. The trees on the boulevards sparkled with twinkling lights, and the city was alive with shoppers, carolers and corner Santas clanging their bells to help the poor. Decorations in red, green and gold adorned the department store windows and lined the streets. Holiday cheer graced the faces of everyone she passed. She passed families with little children awed by seeing Santas on every corner, teens kissing in doorways and even a few senior citizens holding hands, a testament that love really could last a lifetime.

Everyone loved the holidays.

And there, standing on the streets of Houston, among a sea of smiling faces, Crista felt a piercing loneliness and was overwhelmed by grief.

Everyone was gone. Even Diego was gone. He'd been spirited away into protective custody until the trial, and she was going to be spending her Christmas with Calvin.

She lifted her chin, straightened her shoulders and kept moving. Enough of that pity party. She turned and ducked into the first department store she came to.

An hour later, she came out of the store with three bags of gifts, and with her spirits buoyed, she was ready for another store. The revolving door swished behind her as she stepped outside and stood for a moment in the brisk air deciding which one to hit next.

"Crista. Crista!" a child's voice called out.

She turned to see Sam running toward her with Alex trailing behind. Oh, Lord. Her heart wrenched as Sam threw herself into Crista's arms.

"We were shopping," Sam said, her voice ringing with excitement. "I bought you a present."

Crista glanced at Alex.

"Sam bought all her presents tonight."

"Are you coming over for *Noche Buena?*" Sam's eyes lit with excitement. "You hafta come because we have presents for you. Isn't that right, Daddy?"

The surprise on Alex's face made Crista's words freeze on her tongue.

"Yes, of course. We'd all like you to come," Alex said.

She didn't think so. Alex had probably agreed because he didn't want to hurt his daughter's feelings. And because he was a gentleman and didn't want to put

Crista in an awkward situation, either. "Gosh, Sam. Y'know, I think I have to work on Christmas Eve."

Sam's face drooped.

Seeing the child's disappointment, Crista said, "But I'll check my schedule, and then I'll call your daddy and tell him. How's that?"

Sam cheered. "You can call me, too. I answer the phone sometimes now."

"She's growing up too fast," Alex said.

Crista caught his gaze and smiled. "Kids have a tendency to do that, don't they."

Sam stood arms akimbo and said to Alex, "I keep telling you that if you got me a sister or a brother, then you'd have another baby to take care of when I'm all growed up."

Alex coughed. "Uh…I think we better get home now. It's getting late and your grandmother is waiting with that cocoa."

Sam gave Crista another hug, and they waved goodbye. A lump formed in Crista's throat. Tears welled as she watched the two of them head down the street. She kept watching until they disappeared around the corner and only then did she let the tears fall. Standing like a zombie, a soul-deep sob wrenched from deep inside her.

ALEX TUCKED Sam into bed, said good-night and went to the library for a drink. Seeing Crista had only reminded him of how much he missed her.

Since the shooting, his life had been turned inside out and upside down. But he'd come out of it and was even more determined to clean up the gangs in the barrio.

Taking down the TS didn't mean that the gangs

would disappear. It didn't mean the Syndicate wouldn't make a comeback. It was a start. That's all. It was all he could expect.

Uncovering the corruption in Crista's department had created a feeding frenzy among the local media, and no one was immune. Captain Englend, Hanover, the Texas Syndicate and the Houston Police Department were under fire. Even though Crista had been the one to uncover the corruption, her life had become an open book, as well.

Prior to reading those stories, Alex had already come to the conclusion that whatever had happened in Crista's life didn't matter. He'd fallen in love with her before he knew any of it, and, he realized, knowing it now hadn't changed his feelings.

He'd been shocked and hurt. But now he understood her reluctance to get emotionally involved. He understood her need to help others. Her independence. But all the understanding in the world on his part didn't change things between them. They were different, as she'd said. He had Sam to think of, and he had to be sure the decisions he made for his family were the right ones.

But seeing Crista made him want her more, and when Sam had invited her for *Noche Buena*, he couldn't think of anything he'd like better. He knew from her answer though, that Crista had no intention of coming, no matter what she'd told Sam.

The next thing Alex knew, he was knocking at Crista's door. He heard rustling inside and stood where she could see him through the security hole. With a click, the door slowly opened.

"Alex?" she said softly. "Is something wrong?"

She wore gray sweatpants and a black T-shirt with

a Kung Fu logo, her hair was messy, and her eyes were pink and a little puffy. "Yes. Everything is wrong. Can I come in?"

She opened the door wider.

He went inside, slipped off his jacket and tossed it on the back of a chair. She motioned to a seat, but he was too agitated to sit. For a week now, he'd been ruminating about everything that had happened and he had to get it off his chest.

She combed a hand through her long hair, flipping it back behind her shoulders and then sat on the couch herself. When she looked up at him, the sadness in her eyes robbed him of words.

"What is it, Alex?"

"Crista…" He stuffed his hands into the front pockets of his jeans, then moved closer. "I don't know where to start."

She straightened her shoulders, as if to steel herself, and then said, "Why don't you let me say a few things first." Without waiting for his answer, she continued. "I can only imagine how shocking it was to hear about my…past, and I wish I'd been able to tell you about it first. But I didn't and I feel you deserve an explanation."

"No, No," Alex said quickly. "It isn't necessary. I came here to talk to you, not for you to explain anything." He crossed over and slipped onto the couch beside her. "If any explanations are necessary, then it's me who should be making them."

A frown creased her forehead.

"Yes, I was shocked when I heard about you and that creep. It was a natural jealous response—a carryover from the stone ages or something. And yes, I was hurt and disappointed that you hadn't felt close enough or trusted me enough to tell me about it. During this past week, I started second-guessing myself about everything. Was I stupid to think I could protect my family? Was it futile to think I could change things in the barrio? Was it unrealistic to think that two people who loved each other could make things work, no matter how different they were?"

He hesitated, not knowing how much to say, how much would be too much. "The one thing I never questioned, regardless of anything that happened recently, is how I feel about you. I was a jerk to stay away. I should have supported you through all this press garbage. I should've been there for you because I know the kind of person you are. I love who you are. I love your independence, your integrity and belief in your convictions. I wouldn't want you to change for me or anyone. I still believe we can have a future together."

Crista's heart leaped. Could they get past their differences? Alex might believe love solved everything, but she knew better.

Searching for an escape from her horrible stepfather and her dismal, hopeless life, she'd married Trini. Somewhere in her seventeen-year-old mind she'd thought he'd love her and take her away and she'd be happy for the first time since her father died.

But Trini hadn't loved her, and no man after him had ever *really* loved her. After a while she learned it was easier not to get involved. Opening her heart was a recipe for disaster and love was a synonym for pain.

"It still won't work, Alex. You need someone who can be there for you. For you and Samantha. I'm not that person. I couldn't leave my job and you couldn't live with a wife whose life is in danger every time she goes out the door to work. You couldn't live with the thought that your wife may not come home in the evening. You told me that yourself."

"That was before I knew you. I fell in love with a cop and I'm just going to have to deal with it."

"What about Sam? She's lost one person she loved, you couldn't put her through that all over again, could you? I'm being realistic, it's dangerous out there. I could get injured or killed. One slipup. One crazy person. Anything could happen."

"And I could cross the street and a drunk driver could take me out in a flash. I could slip and fall and hit my head and die. That stuff happens far more often than a cop getting injured or killed. I know. I checked the statistics."

He'd actually looked up statistics? But of course he would. He had a daughter to consider. He'd look at all the angles.

"And you know what? All the statistics in the world, good or bad, aren't going to change how I feel about you, Crista. All I know is that I'd rather have you in my life, than not have you at all."

Tears welled in Crista's eyes. She loved him, too, but love couldn't be all that mattered. Could it?

"You've made me see more clearly what I want, and what I want is us. I truly believe you want the same things I do, but you won't let yourself admit it. I don't blame you for being afraid to take a risk. You've been through so much, but if you won't open yourself to love, we'll never know what the future holds for us. Don't run away from me, Crista. Give us a chance."

Was she running from Alex's love? Was she using their differences as a buffer against getting hurt again? Was she afraid to take the risk? The answer, she realized was yes.

"I can't make you love me if you don't, Crista."

Crista closed her eyes. She'd worked so hard for everything she had, overcome so many obstacles. And everything she'd done was to feel safe, so that no matter what happened, she could take care of herself.

All her life she'd fought to stay strong enough to never need anyone. Because when you needed someone—loved someone—that person had the power to hurt you in ways no one else could. Giving someone that power meant she'd no longer be in control. She'd worked all her adult life to have control.

Loving someone meant trusting that they wouldn't hurt her or take advantage of their power over her.

But she trusted Alex. She would trust him with her life if she had to.

Taking Alex's hand in hers, she said softly, "I do love you, Alex. I love you more than I ever thought possible."

As she said the words, panic seized her. She pulled her hand away and stood up. God, this was so hard. Admitting she was vulnerable made her feel so exposed. And…he might not like the real Crista Santiago.

Steeling her resolve, she went on. "You're right. I'm afraid. I was afraid all my life until I took some control over my own destiny. And loving you…" She forced herself to go on. "Loving you makes me feel like I have no control. And I—I don't know how to deal with that."

There, she'd said it, but didn't know what to do next. So she just stood there waiting for him to say something.

He stared at her, thoughtful, and then after a moment he reached out and pulled her back down to sit next to him. Cupping her face in his hands, he said softly,

"Love does that, you know. I haven't felt in control from the minute I met you. But it's a wonderful and exciting feeling to know that someone can affect me that much."

Crista wanted to affect him as much as he affected her. And if she was honest with herself, that edgy out-of-control feeling *was* pretty exciting and wonderful— most of the time. But it was also scarier than going undercover in a drug sting.

She'd never felt more out of control than when she and Alex had made love. She'd forgotten every inhibition she'd ever had and he could've done anything, asked anything and she would have complied like a deprived animal. Or was that depraved? Just thinking about their lovemaking made her face hot and her breath short.

He leaned closer and kissed her softly, gently. She wanted to melt into him, become part of him. She kissed him back, and suddenly she felt free, free of the constraints she'd put on herself. "I love you, Alex. I love you so much it hurts."

He drew back and looked into her eyes. "Thank you. Thank you for loving me and for saying so." He smiled. And a second later, his smile turned into a big mischievous grin. "So does this mean you'll spend Christmas with us?"

Crista laughed from her gut. And then she was laughing and trying not to cry at the same time, and she didn't know what was wrong with her. She finally managed to say, "I'd love to spend Christmas with you, Alex." She couldn't think of anything better than being with his family at Christmas.

"And the rest of your life? Can you think about that, too?"

Her heart swelled. "I'll think about it."

"Seriously?"

"Seriously."

And when he kissed her again, she believed everything he'd said about love and the future and she knew she could never close her heart to love again.

EPILOGUE

"You gotta sit here," Sam told Crista, pointing out a seat on the couch. "And you sit here next to her, Daddy. *Abuela* can sit by the tree and help me with the presents because I don't know how to read yet."

They all did as they were told and Sam started taking the presents from under the enormous and elegantly decorated tree to her grandmother. Crista wasn't quite sure of the *Noche Buena* protocol in the Del Rio household. Every family seemed to have their own version.

"And then what do we do?" Crista asked.

"Tonight we open our presents to each other," Sam explained. "After I go to bed, Daddy goes to midnight mass, and he said maybe he'll take you along if you want to go. When I get to be ten, he said I can go, too. Then—" She stopped to take a breath. "Then in the middle of the night Santa brings presents to kids who've been good all year and I get to open them in the morning!"

"And I'm sure you've been good," Crista said.

"My daddy says I have, so Santa will probably bring me what I want." Elena gave Sam a present and indicated that she take it to Crista.

"Thank you, sweetie. And what did you tell Santa you wanted?"

"A mommy named Crista." The child beamed. "But Daddy says that's not something Santa can bring. Only—"

"Okay, okay." Alex interrupted deflecting the conversation. "Let's get this show on the road. You're dillydallying and it'll be midnight before you get to bed."

"What did *you* ask Santa for?" Sam handed Crista another present.

"I didn't, because being here with my favorite people is the best present anyone could have."

Sam's grin was wide. "Then you're really gonna like Daddy's present."

Crista glanced at Alex. She'd bought him an engraved pen set that held a framed picture of Alex and Sam that she'd taken at the beach. She hoped he hadn't gotten her anything too expensive, even if he could afford it.

"This one's for Diego. Why didn't he come?" Sam asked. Another present went into Sam's pile, and then another to Alex.

"He's busy right now, working on something," Crista lied. She wished Diego was here, too.

"But," Alex said, "when he's done with that job and he comes back, he's going to work for me teaching art at the center."

Crista jerked around to look at Alex. "Really? When did he agree to that?"

"We talked at Thanksgiving and he said he'd consider it. Before he went...away, he confirmed with me."

"Oh, Alex." Crista leaned over and hugged him. "I can't tell you how much that means to me." She'd come full circle in her views about staying in the community.

She'd learned change *was* possible, and like Alex, she now realized that if she wanted to see that change, she had to be a part of the process.

Alex hugged her back. "There's no need to thank me. He's going to work hard and he'll earn every penny he makes."

Crista's heart was so full of love, she thought she might burst.

"Can we give Crista her present now?"

"Sure," Alex said and Sam quickly ran over and gave Crista a small elongated box.

"It's from me and Daddy."

Crista's stomach fluttered. Her fingers picked at the bow and the tape holding the decorative paper in a million places.

"I wrapped it," Sam said.

"And what a beautiful wrapping job you did. I almost don't want to unwrap it."

"Here, just do it like this." Sam's tiny fingers ripped the paper off in one quick movement.

Crista stared at the black velvet box and then slowly opened it. Inside was a silver chain and hanging on it, a St. Michael medal.

"He's the angel to keep you safe when you go to work," Sam said, bouncing up and down, so full of energy she couldn't sit still.

"The patron saint of law enforcement." Crista bit back the tears that threatened.

"Gotta find some way to keep you safe," Alex joked.

Crista's heart filled with joy. It wasn't a joke to her. It meant that Alex had accepted her decision about staying on the Chicano Squad, even though it could be more dangerous than the job she'd been offered in Special Ops. It meant he loved her enough to respect what she wanted—not what he wanted or what he thought best for her.

"And Daddy has another present for you, too." Sam picked up another box in Crista's pile.

Alex frowned. "Samita, some things don't include kids. And this is one of them. Crista will do that one later."

Sam's bottom lip protruded.

"I don't mind, Alex. Really. But why doesn't someone else open something."

"I will," Sam said and ripped into a box that held a doll of Dora the Explorer. "Thank you, Daddy," Sam said and held the doll at arm's length. "But I hope Santa brought me a Barbie doll."

They all laughed and then Sam said to Crista, "Okay, now you hafta do the other present."

Alex looked to the ceiling and rolled his eyes. "This was not how I had things planned."

Sam waited expectantly as Crista slowly opened the tiny box, and lifting the top, Crista stared at a beautiful emerald-cut diamond ring. Joy bubbled up inside her. "As far as I'm concerned, it couldn't have been planned any better."

Alex removed the ring from the box, bent down on one knee and gazed into Crista's eyes. His hands were shaky and his forehead was moist with perspiration. "I know I'm probably rushing you, and I know you want more time, so we can have a long engagement if you'd like, but I have to say this now. I would be honored if you'd marry me, Crista."

"Us," Sam chirped. "She's gotta marry us."

Crista gazed at the two people she loved most in the world. Even if she hadn't been able to admit it in the beginning, she'd known all along that Alex was the

one. And she wasn't going to let her heart go unfulfilled
another moment.

She kissed Alex and then pulled him and Sam into
a group hug. "I'd be honored to marry both of you."

* * * * *

*Please turn the page for an excerpt from
Anna Adam's HER LITTLE SECRET—the fourth
title in Harlequin Superromance's
WOMEN IN BLUE series.*

Watch for it next month.

CHAPTER ONE

OLD HABITS died hard.

Thomas Riley parked his rental car a block from Abby Carlton's house. Ambling—no more dangerous than a guy out for a walk—he reconnoitered the area. A middle-class neighborhood, not shabby, not chic.

Cars whizzed past. Tree branches hung too low over the cracked sidewalks. Children had tossed their bikes and basketballs and Big Wheels into heaps on their front yards. One family's oversize garbage cans wore a coat of rain and mud from a recent, obviously violent storm.

Thomas tracked the house numbers without looking directly at them. As he neared Abby's house, a cracked, off-key voice cut the air. Despite being totally tone deaf, Abby Carlton sang whenever she felt like it.

Only a glass storm door stood between the house and the rest of the world. Even the windows on the ground floor were open just begging someone to rip off a screen and climb into the small green house.

Abby increased her volume, reaching a powerful point in a song Thomas had never heard. He spent too little time in the States to recognize the Top Forty.

Her singing nearly drove him back to his car. Not because she stank, though she'd be wise to keep her job as a cop, but Thomas hated to ruin her good mood.

He'd come to beg for help from the one woman on earth who might hate him too much to care.

He twisted his neck. Children's voices, birdsong, racing car engines all faded, leaving Abby's tuneless joy and the pain that rode up his spine to knot at the back of his head.

She drew nearer. He'd thought he was ready to see her, but he was wrong. Thomas stared at her through the closest window.

Six years after she'd left she remained unfinished business. But no one else could help him.

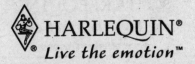

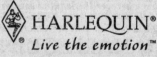